Alan Hunter was born
He left school at the age of fourteen to
father's farm, spending his spare time sailing on the
Norfolk Broads and writing nature notes for the *Eastern
Evening News*. He also wrote poetry, some of which was
published while he was in the RAF during the Second
World War. By 1950, he was running his own bookshop
in Norwich and in 1955, the first of what would become
a series of forty-six George Gently novels was published.
He died in 2005, aged eighty-two.

The *Inspector George Gently* series

Gently by the Shore

Alan Hunter

ROBINSON

Constable & Robinson Ltd
3 The Lanchesters
162 Fulham Palace Road
London W6 9ER
www.constablerobinson.com

This paperback edition published by Robinson,
an imprint of Constable & Robinson Ltd, 2010

A copy of the British Library Cataloguing in
Publication data is available from the British Library

ISBN: 978-1-84901-499-1

Typeset by TW Typesetting, Plymouth, Devon

Printed and bound in the EU

1 3 5 7 9 10 8 6 4 2

In Memoriam

H.E. Hunter
I. Hunter

CHAPTER ONE

E VEN THE SEA which lapped the August beaches of Starmouth looked grey at that hour of the morning. There was something mournful about it – it seemed to be grieving for the thronged crowds of noonday. Northwards it was embraced by the sprawl of the Albion Pier, much destroyed, much reconstructed, south-wards by the elegant iron-work of the Wellesley with its Winter Gardens, while facing it, across the wide promenade, lay the hectic holiday face of the town, a Victorian foundation in evil, dark-red brick with overlays of modern Marine Baroque. And the prevailing note was sadness. The dawn refused to ratify what man called gay. At this solemn hour, when PC Lubbock was observing his regulation speed between pier and pier, the Seaside Of The Midlands looked like a sleeping drunk stretched by the disapproving main.

He stopped, did PC Lubbock: he checked his well-regulated 2mph and conducted a survey of the morning scene. All was quiet, and most was still. On the pale-looking beach below him two or three figures were moving, slow, intent, each with a stick with which he occasionally stirred the marble-cold sand. Beyond them some sandpipers worked along the tide-line, further out some terns, and further still the gulls. Scavengers all were they, men and birds. PC Lubbock marked them with a permitting eye. He had seen them upon their lawful occasions for many a long year now and he gave them a favouring nod as he turned to pursue his jaunt.

But before he could get under way a change took place in the peaceful scene. A movement occurred, quite other than those he had come to expect from the deliberate trade of beach-combing. Towards him came leaping and capering, more animal than human, a strange, chattering figure, a figure that flailed its arms, a figure from whose splaying heels the sand shot up in clouds. PC Lubbock hesitated in his stride. There was something mindless and rather horrible about this bounding creature. Although he recognized it as Nits, a local halfwit, he couldn't help falling back a pace as it vaulted over the balustrade and dropped crouching at his feet.

'Well . . . and what d'you want, m'lad?' he demanded sternly, fixing his gaze on the halfwit's protruding green eyes.

They stared at him silently, seeming to strain towards him: the rest of the face sank backwards towards a toothy gape.

'What is it?' reiterated the Police Constable, raising his voice a degree.

Nits sucked in his lips as though preparing them for articulation. 'He . . . don't wake up,' he blurted in his slurring pipe.

'Eh? Who doesn't wake up?' asked the constable.

'The man . . . he don't wake up.'

Nits made an orang-outang-like gesture towards the direction from which he had come. 'All wet!' he whimpered, 'no clothes on . . . don't wake up.'

There was a pause while the trained mind arranged this information.

'You say it's *a man?*' PC Lubbock demanded suspiciously.

'A man – a man – a man!' Nits nodded his head with astonishing rapidity.

'You mean one like me?'

The head bobbed on as though worked by a piston.

With a stately cock of his leg, PC Lubbock stormed the balustrade and descended to the beach below. Through sand and through shingle went his boots, through shells and through seaweed, till he stood at last where the low slack water played old Harry with his spit and polish. And there he saw him, the man who didn't wake up, the man without clothes, the man who was all wet.

He had stood about five feet ten. He had weighed about 185. His hair had been pale brown, his eyes blue, his eyebrows slanting, his heavy features decidedly un-English. And he had acquired, probably rather late in life, a feature of the keenest police interest: a collection of four stab-wounds in the thorax.

PC Lubbock remarked a high percentage of these details. He glanced sharply at Nits, and sharply at the sea. Then, drawing his whistle with a flourish of professional adroitness, he blew a wailful blast to wake the morning air.

★　★　★

'There seems,' said Chief Inspector Gently, Central Office, CID, sagely, 'to be some as-yet-undiscovered connection between coastal resorts and homicide, Dutt. Have you noticed it?'

Detective Sergeant Dutt nodded dutifully, but without really listening to his senior. It had been hot in the train coming up. It was still hot in the train. Their third-class compartment was a little oven, and its atmosphere wasn't improved by the haze contributed by Gently's pipe.

'You've only to go back to the 'twenties,' continued Gently, with a damaging puff. 'There were the Crumbles murders – Field and Gray in '20, and Mahon in '24. Both classics, Dutt. Especially Mahon.'

'I was bashing me first beat in '24,' said Dutt reminiscently.

'Then there was Smith and the Brides in the Baths – Blackpool and Herne Bay were two of his spots – and coming the other way there's the Brighton Trunk Murders and Sidney Fox at Margate, and that other Starmouth business – slaughter in all shapes and sizes, and all of it going on by the sea. There's a link there somewhere, Dutt, you mark my words. The sea has a bad influence on potential homicides, whether it's recognized or not.'

'Dare say you're right, sir,' replied Dutt, staring out of the window.

'When I retire I shall write a monograph on it,' added Gently. 'There may be some implications which would help a good defence.'

He sank back into his seat and puffed away in silence.

4

The train clattered on, wearying, somnolent. They were nearing the end of the run, four sun-beating hours of it, and both of them felt jaded and grimy. Outside stretched the marshes of East Northshire, very wide, very flat, their distance broken by nothing except the brick towers of windmills and the white handkerchief sails of yachts. Inside there was Gently's pipe and the sooty smell of third-class cushions . . .

'Well, it won't be so bad, sir,' said Dutt, trying to cheer himself up, 'it can't be worse than Southend or Margate.'

Gently smiled at a distant cow. 'It isn't,' he said, 'there's parts of it one grows to like.'

'You know the place, sir – you've been there before?'

'When I was ten,' admitted Gently, 'and that's further back than I like to remember.'

He thought about it, nevertheless. He could see himself now as he was then, a thoughtful child with sunburn and freckles, and those damned knickerbockers. A solitary child he had been, a bad mixer. It may have been the knickerbockers that made him antisocial.

'There isn't much difference between criminals and policemen,' he said, surprising Detective Sergeant Dutt.

They pulled in at Starmouth Ranelagh, a gloomy terminus where the smell of fish blended into a neat olfactory cocktail with the smell of soot, steam and engine oil.

'It hasn't changed,' mused Gently, 'that's just the smell it used to have.'

He reached down a battered leather suitcase and deposited himself and it upon the platform. Sergeant

Dutt followed, carrying a similar case, while in his other hand he clasped the 'murder bag' with which a careful Central Office had equipped the expedition. Outside in the station yard the afternoon sun burned down stunningly. There was a taxi rank, and co-passengers clad in summer dresses and open-necked shirts were streaming towards it. Sergeant Dutt looked longingly, but Gently shook his head.

'It isn't far,' he said, 'they've got their headquarters just off the quay.'

'Don't know what they've gone and packed in the bag,' said Sergeant Dutt reprovingly, 'it's like a ton weight.'

'Probably a ball and chain for when we make the pinch,' replied his senior unfeelingly.

They left the station and plodded over a lift-bridge which carried the main road into the town. Below them a cloudy muddy-banked stream flowed pacifically, bearing on its bosom tugs with barges and smaller traffic. Further down two torpedo boats were moored at the quays, opposite them a lightship undergoing a refit, and one or two stream-drifters. Above the bridge was the yacht station, its staithe packed three-deep with visiting holiday-craft.

'It's a ruddy port!' exclaimed Sergeant Dutt, dropping his bags gratefully as Gently paused to admire the scene.

'Of course it's a port,' said Gently, 'where do you think your breakfast bloater hails from, Dutt?'

'Yus, but I thought it was like Margate – not like flipping Pompey!'

Gently grinned. 'There's a Margate side to it too,' he said. 'Look, Dutt – a ship-chandler's. Have you ever seen a ship being chandled?'

'Can't say as how I have, sir, come to think of it.'

'You should,' said Gently, 'your education is lacking. It's the duty of every intelligent citizen to see a ship being chandled, at least once . . .'

They proceeded across the bridge and down into the sun-baked street leading along the quays. Ahead of them now was the Town Hall, a handsome red-brick building in a style that was purely Dutch. In fact, the whole thing might have been Dutch, thought Gently, there was a strong Continental atmosphere. Coming in, now, through all those marshes with their cattle and windmills and sails . . . And then again it was full of overtones which kept him in a strange frame of mind. He couldn't settle himself to the idea of being out on a case. It was having been here so long ago that upset him, perhaps, the having known the place as a child his mind was baulking and refusing to come to grips with what he was doing. It showed itself in his facetiousness, in the way he twitted Dutt.

But it was no good: he was here on business only. Nostalgic memories didn't mix successfully with homicide, and he just had to shake himself into an alert and receptive state of mind.

'There's a cafe over there,' he said to Dutt, 'let's drop in for a cup of tea before we check in.'

'I was just going to mention it, sir,' panted the sweating Dutt, 'only you seemed to be in such a hurry!'

Gently clicked his tongue. 'I'm not in any hurry,' he

said. 'There's nobody as patient as corpses, Dutt, especially when they've come out in a rash of stab-wounds . . .'

Superintendent Symms of the Starmouth Borough Police paced his office with military stride, a tall, spare man with close grey hair and a little clipped moustache. Inspector Copping, his man of parts, was being strong and silent in a corner.

'And that's it, gentlemen,' said the super, in tones as clipped as his moustache, 'we know nothing – we can find out nothing. We've got a corpse, and absolutely nothing else. There were no clothes and hence no laundry marks. You've had the prints and they're not on record. We've checked the Missing Persons' list for months without getting a lead and we've shown a slide at all the cinemas in town with no better result. In fact, gentlemen, it's a sticky sort of business, and I feel I ought to apologize for calling you in at all. But you understand how I'm placed. There are people above me who pretend to believe in miracles.'

Gently nodded gravely. 'It's our principal business to carry the can.'

'And you were specifically asked for, Gently – after that Norchester case of yours Central Office means only one person around here.'

'It was one of my luckier cases,' agreed Gently modestly.

'So you see, it was out of my hands.' The super paused, both in stride and speech. He was genuinely grieved at having to pass on such a stinker.

'It's a job for the file,' put in Inspector Copping from his corner, 'there's just no angle to it. He might have been jettisoned from a ship, or dumped there, or dumped somewhere else and washed up there. He might even have been shoved out of an aircraft and finished up there. There's no end to the ways he might've come – I've put in hours thinking up new ones.'

Gently nodded a mandarin nod and stuffed a clumsy hand into his pocket. They had some peppermint creams in that cafe, and he had bought a whole pound.

'The body was even *discovered* by a halfwit . . . so far as we can make out he chivvied it around trying to wake it up.'

Gently made sympathetic noises over a peppermint cream.

'And then this blasted Lubbock got the seconds on him and tried three methods of artificial respiration.'

'He's been reprimanded,' said the super grimly, 'there'll be no more of that sort of thing from Lubbock.'

'And all the beachcombers for miles jamming around . . . it was like Bertram Mills'.'

There was a silence, during which the only sound was a sugary chewing from Gently.

'So you see that calling you in is simply a face-saver,' went on the super, recommencing to stalk. 'The lads higher up know there's no chance, but the thing got too much publicity. They daren't just sit tight and let it fade away.'

Gently shuffled a foot. 'Well, as long as you aren't expecting too much . . .'

'We aren't.' Inspector Copping laughed with a little conscious bitterness.

Gently laid a peppermint cream on the super's desk and appeared to study it, as though seeking inspiration. 'This halfwit who found him . . .' he began vaguely.

'They call him Nits,' supplied Copping. 'He's cracked all right – ought to be in a home. Real name's Gibson. Lives with his mother in one of the Grids.'

'And you checked up on him?'

'Naturally.'

'He wouldn't have been carrying a knife of any sort?'

Inspector Copping hesitated a moment and then plucked something from his pocket and threw it down on the desk in front of Gently. It was a cheap one-bladed penknife, and its one blade was broken. Gently poked it with a stubby finger.

'Of course there's no connection . . .?'

'None,' rapped Inspector Copping.

Gently picked it up. 'I'd like to keep it for the moment, all the same . . .' He opened and closed the little blade with a naïve curiosity. 'Did you find out anything else about him?' he asked. 'Has he got any friends – does anybody employ him?'

Inspector Copping grunted. 'He isn't employable. He hangs around the beach and people give him money, that's all. He spends it in the cinemas and amusement arcades. Everybody knows him, but nobody wants anything to do with him.'

'Has he ever given any trouble?'

'A visitor made a fuss about him once and we pinched

him for begging. It took three men to bring him in. He's stronger than he looks.'

Gently revolved the peppermint cream with care. 'About the deceased,' he said, 'when did he die?'

'The report says between eleven and twelve p.m. on Tuesday.'

'When did you find him?'

'Lubbock saw him at five-ten a.m. on Wednesday.'

'So he'd only taken five hours to get where he was . . . it isn't very long. What was the state of the tide?'

'Low slack water. If he came in on the tide he must have grounded at about four.'

'That cuts it down another hour . . .' Gently stared at his white sugar tablet with elevated brows. 'The local currents . . . the ones just off-shore . . . what's their direction?'

Copping glanced at his superior.

'There's nothing just off-shore,' supplied the super, 'it's a perfectly safe beach at all states of the tide. There's a north-south current further out, about half a mile. It accounts for a few damn fools every season.'

'Do you know the speed of it?'

'Not precisely. Maybe six or seven knots.'

'So you give him an hour to get into the current and another hour to come back ashore he might have been put in eighteen miles north.'

'No.' The super shook his head. 'If he was put in from the shore it couldn't be more than five or six. The shore starts in westward just north of the town, and six miles up the coast is Summerness, beyond which it recedes very sharply. At Summerness the current would be two miles off-shore.'

'Two miles . . .' mused Gently. 'He wouldn't drift out that far in the time. It'd have to be lower down. What's up there in that direction?'

The super shrugged. 'It's a wide sand beach all the way, backed with marram hills and freshwater marshes. There are three villages and a lot of bungalows. A little way out of town there's the racecourse.'

'Has there been racing lately?'

'No. It's not due till next Tuesday.'

'I suppose you didn't do any checking up there?'

'What's the use?' interrupted Inspector Copping. 'It's a hundred to one against him having been put in there, and even if he was, what would we be looking for?'

'Someone might have seen something,' suggested Gently mildly, 'there's never any harm in asking questions.'

Inspector Copping's heavyish features flushed. 'The case has had publicity,' he said, 'we've asked for information both in the cinemas and the press. If anyone knew anything we should have heard by now – we've looked into everything that's come our way.'

'Please don't get the impression that we've been asleep,' said the super snappily, 'we may not be homicide experts, but at least we carry out our police duties with strict care and attention. You have made the suggestion that the body of the deceased was put into the sea somewhere between here and Summerness, but the suggestion rests merely on the fact that there is a north–south current. And the current may have brought it from some point at sea, and then again it may never have been in the current at all. It could even have drifted up from a southerly direction inside the current.'

Gently hunched his shoulders chastenedly and made a chessmove with the peppermint cream. 'It could even have been dropped off the pier,' he murmured.

'My guess is it came off a ship,' said Copping. 'There's no doubt about the fellow being a foreigner. Anyone could see that at a glance. The ethnologist who saw him reckoned he was a Slav of some sort, Central European. He could have gone overboard in the Wash somewhere and hooked on to that current.'

'And that would mean trying to pinpoint a ship of some or any nationality which was in the Wash about midnight on Tuesday,' said the super, 'and just suppose we found it, what good would it do us?'

'It'd be outside our jurisdiction,' said Copping brightly.

'Unless it was a British ship,' hazarded Gently.

'In which case we would have heard something before now,' said the super with a note of finality. 'No, Gently. I appreciate your attitude. It's your business to see that no stone is unturned and I can see that you propose to carry it out. But I think you'll have to agree in the long run that everything that can be done has been done. Where there's no identity, no apparent motive and no hopeful line of inquiry, then to proceed with a case is simply a formality. You must do it – that's your business: but I'm afraid that in this instance it will be a very thankless task.'

'And yet this man was murdered,' said Gently slowly. 'Somewhere there's someone who will kill more readily another time if we don't put a finger on him . . .'

'I know, I know!' snapped the super, 'but idealism is no use if there's no prospect of implementing it.'

Gently sighed and heaved himself out of the rather bleak chair which was maintained for visitors. 'There's nothing else you want to tell me?' he inquired.

'I've told you everything that we know.' The super paused, frowning. Then he looked at Gently a little more kindly. 'Don't think we're against you . . . I assure you it isn't that. If you can do anything with this affair I shall be the first to congratulate you, and Copping here will be the second.'

'Hear, hear,' responded Copping, though perhaps more from duty than conviction.

'I've arranged lodgings for you and the Sergeant in Nelson Street. There's a private office here you can use for interrogations. If you need a car you have only to ask for it, and any other assistance we can give.' The super stalked round his desk and held out his hand. 'The best of luck, Gently,' he said warmly, 'I only wish it had been someone with no reputation to lose.'

Gently shook the extended hand woodenly. 'I'd like to see the body,' he said.

'I've a full set of photographs and a copy of the pathologist's report for you,' replied the super. 'Copping will give them to you along with his own report.'

'I still want to see the body,' said Gently.

The super shrugged. 'Very well, then. Copping will take you round.'

They filed out in strict order of rank, Gently, Copping and Dutt, the latter having been a silent and respectful auditor of the conference in the office.

'We'll take a car,' said Copping, 'it isn't far to the mortuary, but you can put your bags in and I'll drop you at your lodgings.' He dodged into his office and came out with a file. 'These are the reports and the photographs – for what they're worth.'

Gently took them with a solemn nod.

The mortuary was a neat modern building of pastel-tone brick and had double doors of a reddish wood with lavish chromium-plated fitments. But it smelled exactly like all other mortuaries. Copping explained their errand to the sad-faced attendant. They were ushered into the dim and odoriferous interior.

'He's had company,' observed the attendant, indicating a second draped form, 'they pulled her out of the river up by the yacht-station.'

'You'd better watch they don't get into mischief,' said Copping callously.

The attendant laughed a ghoulish laugh and twitched the sheet from corpse number one.

'*Voilà,*' said Copping, 'the cause of all the trouble.'

Gently stepped forward and conducted a stolid examination of the wax-like body. It had no humanity now. There was nothing about it to suggest the warmth of life, the kindling of a soul. And the attentions of the pathologist had done little to help matters, though he had tidied up afterwards with needle and gut.

Sergeant Dutt made a hissing sound. 'No doubt about him being a foreigner, sir,' he said, 'there's a bit of the old Eyetye about him, if you ask me.'

'Age?' demanded Gently through his teeth.

'Early forties is their guess,' returned Copping.

'Much force?'

'One stab busted a rib. There's three in the lung and

one in the heart. Penetration about four inches. Double-edged blade about three-quarters of an inch wide. And his wrists had been tied.'

'Poor beggar!' exclaimed the warm-hearted Dutt, 'they never give him a chance.'

'And those?' jerked Gently, indicating a group of brownish marks just above the pathologist's neat stitches.

'Burns,' said Copping, 'that's what the report says.'

Sergeant Dutt caught his breath. 'I've seen burns like that before, sir . . . during the war when I was in France . . .'

'I know,' said Gently, 'I've seen them too.'

He turned away from the slab and stood looking at the narrow window with its bar and pebble-glass pane.

'They didn't just want his life, they wanted something else too. I wonder what it was . . . I wonder why it was so important?'

Copping laughed harshly. 'When you know that you'll have solved the case,' he said. 'Let's get out of here. The smell gets on my stomach. You've done me out of my tea, bringing me to this place just before I knock off.'

CHAPTER TWO

B ODY ON THE BEACH: YARD CALLED IN, ran the
headline of the evening paper, Chief Inspector Gently
To Take Charge, New Move In Riddle Of The Sands. It
continued: 'There were fresh developments today in the
murder mystery which has come to be known as "The
Body On The Beach Murder". The Starmouth Borough
Police acknowledged the gravity with which they view the
case by calling upon the services of Scotland Yard. Chief
Inspector Gently, well known in Northshire for his
handling of the Sawmill Murders, has been assigned the
task and this afternoon he arrived in Starmouth to take
over the investigation. Superintendent Symms told our
reporter in an interview today that sensational developments in the near future are not expected and that the
arrival of Chief Inspector Gently was purely a routine step.'

There was also a photograph of Gently which the
Norchester Evening News had kept in cold storage from his
last visit, but fortunately it wasn't recognizable . . .

All along the Front they were talking about it, from
the bowling greens in the north to the funfair in the

south. It was really making the week for them, holidaymakers and residents alike. Publicity it was, Publicity with a capital P – it dragged in excursionists to be plucked and made the holidaymakers feel that their stay would be truly memorable. For how often does a first-class murder turn up on one's doorstep during a holiday? A classic murder with stabbing, mystery, the Yard, and all that? They even had the spot marked X for them, thought Gently, as he turned away from the crowd which still milled excitedly on the beach: the Starmouth Borough Police, nothing if not thorough, had set up a ponderous post to mark the site of the discovery. Nobody took it seriously, that was the trouble ... the police had already written it off as unsolvable, and everybody else looked on it as a bigger and better side-show. Even Gently himself was being infected by the feeling. He had been practically tipped off that he didn't have to exert himself.

And yet it was still there, up in the mortuary. That shrunken husk of what had once been a man. A foreigner, they all said, as though it were something subhuman – a foreigner whom they couldn't really care about, though he had been tortured, killed in cold blood and thrown into the sea, to be washed up, troublesome and unwanted, on their holiday shore ... just a foreigner: one didn't bother too much about him.

But suppose one did bother, thought Gently, where did one begin on such an impossible business? He had taken the only step that suggested itself. He had got Dutt to phone headquarters to have the prints transmitted to Paris. Where did one go from there – what was one to try that the so-efficient Starmouth BP hadn't tried already? He sighed, and sat down heavily in a deckchair which still remained on the evening sand. He was still baulking, and he knew it. He still couldn't get his shoulder under the thing. There was something about just being in Starmouth, quite apart from anything else, that sapped his power of concentration. Those tight-fitting knickerbockers, for instance . . . And where were the donkeys . . .?

Behind him the lights blazed and jewelled as far as the eye could see, outlining buildings, flashing on signs, revolving on the sails of the windmill which reared further down. The two piers presented a strong contrast. The virile Albion seemed to burn and throb with illumination, to assert itself by sheer candlepower; the Wellesley contented itself with graceful and glittering outlines, making it appear, with its Winter Gardens, like an iced-cake shored-up above the sea. And there was the great evening medley of the Front, the undertone of the traffic, the beat of ten thousand feet, the shrieks and cries of ragamuffin children, the tinkle and soughing roar of mechanical music and the intermittent spang and crash of a shooting saloon not far away.

And then, of course, there was the sea, the sea that knew the secret, the heavy-looking evening sea that hissed and chuckled near that solitary post.

Gently took out his pipe and lit it. There had to be something, he told himself obstinately. After all, that man must necessarily have been murdered not very far away and murder under the best conditions is apt to leave traces. He blew out the match in a gust of smoke and held it poised in the air beside him. Except if it were done at sea, of course . . . but one mustn't begin by assuming that.

Suddenly, the match disappeared from his fingers. It went so quickly and so silently that for a moment Gently simply sat still in surprise. Then he jerked his head round to see by what agency the match had taken flight. But there was nothing to be seen. There was nobody within yards of the back of his chair. The nearest people to him were two uniformed Americans with their inamoratas and they were patently occupied with quite other things. Puzzled, he returned to his meditations. He puffed at his pipe, his empty fingers taking up the same position as before. And then, just as suddenly, with the lightest of twitches, the match reappeared in its former situation.

This time Gently got up. He got up with an alacrity unexpected in a bulky man of fifty summers. But his haste was quite needless, because the worker of these miracles was merely crouching behind the chair and it made no attempt at flight when Gently pulled away the chair and exposed it.

'And who may you be?' demanded Gently, realizing then whom it could be no other.

'I'm Nits – I'm Nits!' piped the halfwit, staring up painfully with his bulbous eyes. 'I know who you are, they told me who you are! I know – I know!'

Gently released the chair slowly and reseated himself, this time with his back to the sea. 'So you do, do you?' he said, 'and who did they tell you I am?'

'You're a policeman!' chattered Nits, 'you're a

policeman, though you haven't got a hat. I know! They told me! You want to know about my man who wouldn't wake up.'

Gently nodded profoundly, keeping his eyes fixed on the halfwit's. 'And what else did they tell you about me?' he queried.

'They said I mustn't talk to you – ha, ha! – they said you might take me away and lock me up. But' – Nits assumed an expression of exaggerated cunning – 'I know you won't do that.'

'And how do you know I won't do that, Nits?'

'Because I haven't asked for any money. That's why they locked me up!'

Gently puffed at his pipe, still keeping the staring green eyes engaged. This was it, the solitary link – an idiot who ought to be in a home. Not even a rational creature, however stupid. Just an idiot, someone who couldn't testify anyway. As he sat there, smoking and brooding and watching the ragged Caliban crouched in the sand, he seemed to hear a mockery in the tinkled outburst of music and a laughter in the shuffling of feet on the promenade. What was the use of it? And who cared two hoots, really?

'So you found the man who wouldn't wake up . . .' he murmured.

Nits nodded in energetic glee.

'Just there, where they've put the post.'

Nits's head bobbed ceaselessly.

'And you tried to wake him up . . . then you went and told a policeman . . . and the policeman tried waking him up too.'

The head never wavered.

'You've no idea how he got there?'

The head changed direction agreeably.

'You didn't see anybody around before you found him?'

'My part,' said Nits, his features twisting into an absurd mask of aggression, 'nobody come on my part of the beach.'

It was just what was in Copping's report. The efficient Inspector had covered the ground admirably. Nits had told what he knew, and he didn't know anything: it just so happened that the corpse had been washed up on 'his' part of the beach.

'You were told not to talk to me,' said Gently wearily, 'who was it told you that?'

Nits grinned and chattered but made no intelligible reply.

'And why *did* you talk to me, after being warned not to?'

The halfwit frowned ferociously and turned his trouser-pockets inside-out. 'The other man – he took it away!'

'Took *what* away?'

'My knife – he took it!'

Gently smiled and felt for the little broken-bladed penknife. Nits gabbled with joy and snatched for it with the speed of a striking snake. But Gently had already experienced a sample of the halfwit's snatching and he held the knife carefully out of range.

'Who was it told you not to talk to me?' he demanded.

Nits chattered and tried another sudden grab.

'You get it when you tell me, not until.'

Nits made all sorts of fierce faces, but Gently merely made as if to return the knife to his own pocket.

'Jeff!' piped the halfwit suddenly, 'it was Jeff and Bonce – they told me.'

'And who are they?'

'I don't know – I don't know!'

'You know their names – you must know something else about them.'

'I just see them, that's all.'

'See them *where*?' persisted Gently, 'see them here – on the beach?'

But the halfwit relapsed into a mewing and gabbling, and refused to make himself any further intelligible. Gently sighed and tossed him the knife. It was plucked out of the air as though by the lash of a whip and Nits capered off, clutching it to his bosom, his two trouser-pockets still turned inside-out.

'Whoa – wait a minute!' called Gently, rising to his feet.

He produced a florin and held it out between thumb and finger. The halfwit paused in his flight, hesitated, and then came sidling back, spaniel-like, his chin tucked in until there seemed nothing of his face below the two bulging eyes. He didn't snatch at it, as Gently expected: he reached up and took the coin quietly from Gently's hand. Then he crept closer still, crouching, cringing almost, and stared up with his faceless eyes.

'The man who wouldn't wake up!' he piped, but in a sort of whisper.

Gently nodded silently.

'Different . . . different!'

'Different from . . . what?' murmured Gently.

'From when he was awake.'

'From when he was awake!'

Nits went into one of his fits of nodding.

'Hold it!' exclaimed Gently, feeling his universe beginning to rock, 'did you know him, Nits – did you know him when he was awake?'

'I knew him – I knew him!'

'But when did you know him – and where?'

Nits screwed his face up into an expression of rage and shook his head. Then he pointed to the tip of his almost non-existent chin.

'Hair!' he chattered, 'hair – when he was awake!'

The next moment he was capering over the beach again, leaving Gently with his eyebrows hoisted in almost comical surprise.

Twilight had become dusk and the lights which had sparkled like fugitive jewellery were now glowing and full. The blazing Front had a strange glamour about it, as though it belonged to a different world, and the holidaymakers too seemed to partake of the strangeness. Perhaps it was simply the multiplicity of lights destroying the shadows, perhaps only the sense of anonymity and freedom . . . they felt changed and in some way abnormal.

Gently picked his way through the promenade crowds and paused at the edge of the carriage-way. He felt changed also, though his changedness was due to something quite different. He'd got a lead, that was it. He'd found something to hang on to in this slippery orphan of a case.

Almost jauntily he crossed the carriage-way and directed his steps to a phone-box on the other side.

'Chief Inspector Gently . . . is Inspector Copping in, by any chance?'

The switchboard girl thought he might be if Gently would kindly hang on. Gently grunted and wedged himself into a supportable position in the corner of the box. Outside he could see the front of the amusement arcade from which blared much of the canned music which disturbed that part of the promenade – a striking blaze of light in the shape of three feathers, with a lurid red arrow snapping backwards and forwards as though working up to burst in through the door. And there was some jutting neonry which said LICENSED BAR . . . a ritzy sort of touch for an amusement arcade, thought Gently.

'Inspector Copping,' said the switchboard girl.

Gently jammed the door yet tighter-shut on the racket without. 'Gently here . . . I want something done,' he said. 'Look, Copping, can you get on to the pathologist who did the post-mortem? I want him to have another check.'

'Can't see what that's going to buy,' came Copping's voice plaintively, 'he didn't die of asthma.'

'I'm not interested in the way he died. I want a thorough examination of the skin of the face for spirit gum.'

'Spirit gum!'

25

'Or any other mucilage that may be present,' added Gently generously.

There was a pause at the other end, and then Copping came back: 'But what's he supposed to be now – a member of a touring company?'

Gently smiled at the leaping red arrow. 'Your guess is as good as mine . . .'

'And where did you dig up the idea, anyway?'

'Oh . . . it was a present for a good Central Office man. And by the way, Copping, you wouldn't know anything of two characters called Jeff and Bonce, would you?'

'Not to my knowledge. Are they hooked up to this business?'

'Could be,' admitted Gently, 'it's an even chance . . .'

There was a noise like a snort at the other end. 'But how do you *do* it? I've been three days on this case!'

'Just luck, you know . . . you need it in homicide.'

'It looks like all the breaks were being saved up till you came. Are there any other small ways I can help?'

Gently brooded a moment. 'There's an amusement arcade down here . . . it's called "The Feathers" and it sports a licensed bar. What do you know about that?'

'Is that in the case too, or are you just being curious?'

'I've been tailing Nits . . . when he's finished collecting he makes for "The Feathers" like a homing pigeon.'

'Well, it's got a clean record. The proprietor is a man called Hooker – Louey Hooker. He lives in a flat at the back of the building, and he runs a bookie's business too. The office is under the flat and fronts on Botolph Street, which runs parallel with the Front.'

'A bookie's business.'

'That's right. They're still legal in this year of grace.'

Gently nodded at the undiscourageable arrow. 'Well . . . send me Dutt along, will you? And drag that pathologist away from whatever he's doing and put him to work.'

'You mean tonight?' inquired Copping in surprise.

'We're working, aren't we?' retorted Gently heartlessly.

He hung up and levered open the door of the phone-box. The year's hit-tune, mildly interruptive till then, leaped to meet him with a vengeful roar. Gently frowned and felt in his pocket for a peppermint cream. Mr Edison, he felt, hadn't been an unmixed blessing to mankind.

The interior of the amusement arcade was as aggressive as the exterior had promised. It was lit with a farrago of fluorescent tubes and popping bulbs, and the walls were panelled in a gooey pink plastic relieved by insets of 'teinte de boiled cabbage'. And there was a vigorous use of chromium plate in all departments. The décor man had obviously had a flair for it. Left and right of a central aisle the machines were deployed – all the latest attractions, space-flights, atom-bombing and the rest, with a few tried favourites still making a stand against the march of science. There was the crane that picked up a prize and dropped it down a shoot, Gently noticed . . . at least, it picked up a prize when Nits was operating it. The halfwit had apparently got the low-down.

Stationed behind a punchball machine, Gently watched the crouched, ragged figure insert coin after coin. Each time the descending grab would seize on one of the more substantial pieces of trash in the glass case. Sometimes it failed to grasp securely and nothing would rattle down the shoot except a few gaudy-coloured sweets, but always the grab dropped plumb on a prize in the first instance.

Gently lit his pipe and continued to watch. All round him machines were ringing and clattering. Any two of that crowd could be the two in question . . . at any moment they might spot Nits, or Nits them. And what then? he asked himself. Suppose he was lucky and stumbled on them? What they had said to Nits might have been no more than a joke, the sort of silly thing to be said to a halfwit. Of course it was odd that they had known him, Gently, on sight . . . but then, the picture in the evening paper might have jogged their memories. There had been bigger and better pictures of him in the same paper the year before.

No, he told himself, it wasn't much better than a hunch, after all . . .

The music changed to something plaintive and caressing, and as though it were a signal Nits crammed his collection of ballpoints and flash jewellery into his pockets and darted to the door. Gently moved forward also, but the halfwit came to a standstill short of the entrance, so he slid back again into the cover of the punch-ball machine. Was Nits expecting someone? It rather seemed like it. He stood by the door, apparently trembling, and strained his protruding eyes in the direction of the Wellesley Pier. Several people came in, but these were ignored. Nits didn't even glance at them as they pushed past. Then he gave a little whimper and a skip, like a dog sighting its master, and a moment later the object of his vigil appeared.

She was a blonde, a tall, big-bodied blonde. She didn't have to broadcast her vocation, either to Gently or the world. She wore a sleeveless green silk blouse, high-heels and a black hobble skirt, and walked with a flaunt that looked vaguely expensive.

'Geddart,' she said to Nits in the husky voice of sin, 'keep away from me, you dirty liddle so-and-so – how many more times must I tell you?'

'I've been a good boy!' piped Nits, frisking and cringing beside her as she hipped down the arcade.

'I don'd care – jusd keep away from me.'

'I got something – I got something! Look for you!' Nits pulled out his hoard of swag and tried to thrust it into the blonde's hands, but she snatched them away and the stuff tinkled on to the floor.

'I don't wand it!' she yelped, 'keep your dirdy muck to yourself! Don'd ever come near me again!' And she bustled away through the grinning crowd, leaving Nits to scrabble amongst the feet for his scattered treasure.

'That's my gal, Frenchy!' shouted someone, 'don't you have him if you don't fancy him!'

The blonde turned back and said something so filthy that even Gently was taken aback, then she swaggered through the swing-doors of the bar.

'Whoo-*whoo*!' was the cry, 'Frenchy's got the answer, don't you forget it!'

On the floor Nits chattered and sobbed with rage. 'I'll

kill you – I'll kill you!' he babbled, 'I've been a good boy – I have – I have!'

Gently stooped and rescued a plastic ballpoint from under the heel of a bystander. 'Here,' he said, 'one you missed.'

Nits seized it and stuffed it into his pocket after the others. 'I'll kill you!' he whispered in an ecstasy of passion.

'Did she know him?' asked Gently, 'did she know the man who wouldn't wake up?'

Nits's green eyes burned at him like two malignant lamps and Gently, moving swiftly, moved only just in time. As it was the leaping halfwit sent his trilby flying. Then, recovering himself, Nits dived for the door and his turn of speed was something that Gently could only have sighed for in his palmiest days . . .

CHAPTER THREE

T HE BAR WAS rather a contrast to the rest of the establishment. It had got missed out when the wielder of plastic and chromium-plate had gone his merry way. It was quite a large place and its dim, parchmented lighting made it seem larger still. It was also irregular in shape. There were corners of it that tucked away, and other corners which had been given an inglenook treatment. Opposite the swing-doors ran the bar counter, its supporting shelves well fledged with opulent looking bottles, and to the left of the counter was a door marked 'Private'. Further left again was a small exit door, leading probably into a side-street.

Gently eased himself through the swing-doors and stood still for a moment, adjusting his vision to the drop in candle-power. It seemed a fairly well-patronized place. Most of the tables and nookeries were occupied, and there were several customers perched on high stools at the counter. Also it seemed quiet in there, but that may have been due only to comparison with the racket going on outside the swing-doors.

He strolled across to the counter, where the blonde was taking charge of a noggin of straight gin.

'Chalk id up, Artie,' she crooned, 'and no chiselling, mind.'

'Who shall I chalk it up to?' asked the ferrety bartender with a wink.

'Don'd be cheeky, Artie – Louey don'd like it!'

She slunk away from the counter, and her eye fell on Gently for the first time. She recognized him, he knew – there was just that much of alert interrogation in her glance – and for a moment he thought she would say something. Then she shrugged a scantily-clad shoulder, gave her head a little toss, and swung away across the room to one of the nookeries.

Gently seated himself on a high stool and ordered an orange-squash.

'Who is she, Artie?' he asked the ferrety bartender.

Artie gave the squash-bottle a practised twist. 'Don't ask me – ask her,' he retorted sullenly.

'But I am asking you. What's her name?'

'It's Frenchy – and I'm not her boyfriend.'

'Her other name, Artie.'

'I'm telling you I don't know!'

'She mentioned a Louey . . .'

'What's that got to do with me?'

'She spoke as though you knew him . . .'

'Well, I don't. He must be someone new.'

Gently drank a mouthful of orange-squash and appeared to be losing himself in contemplation of the fruit-scum collected at the mouth of his glass.

'That'll be a bob,' said Artie, '*if* you don't mind.'

Gently drank some more and was still interested in the fruit-scum. 'You know, it's amazing,' he said casually, 'the number of people round here who know me without me knowing them . . . you seem to be the fifth, Artie, by my computation.'

The ferrety one stiffened. 'Don't know what you mean by that . . .'

'Never mind, never mind,' said Gently soothingly, 'we'll go into it some other time, shall we?' He slid off his stool and picked up the part-drunk glass of orange-squash.

'Hey!' clamoured Artie, 'that's still got to be paid for . . .!'

'Chalk it up,' returned Gently, 'and no chiselling, mind. Louey don'd like it . . .'

He ambled over to a small table by the wall and pulled up a seat with better padding than the high stool. There were other eyes on him besides Artie's; several customers at the counter had heard the conversation, and now turned to watch the bulky figure cramming itself into its chair. Not only at the counter either . . . out of the corner of his eye Gently could see Frenchy in her nookery, and two other figures near her. They were all giving him their attention . . .

''Ere!' whispered a sporty-looking individual to Artie, 'is that geezer a busy?'

'Yard,' clipped Artie from the corner of his mouth.

The sporty-looking type favoured Gently with a bloodshot leer. 'Nice bleedin' company we get here these days . . .'

Gently quaffed on imperturbably. He might have

been entirely alone in the bar, so oblivious did he seem. He took out his pipe and emptied it with care into the ashtray; then he took out his tobacco and stuffed the bowl with equal care.

''E's set in for the night,' said the sporty-looking individual, 'blimey, you'll have to look sharp with them shutters at closing-time . . .'

'Why don't you offer him a light?' quipped his neighbour.

'What, *me* – and him a busy? Give us another nip, Artie . . . there's a smell round here I don't like . . .'

Gently, however, lit his own pipe, and having lit it he entertained his audience with a scintillating display of smoke-rings. He could blow them single, double and treble, with combinations and variations. He had infinite patience, too. If one of his airy designs went wrong he had all the time in the world to try it out again . . .

The private door beside the bar opened and a man in seedy evening-dress appeared. He was a heavily built type of about forty with dark hair, a parrot-shaped face, and little pale eyes set very close together, and he smoked a cigarette in a gold-plated holder about as long as his arm. Gently surveyed him with mild interest through a pyramid of smoke. Faces of that shape must at all times be rarities, he thought.

'Oi – Peachey!' yipped the sporty-looking individual, and made a cautionary face while he thumbed over his shoulder in Gently's direction. Artie also hastened to breathe a word in the newcomer's ear. The man's two pale eyes reached Gently, paused and strayed uneasily

34

away again. Gently's own slipped round to Frenchy. She was sitting up straight and shaking her peroxide head.

'Louey wants a fresh bottle,' said the newcomer hoarsely, 'gimme a white-label.'

Artie produced one from under the counter and handed it to him. He dived clumsily back through the door. Artie returned to his business of serving drinks without a further glance at Gently; there was an expression of satisfied malice on his face . . .

'You loog lonely for a big man,' said a voice at Gently's elbow, and he turned his head to see that Frenchy had slunk over to his table. She was smiling, at least with her mouth. Higher up it didn't show so much – by the time one got to her rather pretty warm-brown eyes it had gone completely. But she was smiling with her mouth.

Gently smiled too, somewhere between the South Lightship and Scurby Sands.

'I'm not lonely,' he said, 'there's too many people around who know me.'

Frenchy laughed, a throaty little gurgle. 'Thad's because the big man is famous . . . he geds his picture in the paper.'

'You think that makes people notice? Such a bad picture?'

'But of course . . . nobody talks about anything else except whad the police are doing.'

She pulled up another chair and sat down, not opposite Gently but to the side, where the table didn't hide anything. She slid forward and crossed her legs. They weren't terribly attractive, he noticed. The skin

35

was a trifle coarse and the contours inclined to be knobbly – they were designed for strength rather than quality. But she managed them well, they were crossed with great competence. And the hobble skirt contrived to lose itself somewhere above the knee.

'Id musd be exciding,' she crooned, 'hunding down a murderer . . .'

Gently breathed an unambitious little smoke-ring.

'And difficuld too . . . especially one like this.'

Gently breathed two more, one exactly inside the other.

'I mean,' she continued, 'where does one begin to loog if one doesn'd know his name . . .?'

'What's *your* name?' inquired Gently suddenly; 'all they call you round here is Frenchy.'

The brown eyes opened wide and the smile tailed off: but it was back again in a moment, and wider than ever.

'Surely you don'd suspecd me, Inspecdor . . .'

'I'm just asking your name.'

'Bud why should you wand to know thad . . .?'

'I'm curious, like all policemen.'

Frenchy seemed to consider the matter between half-closed lids. Gently stared at the table and smoked a few more puffs.

'If you wand to ask questions . . .' she began.

Gently favoured her with a glance.

'There are bedder places than this to ask them . . .'

She leaned forward over the table and balanced her chin in the palm of her hand. In effect the green silk blouse became an open peep-show.

'Afder all, it's your dudy,' she melted, 'and you know when girls dalk the besd . . .'

Gently sighed and felt in his pocket for a match. 'You're not local,' he said, 'you've had West End training . . . who brought you down here?'

For a moment he thought her scarlet nails were going to leap at his face. They angled for a strike, and the brown eyes burned with the merciless ferocity of a cat's. Then the fingers relaxed and the eyes narrowed.

'You filthy b— cop!' she hissed, all accent spent, 'I wouldn't let you touch me if you were the last bloody screw on God's earth, and that's the stinking truth!'

Gently shrugged and struck himself a fresh light. 'Where do you live?' he asked.

'Bloody well find out!'

'Tut, tut, my dear . . . it would save unnecessary police-work if you told me.'

'Well I'm not going to . . .!'

Gently held up a restraining hand. 'It doesn't really matter . . . now about our friend with the beard.'

She stopped in mid-flow, though whether on account of his casual remark or not Gently wasn't able to decide.

'Where did you meet him – here or in London?'

'Who?' she demanded sullenly.

'The deceased – the man who was stabbed.'

'Me!' she burst out, 'what have I got to do with it?'

'I don't know,' murmured Gently, 'I thought perhaps that was what you came across to tell me . . .'

Frenchy riposted with a stream of adjectives that fairly blistered the woodwork.

'Still, you might like to tell me about your movements on Tuesday night . . .' added Gently thoughtfully.

37

There was a pause, pregnant but not silent – silence was a strictly comparative term when only a pair of swing-doors separated them from the uproar without – and Gently occupied it usefully by prodding around in his pipe, which wasn't on its best behaviour. Over at the counter, he noticed, they were straining their ears to catch a word of what was taking place. And in Frenchy's nook two figures in the shadows leaned intently in his direction . . .

'You can't drag me into this, and you bloody well know it!' seethed Frenchy, with the aid of two other words. 'I never knew him – I didn't do nothing – I don't know nothing!'

Gently tapped his refractory pipe in the ashtray and drew on it tentatively.

'It's true!' she spat, 'why do you pick on me – who's been lying about me?'

'Who *might* lie about you?' inquired Gently absently.

'How should I know? – anyone! A girl's got enemies. And I've got a right to know, haven't I? If someone's been making accusations—!'

'Nobody has accused anybody . . . yet.'

'Then what's it all about?'

Gently shrugged and forked about in his pipe again. 'If you're so far in the clear you shouldn't be afraid to tell me what you were doing on Tuesday night . . .'

'It's got nothing to do with it – I can't tell you plainer than that, can I?'

'Of course, if it's something you'd rather not officially acknowledge . . .'

Again the scarlet nails flexed and a flicker went over

the brown eyes. But once more Frenchy controlled herself.

'I haven't got to tell you, flattie . . . you've got nothing on me!'

Gently nodded and turned out the fragments from his pipe. 'Between nine, say . . . and midnight . . .'

'All right, you bleeding copper!' Frenchy jumped to her feet and raised her voice to a scream. 'So he wants to know . . . he wants to know what I was doing on Tuesday night when someone was doing-in the bloke they found on the beach . . . I'm a naughty girl, and of course he picks on me!'

'That's right!' bawled the sporty-looking individual, sliding off his stool, 'you tell him, Frenchy, you tell him where to get off!'

'He doesn't know anything . . . he's just picking on me . . . maybe he's after something else too, the dirty so-and-so!'

'He wouldn't be the first, either!'

'And now he's looking for a chance to run me in . . . that's what it is . . .'

'Shame!' welled up from all over the bar.

'He comes from tarn just to pinch our Frenchy!' yapped the sporty-looking individual.

'They're a dirty lot . . . there isn't a man I'd call one amongst them . . . they're sent down here to find a murderer and all they can do is make trouble for girls like me.'

'It's all they're good for, chasing-up women!'

Gently looked up mildly from the refilling of his pipe. 'We don't seem to be getting very far with what you were doing on Tuesday night ...' he murmured.

Frenchy rocked on her heels, fuming at him. 'I'll *tell* you!' she screamed. 'I'll tell everybody, and they can bear me out. I was right here, that's where I was. I didn't shift an inch from this bar, and God help me!'

'It's the truth!' barked the sporty-looking individual, coming up, 'we saw her here, didn't we, boys?'

There was a unanimous chorus of assent.

'And after half past ten?' proceeded Gently.

'I was outside playing with the machines.'

'And after that?'

'Christ, can't a girl have any private life these days?'

'What was his name?' asked Gently amid laughter and jeering.

'Jeff!' shouted Frenchy, 'come and shake hands with a chief inspector.'

Gently glanced sharply at Frenchy's nook, where one of the two shadowy figures was getting reluctantly to his feet. He was a tall, well-made youth of sixteen or seventeen, not unhandsome of feature but with a weak, wide, thin-lipped mouth. He wore a Teddy boy ensemble of all one colour – plum red. It began with his bow tie and collar, descended through a straight-cut narrow-sleeved jacket and reached the ground via drain-pipe trousers and spats – a red of the ripest and fruitiest.

Gently eyed this vision curiously. It hovered uncertainly at some little distance.

'It was him?' inquired Gently, a shade of incredulity in his tone.

'Of course it was bloody well him . . . they all have to make a start, don't they?'

Gently beckoned to Jeff. 'Don't be frightened,' he said, 'it wasn't indictable . . .'

The Teddy boy came forward, flushing.

'Can you confirm what this woman says about Tuesday night?'

'I suppose so.'

'Would you care to describe it . . . I mean, the relevant parts?'

'There isn't anything to describe!' scowled Frenchy, 'he met me in the bar, that's all.'

Gently glanced at Jeff interrogatively.

'That's right . . . in the bar,' he said.

'And then?'

'And then we went to her . . . place.'

'Where is that?'

'It's a flat in Dulford Street.'

'And you spent the night?'

'I . . . actually . . . you see . . .'

'Of course he didn't!' Frenchy broke in, 'did you think I wanted his old man on my barrow? I turned him out at half past twelve . . . he'd done enough by then, anyway!'

There was a roar of laughter.

'And who is his old man?' inquired Gently smoothly.

'He's Wylie of Wylie-Marine.'

'You mean that big factory on the quays near the station . . .?'

'That's right, copper,' Frenchy sneered, 'you're good, aren't you?'

Gently drew a few slow puffs from his newly-filled pipe. Most of the occupants of the bar seemed to have drawn closer to a centre of such absorbing interest. But the second figure in Frenchy's nook wasn't joining in the general enthusiasm. On the contrary, he had shrunk back almost out of sight.

'And Bonce?' inquired Gently, inclining his head towards the nook.

'Bonce?' queried the Teddy boy. He had stuck his hands in his jacket pockets and seemed to be screwing himself up to an air of toughness.

'If you're Jeff, I take it that your shy friend is Bonce. What was he doing while you were getting off with Frenchy here?'

'Bonce!' shouted Frenchy, 'stop hiding yourself . . . the big noise is on to you too.'

All eyes turned towards the nook, where there was an uneasy stirring. Then there ventured forth a second version of the plum ensemble, shorter, clumsier and even more youthful looking than its predecessor. Bonce was no beauty. He had carroty hair, round cheeks, a snub nose and an inherent awkwardness. But he was sartorially correct. His outfit matched Jeff's down to the tie of the shoes.

'And what's *your* name when you're at home?' queried Gently.

Bonce licked his lips and stared agonizedly. 'B-Baines, sir,' he brought out, 'Robert B-Baines.' He spoke with a Starmouth accent.

'And where do you live?'

'S-seventeen Kittle Witches Grid, sir.'

'Well, Baines, you've heard the account of Tuesday night your friend has given . . . I take it that you can endorse it?'

'Oh yes, sir!'

'You came here with him, in fact?'

'Yes, sir!'

'And you were with him until he departed with this woman here?'

'Yes, sir!'

'All the time?'

'Yes, sir!'

'Even when he was ingratiating himself with her?'

Bonce stared at him round-eyed.

'When he was getting off, I mean?'

'Oh yes, sir! . . . I mean . . . no, sir . . .'

'Well . . . which is it to be?'

'I . . . I . . .!' stuttered Bonce, completely floored.

'And when they had gone,' pursued Gently affably, 'what did you do then . . . when you were left on your own?'

'Don't you tell him!' screamed Frenchy before Bonce could flounder into a reply, 'it's all a have — you don't need to tell him nothing.'

'No, we haven't done anything,' blurted Jeff, trying to swagger, 'you keep quiet, Bonce.'

'He just comes in here trying to stir something up, trying to get people to say something he can pinch them for . . . that's how they work, the bleedin' Yard! I—!'

'CLOSING TIME!!!' roared a stentorian voice, a voice which drowned Frenchy, drowned the jazz and rattled empty glasses on some of the tables.

43

Every head spun round as though jerked by a string. It was as though a bomb had exploded over by the counter.

'FINISH YOUR DRINKS!!!' continued the voice, 'IT'S HALF PAST TEN!!!'

Gently peered round Frenchy's shapely form, which was hiding the owner of the voice from his view.

'DRINK UP, LADIES AND GENTS. YOU WOULDN'T WANT ME TO LOSE MY LICENCE!!!'

He was an enormous man, not so much in height, though he topped six feet, but enormous in sheer, Herculean bulk. His head was bald and seemed to rise to a point. His features were coarse and heavy, but powerful. There was a fleck in the pupil of one of his grey eyes and he had, clearly visible because of the sag of his lip, a gold tooth of proportions to match the rest of his person.

'BREAK IT UP NOW, LADIES AND GENTS. YOU CAN STILL AMUSE YOURSELVES WITH THE MACHINES!!!'

About fifty, thought Gently, and still in good fighting trim.

The owner of the voice moved ponderously across to Gently's table. He glowered at Frenchy and nodded towards the door.

'Get out!' he rumbled, 'you know I don't encourage your sort.'

Frenchy glared back defiantly for a moment, but she waggled off all the same; her parting shot was at Gently, not the gold-toothed one. It was unprintable.

'GET OUT!!!' detonated the big man, and Frenchy got.

His next target was Bonce.

'*How* old do you say you are?'

'Eight–eighteen!' burbled Bonce.

'When was that – next Easter? Don't let me find you in this bar again.'

'B–But Louey, you never said anything before!'

'GET OUT!!!'

Bonce faded like a cock-crowed ghost.

Louey sighed draughtily. He picked up Gently's empty orange-squash glass and gave it his sad attention. Gently looked also. The hands that held the glass were like two hairy grappling-irons. On one of his crooked fingers Louey wore an out-size solitaire, on another a plain gold ring engraved with a bisected circle.

' 'Night, Louey,' leered the sporty-looking individual, passing by on his way to the door, 'watch your company – it ain't so healthy as it might be!'

Louey rumbled ominously and set down the glass again. 'Can't help it,' he said, turning apologetically to Gently, 'this time of the year you're bound to get some riff-raff . . . the best you can do is to keep kicking it out.'

Gently nodded sympathetically. He found Louey's gold tooth fascinating.

'There's girls like Frenchy . . . we know some of them, but there's fresh ones come up every summer. If they don't solicit you can't make too much of a fuss.'

Louey permitted himself a searching glance at Gently.

'And those kids . . . I suppose it's asking for trouble to have an arcade next to a bar.'

Gently rose to his feet and felt in his pocket for a coin.

'Here,' he said, 'I haven't paid for my drink.'

'Oh, never mind that!' Louey laughed comfortably,

easily, as though he felt Gently to be an equal. 'Only too pleased to see you in here, Inspector . . . sorry if anything happened that shouldn't have done . . .'

'You needn't worry about that – it was nothing to do with you.' Gently paused and looked into Louey's deep-set eyes. They wore a deferential smile, but because of the fleck breaking into one of them the smile had a strangely hard quality, almost a sinisterness.

'There's only one thing bothers me,' mused Gently, picking up his shilling and re-pocketing it.

'And what is that, Inspector?'

'The way everyone around here knows me on sight . . . you, Mr Hooker, amongst the others.'

There was a rowdiness now along the promenade. There were drunks and near-drunks, quarrelsome and loutish roisterers. Alcohol had been added to the heady mixture of humanity about its annual purgation . . . the beer had begun to sing, and the whisky to argue. And they were largely youngsters, Gently noticed, it was the teenagers who did the shouting and singing. Banded together in threes and fours they swaggered about the Front, stupid with Dutch courage: lords of a pint, princelings of Red Biddy. Did nobody spank their children these days?

A burly figure shouldered across the carriage-way and joined him on the pavement.

'Have any luck, Dutt?' inquired Gently with interest.

'Yes, sir, I did, as a matter of fact.'

'Well, go on . . . don't spoil a good story.'

'I stood where you told me, sir, and kept an eye on the bookie's joint at the back. There wasn't no lights on there, but about quarter of an hour after you went in again the door opens and out hops a bloke in a dark suit.'

'Oh, he did, did he? I suppose he wasn't a freakish-looking cove with a parroty face?'

'No, sir, not this one. I got a good look at him under a street-lamp. He was about middling-size, dark hair, sort of slanty-eyed, and he'd got a long, straight conk. And there was a scar of some sort on his right cheek – knife or razor, I should say, sir.'

'Hmm,' mused Gently, 'interesting. And did you tail him?'

'Yes, sir – at least, I stuck to him all along the prom going south. But then he goes into the funfair and there was such a ruddy crowd there I didn't stand a chance. So after a bit I gives it up.'

'Ah well . . . we do our best,' sighed Gently.

'Do you think there's a hook-up there, sir – have we got something definite?'

Gently shook his head sombrely. 'I don't know, Dutt, and that's the truth. There's some racket goes on there, I'm pretty sure, but whether it connects with ours is beyond me for the moment. Anyway, I threw a scare into them . . . I'll tip off Copping to keep an eye lifting.'

'The bloke I was tailing looked a right sort,' said Dutt sagely.

'There's a lot of right sorts in there, Dutt,' agreed his senior, 'they'd keep the average policeman happy for weeks.'

CHAPTER FOUR

G ENTLY WAS DREAMING what seemed to be a circular dream. It began at the stab wounds in the man who wouldn't wake up, took in all the principal characters at 'The Feathers' and wound up again with that stabbed torso. And it continued like that for round after round. Or was it all going on simultaneously? His dream-self found time to wonder this. There seemed to be two of him in the dream: he was both actor and producer. First (if there was a first), came the chest of the corpse, caught in a sort of golden glow, and he noticed with surprise that, although the stab-wounds were present, the pathologist's carvings were not. Next, his dream-camera lifted to take in Jeff, or rather the top part of Jeff: the rest of him dissolved into the haze which surrounded the corpse. He was shrugging his shoulders and saying something. Gently didn't know what it was he was saying, but he was acutely aware of the implication. Jeff *wasn't* responsible. He might have done it, of course, that was beside the point. But he wasn't responsible. You couldn't possibly blame him.

As though to make it more emphatic the camera shifted to Bonce, who was blubbing and stuttering his innocence in the background. They couldn't help it. Gently fully agreed. They had done it at the behest of some irrevocable Fate, which was curious but in no way blameable. It was just how things were . . . And then Bonce shrank and his blubbing mouth disappeared. He had become Nits, and Nits had become nothing but two protruding green eyes, painfully straining. Gently knew what *he* was saying. The halfwit's words piped clearly in his brain. 'I've been *a good* boy,' they echoed, 'I've been *a good* boy,' and Gently tried to ruffle his hair good-naturedly, but the head sank away under his hand . . .

Then it was Frenchy's rather knobbly knees trying hard to make themselves look attractive: the camera wouldn't lift to her face, it just kept focussed on those unfortunate knees. We aren't bad, they seemed to be pleading (and Gently heard a twang of Frenchy's croon, though there weren't any words): you'll see a lot worse than us on the beach. Of course, you've got to make allowances, but it's the same with everyone . . . honestly now, we aren't bad at all . . . you must admit it. And Gently admitted it. What was the use of struggling? He'd been round before and knew the rules of the game . . .

So the camera faded across to the parrot-faced man and Artie. They'd got a lot of empty bottles, squash-bottles, and Gently only had to see the bottles to know that he was the one who had emptied them. Not that they were being nasty about it, those two. On the contrary, they seemed to be almost sympathetic, in a sad sort of way. Gently had blotted his copy-book. He'd drunk through all those bottles of squash without paying for them. They knew he couldn't help it, but all the same . . . a man of his reputation . . . Gently felt in his pocket for some money. They shook their heads. It wasn't just paying for it that counted. It was the fact that he'd *done* it at all . . .

And now Louey's gold tooth filled all the screen, a huge, glowing tooth with (and it seemed so natural that Gently realized he was expecting it) a glittering solitaire diamond set in the top and a bisected circle engraved underneath it. It doesn't matter, the tooth was saying, the inspector can do what he likes, he's always welcome. It's not the same with the inspector, he's an old friend of mine. Yes, he can do what he likes . . . he can do what he likes . . . it's not the same with the inspector . . . And then the glowing tooth became the glowing chest of the corpse again, and the dream was off anew. Or was it, after all? Wasn't it really simultaneous, flashing on and off like the arrow outside the arcade . . .?

Either way, the dreaming Gently perceived at last a change coming o'er the spirit of his dream. There was a word that kept getting interjected into the mechanism, and for some reason or none he didn't want to hear that word, he kept struggling not to hear it. But he did hear it. It persisted. It paid no attention either to himself or his characters, who were showing similar disapproval.

'Raouls! Otraouls!'

It was making Frenchy's knees jiffle and the empty bottles fall off the counter.

'Raouls! Raouls!'

Gently held Frenchy's knees still with one hand and

tried to pick up bottles with the other, but he didn't seem to be getting anywhere.

'Raouls! Otraouls! Raouls!'

He made a final effort to shore-up his collapsing world, to ward off that frightful trump of doom. It was no use. Frenchy kicked the bottles from under his arm. There was a crash of glass which he knew to be the descent of every bottle in the bar and he was dragged back out of the dark or red-lit tunnel in the nick of time . . .

'Raouls! Otraouls!'

Gently snorted and rubbed his eyes. There really *was* a sound like that. It was coming through his bedroom window, and getting louder every minute. He jumped out of bed and went to have a look. And then he remembered . . . over how many years? It was the boy with the hot rolls, that wandering voice of the morning . . . his very accent had been handed down intact.

Gently hammered on the communicating door. 'Dutt! Aren't you up?'

'Yessir. Been hup half an hour.'

'Half an hour!' Gently glanced at the watch propped up on his dressing-table. 'You're late, Dutt. You should have been up before.'

'Yessir.'

'We aren't on holiday, Dutt, when we're out in the country.'

'No, sir.'

'Discipline,' said Gently, shoving his feet into his bedroom slippers, 'that's the key to success, Dutt. Discipline and luck, but mostly discipline. Is Mrs Davis providing hot rolls for breakfast?'

'Well, sir, I really don't know . . .'

'Then find out, Dutt, find out, and if she isn't go down and buy half a dozen off that expert out there.'

Twenty minutes later a shining morning Gently put in his appearance at the breakfast table. The papers he had ordered lay fragrant on his plate and he turned them over as he stowed butter into his first roll. The case was still making front-page in the local. They had found a bigger and better photograph, one of which Gently was just a little proud. And they were up-to-date on his visit to the mortuary, and especially up-to-date on his calling out of the pathologist.

PATHOLOGIST RECALLED IN BODY–ON–THE–BEACH CASE, ran the local. GENTLY MOVES – PATHOLOGIST RECALLED – SENSATIONAL MIDNIGHT DEVELOPMENT, ran a London paper.

Gently shoved them across to Dutt. 'Nice press,' he said laconically.

'We'll have 'em round our necks today,' grumbled the sergeant.

Gently clipped the top off a boiled egg and took another bite from his roll. 'They make it seem so exciting,' he mumbled, 'as though we were shifting heaven and earth. I wonder what people would think if they knew how simple it all was?'

They were still finishing breakfast when Inspector Copping was ushered in. He bore an envelope in his hand and an almost reverential expression on his face.

'You were right!' he exclaimed, 'my God – and how! There wasn't only traces of gum on the face, there was crêpe hair too, and quite a bit of it considering. The

52

super's blown up the pathy for not finding it the first time and the pathy's as sniffy as hell.'

'Wasn't his fault,' grunted Gently stickily, 'his job is finding out how they died . . .'

He wiped his hands on his serviette and thumbed open Copping's envelope. It contained the pathologist's report. He glanced over it.

'Must have been a full beard,' he mused, 'I'm glad he found some of the hair . . . it might have been a different colour.'

'You were even right about it not being spirit gum. He's going to do a thorough analysis when he's had some shut-eye.'

Gently shrugged. 'Don't wake him up specially. Have you got any artists down at headquarters?'

'Artists?' Copping stared.

'Somebody who can put a beard on some photographs.'

'Oh – *that!* Our camera bloke can do it for you.'

'Then I'll want some copies of the Missing Persons' list and anybody you can spare to help Dutt go the rounds.'

'I'll have them laid on. But' – Copping looked doubtfully at the marmalade Gently was lavishing on his toast – 'what makes you so positive he came from the town?'

'I'm not,' grunted Gently, poising the piece of toast, 'it just seems to fit the picture, that's all.'

'What picture?' queried Copping.

'Mine,' retorted Gently, and he bit largely and well into the marmalady toast.

★ ★ ★

The super seemed a little off-hand that morning. He didn't seem as pleased as he ought to be with the progress being made. He congratulated Gently briefly on his discovery of the beard and asked some terse questions about what he proposed to do. Gently told him.

'You can have a couple of men,' said the super.

'There's something else ... I mentioned it to Copping.'

'If it means more men, Gently, I'm afraid I can't spare them just now.'

'No hurry,' murmured Gently, 'I daresay it will keep. But it might be worth keeping an eye on the amusement arcade called "The Feathers".'

The super frowned. 'Well?' he snapped.

'I don't know quite what ... vice, perhaps, for a start.'

'In that case it will have to wait. Vice is too common during the season in towns like this.'

'Could be something else ... I thought it was worthwhile mentioning it.'

'I'll make a note of it, Gently. Is there anything else you want?'

'Not just at the moment.'

'Then I won't take up any more of your time.'

Outside the super's office Gently shook his head. 'Of course,' he said to Copping, 'I don't expect gratitude ...'

'Oh, don't let the Old Man worry you,' returned Copping. 'He's got something else on his plate now, as well as homicide.'

'It must be fascinating, whatever it is.'

'It's forgery – a faked hundred-dollar bill. The super's panicking in case he has to run to the Central Office again. He's trying like mad to trace it to some American Forces personnel.'

Gently clicked his tongue. 'Why should American Forces personnel forge hundred-dollar bills to work off in Starmouth?'

'Search me – but if the super can get back to one of them he's in the clear.'

'Of course, I appreciate his point.'

Copping led the way to the photographer's shop, where Sergeant Dutt was watching the technician apply the final beard to half a dozen postcard prints. He had made two sets, profile and full-face, and the difference between the face bearded and the face unbearded was certainly striking.

Copping whistled when he saw them. 'No wonder we drew a blank the first time round . . . why do you think he dolled himself up that way?'

Gently shrugged. 'The usual reason – he didn't want somebody to recognize him.'

'But that's fantastic when you come to think of it. Nobody does that sort of thing outside spy thrillers.'

'Could be a spy thriller we're working on,' suggested Gently, dead-panned.

'Could be,' agreed Copping seriously.

It was a Saturday, a day of coming and going. As Gently plodded down Duke Street, which led from the dock side of the town to the Front, he was obliged to thread his way through a stream of parties and individuals lugging bags and suitcases, all of them in a hurry, all of them going one way. He surveyed them lugubriously. They were all good potential witnesses – any one of them might hold the clue he wanted, the unsuspected information. And now they were departing in their hundreds and thousands. They were splitting up and scattering to the four quarters of the Midlands.

On the Front it was the same. The beach had a patchy and unsettled look. Up and down the promenade chased laden cars, taxis and coaches, while the touts stood about in disconsolate groups, their function in abeyance. Everything had stopped. For a few hours the Pleasure Machine stood still. There were those who stayed on, but nobody paid them much attention: they were only there on sufferance, it seemed, until a new lot arrived and the machine began to turn again.

Gently crossed over by the Albion Pier and leaned on the balustrade overlooking the beach. In his breast pocket he could feel the stiff pasteboard of the two doctored photographs, and in the distance he could see the post set up by the Borough Police. If Nits knew him when he was alive, thought Gently, it was at least an even chance he met him here, on the Front . . . and if he met him on the Front it was ten to one he met him on this stretch, between the two piers. Because that was where 'his' part was, and beachcombers were jealous of their territories.

What next . . . where was the best prospect after that?

Did he drink, this false-bearded fugitive? Did he play bowls, or tennis, or eat a sandwich at one of the tea-shacks that prospered along the golden mile? Or buy himself a straw hat or sunglasses? Or an ice-cream?

Sunglasses, mused Gently, rummaging in his pocket for a peppermint cream – he'd want some sunglasses if he were playing hard-to-find. At least, he would if he hadn't bought them earlier, about the same time as he was buying crepe hair and adhesives. But it was no use making difficulties. There was a beach-gear stall only a dozen yards away. Gently swallowed the peppermint cream and presented himself at the counter.

'Police,' he said tonelessly, 'can you remember having seen this man during the last week or ten days?'

By lunchtime he'd got the usual mixed bag of possibles and improbables. There were people who thought they had, and those who weren't quite sure: there were numbers who were determined to recognize nothing shown them by a policeman. One gentleman, indeed, was completely positive. The deceased had been to his stall two days running – he'd bought some sun-tan lotion and a pair of frog-man flippers. 'When was that?' asked Gently eagerly. 'Yesterday and the day before,' responded the helpful one . . .

It was a dispiriting business. He'd been through it before many a time, and with similar results. But here and today it seemed particularly dejecting, as though the whole prospects of the case were tied up with his good or ill success that morning . . .

They weren't, of course. He was only probing a little of the surface. Elsewhere Dutt and his colleagues were at work on the lines of strongest probability. He glanced at his wristwatch and made for a phone-box. By now they ought to have made some progress.

He dialled, and got the switchboard girl.

'Chief Inspector Gently. Give me the desk.'

She gave him the desk and the duty sergeant answered slickly.

'Gently here . . . has Sergeant Dutt reported back yet?'

There was a buzz and a faraway question and answer.

'No, sir,' returned the duty sergeant, 'Bryce and Williams have come in – they're in the canteen having their lunch. I don't think they had much luck, sir. Shall I get them to speak to you?'

'No . . . don't bother them.' Gently made a rapid survey of the terrain without. 'When Dutt comes in get him to phone me at the Beachside Cafe . . . you got that?'

'The Beachside Cafe . . . what is the number, sir?'

'Find out,' retorted Gently peevishly, 'I'm a policeman, not the local directory.'

He hung up frowning and shouldered his way out of the box. So Bryce and Williams had drawn a blank also. Like himself. Like Dutt, probably. And there couldn't be so many chances left on that list . . .

He directed his steps to the Beachside Cafe. It was one of the smaller of the cafes on that part of the Front, a green-painted wooden structure with a sort of veranda that faced the sea. Gently sat himself at one of the veranda tables and ordered a *table d'hôte* lunch. Three out of the four of them had drawn a blank . . . three out of four. Was it going to fold up on him, that little streak of luck – his 'dramatic midnight move', as the paper called it? But he'd been right . . . the man *had* been wearing a false beard. And Nits had known about it, so the man must have been in Starmouth . . .

'Your soup, sir,' said the waiter at his elbow. Gently grunted and made room for the plate.

'Excuse me, sir, but aren't you Chief Inspector Gently?' faltered the waiter, hovering at a respectful distance.

Gently eyed him without enthusiasm. 'I might be,' he said.

'I recognized you from your picture in the paper, sir.'

'You're good at it,' said Gently, 'my mother wouldn't have done.'

'Naturally we're interested, sir, it all happening so close . . .'

Gently sighed and gave the waiter the benefit of a prolonged stare. 'You wouldn't like to be helpful, I suppose?' he asked.

'Of course, sir . . .' The waiter sounded as though he were conscious of being about to buy something.

'Really helpful?'

'If there's anything I can do . . .'

Gently produced his two doctored prints and shoved them under the waiter's nose. 'What did he have for lunch last time he was here, or don't you remember?'

The waiter gulped like a guilty schoolboy. 'Dover sole and chips, sir, and fruit salad to follow.'

'He had *what*—!'

'Dover sole and chips, sir. I remember because it was on the Tuesday, which is the only day we have it.'

★ ★ ★

There was a razor-edged pause while Gently clutched at his chair to prevent it revolving quite so fast. The waiter flinched and edged back a pace.

'Now let's be calm about this,' said Gently sternly, 'it was Dover sole *and* chips – not just Dover sole?'

'No, sir . . . it was always chips. He was very fond of them.'

'You mean he'd been here *before*?'

'Of course, sir. He came here regular.'

'*Regular!* How long does it take someone to become a regular?'

The waiter looked worried. 'I think it was Thursday last week . . . might have been Wednesday. Anyway, he came every day after that, including Sunday . . . he sat at this table, sir. I thought perhaps you knew him.'

Gently laughed with a certain amount of hollowness. 'I do,' he said, 'in a manner of speaking. But I've still a lot to learn. What's your name?'

'Withers, sir.'

'Well, take that other chair, Withers.'

'Y-yes, sir.'

'Don't be nervous – I'll square you with your boss. And you can fetch in the roast beef when I'm ready for it – even Central Office men have to eat.'

'Yes, sir. Of course, sir!'

Withers pulled out the chair and lowered himself dubiously on to the edge of it. He had the unhappy air of someone who had bitten off more than he could chew. Gently crumbled some roll into his Brown Windsor and tested a mouthful. It seemed up to a fairish standard in provincial Brown Windsors.

'So he came here first on Thursday, Withers. Or it might have been Wednesday.'

'That's right, sir.'

'You haven't any preference.'

'N-no, sir . . . I just don't remember.'

Gently nodded intelligently and tried another spoonful of soup. 'Did he have any name that chanced to leak out?'

'He said to call him Max, sir.'

'Max, eh?' Gently rolled the word round his tongue. Now he'd even got a name for the fellow! 'Max anything or just Max?' he asked hopefully.

'Just Max, sir.'

Gently sighed. 'I felt it had to be. He had an accent, though, this Max?'

'Oh yes, sir.'

'What sort of an accent . . . did you recognize it?'

The waiter stirred tormentedly. 'Foreign, I'd say, sir.'

'Was it French, for instance?'

'Yes, sir, it might have been.'

'Or German?'

'No, I don't think so, sir.'

'Russian, maybe?'

'I wouldn't like to say it wasn't, sir.'

'You couldn't imitate something he said?'

The waiter shook his head and sent a haunted look towards the rear of the cafe. Gently shook his head also and reapplied himself to his soup. But why should he complain, he asked himself, why look such a regal gift-horse in the mouth? Ten minutes ago he had begun to despair and now he actually knew the dead man's name . . .!

'Describe it,' he said, 'describe Max coming in here and having lunch.'

'H–how do you mean, sir?' faltered the waiter.

'Tell me, man! Tell it as though he were just coming in at the door.'

The waiter twisted his hands together agonizedly and cleared his throat. 'H–he'd come in . . .' he began, 'he'd stand for a moment looking about . . . as though he expected to see somebody he knew . . .'

'Did he ever see that somebody?'

'No, I d–don't think so, sir.'

'What was he wearing?'

'He'd got a light grey suit, sir. On Sunday he wore a darker one, but the other days it was the light grey. And he had a blue bow tie.'

'Go on.'

'He carried an attaché case, sir, he had it with him every day except the last day . . . then there was his beard, that struck me as being funny . . . and the way he spoke . . .'

'What did he say?'

'When he first came in he asked me my name, sir. Then he sort of laughed and told me to call him Max.'

'Was there any reason for that?'

'It was because I called him "sir," sir. He said they didn't call people "sir" where he came from, and then he laughed again and patted me on the arm.'

'He was a friendly type, was he?'

'Oh yes, sir, quite a gent.'

'So he patted you on the arm. What happened then?'

'He ordered the chicken, sir, and sent me out for a bottle of wine . . . we aren't on the licence here, sir.'

'And what day were you serving chicken last week?'

'Wednesday, sir.'

'Ah!' said Gently with satisfaction. He laid down his spoon. 'We'll pause for a moment on that happy note . . . just pop along and see what the roast beef is doing.'

'Certainly, sir!'

'And fetch me a lager, Withers. The occasion seems to justify it.'

The waiter slipped from the chair and resumed his function with obvious relief. Gently smiled distantly at a paddling child. Another time Withers wouldn't be quite so forward in accosting chief inspectors who got their pictures in the papers . . .

And the name was Max. Max, in a light grey suit with a blue bow tie. Max, who came from somewhere where they didn't 'sir' people. Max, who was friendly. Max, who was quite a gent. Max, who had sat at that same table from Wednesday till Tuesday, eating his chicken, his Dover sole and chips, and drinking the wine Withers brought him from over the road . . . and Max, who had finished up as Exhibit A on the mortuary slab exactly a week after his first appearance. He was getting into focus, that one. Gently was beginning to see him, to fit him in. And over all there was his foreign-ness, pervasive and misty, his Franco-German-Russo-what-have-you foreign-ness . . .

Withers returned with Gently's roast beef and the lager. He seemed to have been gone a good deal longer than was strictly necessary, even allowing for the trip across the road. Gently raised his eyebrows to the unhappy man.

'Talked it over with the boss, Withers?' he inquired affably.

'I–I beg your pardon, sir!' stammered Withers, spilling some lager.

'Never mind, Withers . . . and don't be well-bred about the vegetables.'

The waiter served, and Gently picked up his knife and fork. It was odd, but he hadn't been feeling hungry when he came into the cafe . . .

'Sit down,' he mumbled to Withers, 'you'll give me indigestion, jiffling about like that.'

'I b–beg your pardon, sir, but really I ought to be getting on with my work . . . there isn't n-nothing I haven't told you, honest . . .'

Gently beamed at him over a mouthful of lager. 'Nonsense, Withers, we've only just begun . . .'

'It's making extra work for the others, sir,' persisted Withers, encouraged by the beam.

'Sit down!' retorted Gently with a slight touch of Bogartesque.

Withers sat down at great speed.

'. . . Now,' continued Gently, after a certain amount of plate-work, 'we got to him ordering the chicken and sending out for some wine. What sort of wine did he send for?'

'Just red wine, sir. I got him a brand they specialize in over the road.'

'I don't doubt it for a moment. Did he express his satisfaction?'

'N–no sir, not really.'

'Did he order the same wine the next day?'

'He asked if they hadn't got another brand . . . I couldn't understand the name he gave it.'

'What did it sound like?'

'It just sounded foreign, sir . . .'

'Like what sort of foreign?'

'I d–don't know . . . just gibberish.'

'Did you ask if they'd got it?'

'No, sir. I couldn't say the name.'

'So what did he have?'

'I got him Burgundy, sir, when he wanted a red, and Sauternes when he wanted a white.'

'And that was satisfactory?'

'He seemed a bit surprised at the price, sir.'

'He was a foreigner, Withers.'

'Yes, sir, I dare say that had something to do with it.'

Gently brooded a moment over a roast potato. Then he halved it meticulously and transported one half, suitably garnished with gravy, to a meditative mouth. 'What did he have for sweet, Withers?' he asked through the potato.

'Ice-cream, sir.'

'Not much to be deduced from that . . . was his coffee black?'

'Yes, sir.'

'Did he smoke . . .? Cigarettes . . .?'

'He bought a box, sir.'

'A box, Withers?'

'Twenty-five Sobranie, sir.'

Gently raised an eyebrow. 'And what particular variety?'

'Just Balkan Sobranie, sir. He bought a box every day after that . . .'

'He seems to have been a well-heeled foreigner, Withers.'

'Yes, sir. He never tipped less than half a crown.'

Gently finished his roast beef and motioned to have his plate removed. Withers took it adroitly and produced a cold sweet from a side-table. It was a trifle, a robustly constructed affair involving sliced pineapple, and Gently inserted a spoon in it with unabated gusto.

'Of course, he asked a few questions,' volunteered Withers, beginning to feel that Gently wasn't so bad after all. 'He wanted to know if we got many foreigners in Starmouth.'

'Mmph?' grunted Gently, 'what did you tell him?'

'I told him we scarcely saw one – not a right foreigner . . . just midlanders and such-like.'

'Yanks,' mumbled Gently.

'Well there . . . we don't count them.'

'Was he happy about the situation?'

'It didn't seem to worry him, sir. He said we might have him around for a bit . . . and later on, of course, he picked up with a woman . . .'

Gently made a choking noise over a segment of pineapple. 'What was that, Withers . . .!'

'He picked up with a fern, sir. Brought her in to lunch here on the Tuesday.'

Gently got rid of the pineapple with a struggle. 'So he did . . . did he! Just like that! Why the flaming hell didn't you say so sooner?'

66

'You never asked me, sir!' exclaimed Withers, surprised and apprehensive, 'it wasn't nobody really, sir . . . just one of the girls you get around here during the season . . .'

'Just one of the girls!' Gently gazed at the wilting waiter. Then he took himself firmly in hand and counted ten before firing the next question. 'You know her name? It wouldn't be Yvette, by any chance?'

'No, sir! I don't know her name! I've never had nothing to do with women of that class . . .'

'She's the little dark one with long slinky hair.'

'But this one's a blonde, sir – quite well set-up. And her hair is short.'

'Nice legs – smooth, rounded knees.'

'I d–didn't notice, sir . . .'

'Don't lie at this stage, Withers!'

'I thought they were bony, sir – I did, honest I did!'

'She speaks with an educated accent.'

'Not this one, sir – she's terribly common!'

'You'd recognize her again?'

'Of course, sir. Anywhere!'

A telephone began pealing at the counter inside the cafe and Gently relaxed his hypnotic attention from the freshly-shattered Withers. 'Go and take it,' he purred, 'it's probably for me.'

Withers departed like greased lightning. He was back inside seven seconds.

'A S–sergeant Dutt, sir, asking for you . . .'

Gently made the phone in even better time than Withers.

'Gently . . .!' he rapped, 'what's new with you, Dutt?'

'We've placed him, sir!' echoed Dutt's voice excitedly, 'he was missing from a lodging in Blantyre Road –
disappeared on Tuesday evening and nothing heard
since. The woman who let the room identified him
straight away. His name was Max something – she didn't
know what.'

A faraway look came into Gently's eyes. It was
directed at the ceiling, but in reality it plumbed sidereal
space and lodged betwixt two spiral nebulae.

'Get a car, Dutt,' he said, 'come straight down here
and pick me up . . .'

'Yessir!' rattled Dutt, 'I'll be with you in ten minutes.'

'Ten minutes,' mused Gently, 'that'll just give me
time to drink my coffee . . . won't it, Withers?'

CHAPTER FIVE

B LANTYRE ROAD WAS a shabby-genteel thoroughfare which began at the top of Duke Street and
meandered vaguely in a diagonal direction until it joined
the Front a good way south, where hotels had already
begun to thin out. It was at its best at the top end. Just
there it skirted a small park or garden, and the houses
which faced it, Edwardian Rococo, had a wistful air of
having known better times and more civilized people.

Outside one of these a crowd had collected. It spread
along the pavement in both directions and was a model
of quietness and patient expectancy. On the steps behind
them the careful Copping had stationed a uniform-man,
but his authority was somewhat vitiated by the presence
of three gentlemen with cameras supported by four
gentlemen without cameras – a contingent possessed of
far more glamour than a mere police constable.

'Blimey!' exclaimed Dutt, as he, Gently and Copping
came dramatically on the scene in the back of a police
Wolseley, 'there wasn't a soul about here half an hour
ago.'

'That woman must have blabbed,' snapped Copping, 'I sent Jennings down to try and stop it . . . blast her tattling tongue!'

'Of course, she's got a perfect right to . . .' murmured Gently.

The Wolseley made a three-point landing opposite the door and the police constable marched down to give them his official greeting.

'Sorry about this here, sir,' he apologized to Copping, 'that was all done before I arrived . . .'

'Never mind – never mind!' barked Copping, 'just keep those wolves there out of the house, that's all.'

He strode up the steps, an impressive figure. Gently followed with Dutt at a more sedate pace. The flash-bulbs popped and the crowd rippled.

'How about a statement!' demanded a reporter, pushing up, notebook at the ready.

'Nothing about a statement!' boomed Copping, 'if you want a statement, come to headquarters for it.'

'A statement from you, then,' said the reporter, turning to Gently.

Gently shrugged and shook his head. 'Did you get one from Mrs Watts?' he inquired.

'We were actually getting one when the constable interfered . . .!'

'Then you probably know more than I do just at the moment . . .'

He pushed past and up the steps.

The interior of the house was as pleasingly period as the outside. Inside the front door was a long, narrow, but lofty hall, a good deal of it occupied by a disproportionately wide staircase. At the far end another door led into the back garden, a door equipped with panes of red and blue glass. There was a certain amount of upheaval apparent, quite incidental to the main theme – it was a lodging-house Saturday, one set of guests departed, the other not yet arrived. At the foot of the stairs lay a bundle of dirty sheets, in the dining-room, its door ajar, a heap of tablecloths and napkins . . . *Entr'acte,* thought Gently. The phrase epitomized Starmouth on a Saturday.

Copping had marched ahead into Mrs Watt's private parlour, from whence could be heard issuing the landlady's strident and aggressive tones.

'I don't know why you're making all this fuss *now,* I'm sure . . . I told the man who called round here on *Wednesday* . . . well, is it my fault if you didn't know about the beard?'

'There must be some mistake, mam,' came the discomfited voice of Copping, 'I'm sure O'Reilly . . .'

'Mistake, Inspector! I should just say there was a mistake. My daughter Deanna and my husband Ted both backed me up about it . . . "Beard or no beard," I says, "the man on that photograph is our number seven" . . . and that was on *Wednesday,* Inspector, yet you come worrying me today of all days, a Saturday, and Race Week – it's too bad, it is really! If it's not making me all behind with my work, it's what my people are going to think with all that lot gawping outside . . .'

Dutt gave Gently a knowing wink. 'Aye, aye! I was waiting for him to run into that lot.'

'Somebody's boobed, Dutt.'

'Yessir . . . and it isn't you and me.'

Gently pushed in at the parlour door. It was a small but expensive room. The gilt-edge of Mrs Watts's season expended itself on radiograms, television sets, slow-burning stoves, carpets and furniture notable for its areas of glossy veneer. The available floor-space was a trifle restricted by these evidences of wealth. It occurred, where it occurred in small islands of gold mohair. On the largest of these, which adjoined the multi-tile hearth, Mrs Watts was conducting her attack, while a red-faced Copping had got himself wedged into a triangle between a radiogram and a television set.

'What do you send them round for?' continued the stalwart matron, snaking a glance at the new intruder *en passant*. 'What's the idea of wasting our time asking questions when you aren't going to believe us anyway? Is that how you run the police in Starmouth? Is that why they keep putting the rates up?'

'I assure you, mam, if you'll let me explain . . .'

'Oh, I don't doubt, you'll be a wonderful one for explaining. And I dare say your explaining will get the work done by the time my people start coming in. If you ask *me*, Mr Inspector, we need someone in Starmouth who can teach you your job . . . that body on the beach was a show-up for you, wasn't it just . . .?'

'Ahem!' coughed Gently, appropriating some mohair behind the door.

Mrs Watts shook her platinum locks and presented a square chin at him. 'And who's this?' she demanded of

Copping, 'how many more have you brought down here to waste my time?'

'This is Chief Inspector Gently, mam!' explained the squirming Copping, 'he's in charge of the case . . . he wants to ask you a few questions.'

There was a pause while Mrs Watts digested this information. Then her expression underwent a change, passing from steely aggressiveness to steely affability. 'Well!' she said more placably, 'well! And aren't you the gentleman they've sent from Scotland Yard to clear up this body-on-the-beach business?'

Gently nodded gravely.

'The same Chief Inspector Gently that did that case at Norchester?'

'The same, Madam.'

'Well!' repeated Mrs Watts, 'of course, if I'd known that . . .' She favoured Gently with a smile in which steeliness was still the principal ingredient. 'Do please sit down, Inspector . . . I shall be pleased to be of any assistance. Deanna!' – her voice rose to a shout – 'Deanna, leave what you're doing and make a pot of tea, do you hear?'

There was a faint acknowledgement from without and Mrs Watts, satisfied, ushered Gently to the room's most dramatic and veneer-lavish chair. He contrived to avoid it, however, and it was Copping who became the victim . . .

'Now,' pursued Mrs Watts, 'I'd like you to know, Inspector—'

'Just a minute,' interrupted Gently, 'has the room been interfered with?'

'The *room*, Inspector . . .?'

'Number seven – the room from which this man disappeared?'

Mrs Watts looked doubtful. 'I don't know what you mean, interfered with. I've changed the sheets and pillow-cases, and Ida (that's the maid) has polished and hoovered, but that's all . . . there's nothing been moved about.'

Gently sighed softly to himself. 'Well . . . we'll look in there later, if you don't mind. Now about the man himself. . .'

'I recognized him directly, Inspector. There was never any doubt.'

'You recognized him without the painted-in beard?'

'As soon as I clapped eyes on the photograph . . . "Yes," I says to the man, "that's our number seven. Only he's got a beard," I says, "a lot of it – all over his face."'

'And that was on Wednesday, the day after your lodger was missing?'

'That's right – Wednesday evening. Naturally, I didn't pay too much attention to him spending the night out . . . you can't be too particular about that sort of thing, Inspector. But when it got near tea-time and still no sign of him . . .'

'You rang the police and were shown the photographs. You acted very properly, Mrs Watts.'

'But the man didn't *believe* me, Inspector – I could see he didn't!'

Copping made a rumbling noise. 'It was O'Reilly,' he brought out, 'he was going on transfer to Liverpool the next day . . . he didn't want to believe it . . .'

Gently nodded comfortably to one and the other. 'Everyone is human . . . even the police. And of course you recognized the touched-up photograph, Mrs Watts?'

'Naturally I did – and so did Deanna – and so did my husband Ted, who was in after his lunch.'

'You'd be prepared to swear to the identity in court?'

'I'd take my Bible oath on it, Inspector . . . and so will *they*.'

Gently nodded again and felt absently in the pocket where he stowed the peppermint creams. 'When was it he arrived?' he asked, struggling with the bag.

'It was last Wednesday week – in the morning, just after breakfast.'

'Go on. Describe what happened.'

'Well, I answered the door, Inspector, and there he stood. "I see you've got a room vacant," he says – only he had a queer way of slurring it, as though he were trying to be funny – "do you think I might see it?" he says. I mean, the cheek of it, Inspector! People are usually glad enough to *get* rooms in the middle of the week at this time of the year, without being awkward about it. And him a foreigner too, and smelling as though he'd just walked off a fishing boat . . .!'

Gently paused in the act of transporting a peppermint cream to his mouth. 'A fishing boat?' he queried.

'Yes – that's just the way he smelt. Mind you, I don't want to accuse him of having been a dirty man. It was something that wore off later and the first thing he did was have a bath. But there's no doubt he had a fishy smell on that particular morning . . . well, I nearly slammed the door in his face!'

Mrs Watts pulled herself up in a way which reminded Gently of a baulking mule.

'How was he dressed . . . can you remember?' he asked.

'He'd got his light grey suit on – he nearly always wore that . . . a bit American, it was, with one of those fancy backs to the jacket.'

'Tie?'

'That was a bow.'

'Hat?'

'He never wore one that I can remember.'

'Did he have some luggage with him . . .?'

'He'd got a couple of cases, one bigger than the other . . . the big one is still in his room.'

'How about the other – what happened to that?'

'I suppose he took it with him, Inspector. He always did when he went out . . . he seemed to think there was something very precious about it.'

'Did you see him leave with it the last time you saw him?'

'No . . . I didn't see him after I'd given him his tea. Deanna saw him go out, perhaps she noticed. Deanna!' – Mrs Watts's voice rose piercingly again – 'come in here – the inspector wants to ask you a question!'

'Coming, Ma!' replied a sugary voice just without the door, and a moment later Deanna made her entrance bearing a chrome-and-plastic tea-tray.

'Put it down here, Deanna – I'll pour it out.' Mrs Watts was obviously proud of her daughter and wanted her to be admired. 'This is Chief Inspector Gently down here about the body on the beach . . . don't be afraid of him, my dear, there's no need to be shy.'

Deanna wasn't shy. She beamed at Gently with a mechanical smile which had haunting overtones of Mrs Watts in it, then seated herself next to him. She had a cat-like grace too studied to be pleasing. She was twenty-one or -two.

'My daughter's on the stage, Inspector,' chattered Mrs Watts, sploshing tea into straight-sided cups with lustred rims, 'she was in the pantomime last season . . . just in the chorus, you know.'

'I understudied the principal boy,' beamed Deanna.

'They're going to give her something bigger this year . . . of course, she's home with me during the summer.'

Gently accepted one of the straight-sided cups and stirred it with a spoon that had a knob of black plastic to its spindly shank. 'Getting back to your lodger . . .' he murmured.

'Of course, Inspector.' Mrs Watts handed a cup of tea to Dutt behind the television. 'Deanna dear, you saw him go out on Tuesday . . . the inspector wants to know if he had his case with him.'

'I don't really remember, Ma . . . I didn't know it was going to be important.'

'But it *is* important, dear . . . you *must* try to think.'

'I *am* trying, Ma, but it isn't any good.'

'What time was it when he went out?' asked Gently.

Deanna curled round in her seat to him. 'I just can't remember, Inspector . . . isn't it awful of me?'

'What were you doing when you saw him?'

'Oh . . . I was going up to my room to get ready for the Tuesday dance at the Wellesley.'

'How long would that have taken you?'

'About an hour . . . aren't I terrible!'

'And then your boyfriend called for you?'

'Well yes, he did, Inspector!'

'And what time was that?'

'It was a quarter past eight . . . he was late.'

'Thank you, Miss Deanna.'

In his veneered throne Copping stirred restlessly. 'How about the visitor's book – what did he put in there?' he asked.

Mrs Watts's chin took on an ominous tilt. 'He didn't put anything in there. They don't, most of them, until they're going.'

'They should,' said Copping stoutly, 'they should make an entry as soon as they arrive.'

'Well, they *don't*, Mr Nosey, and that's all there is to it. And if you're going to make trouble out of it you'll have to make trouble for everybody in Starmouth who lets rooms . . .'

Gently made a pacifying gesture. 'But surely he gave a name, Mrs Watts? Naturally, you would ask for that . . .'

'Of course I did, Inspector. And he gave it to me without any hanky-panky – only it was such a peculiar one that I couldn't even say it after him. So he just laughed in that rather nice way he had and told me to call him Max . . . and that's what we all called him.'

'Didn't you inquire his nationality?'

'He said he was an American but if he was, he hadn't been one for long, not with that accent.'

Gently sipped some tea and looked round for somewhere to put his cup. 'How long was he going to stay?' he asked.

'Just on to the end of this week – I hadn't any room for him after that. I'm usually full up right through, of course, but it just so happened through an illness . . .'

'Quite so, Mrs Watts. And did he pay up till the end of the week?'

'He did – it's one of the rules of this establishment.'

'There seemed to be no shortage of money with him?'

'Not him, Inspector. He'd got a whole wad of notes in his wallet – fivers, most of them.'

'Did he ask any questions before he took the room?'

'Well, the usual ones . . . how much it would be, if we'd got a separate bathroom and the like.'

'Did he ask about the other guests, for instance?'

'Yes, he did, now you come to mention it. He asked if they were all English and if they had all arrived the Saturday before.'

'And did that suggest anything to you?'

'He seemed a bit anxious about it . . . I thought he might be expecting to run into somebody he knew.'

'Somebody pleasant or somebody unpleasant?'

'Unpleasant, I suppose . . . if he really is the one you picked up on the beach.'

'Did he suggest that from the way he spoke?'

'Well no, Inspector, he didn't actually . . .'

Gently prized up a peppermint cream from the dwindling stock in his pocket. It induced that faraway look in his eye which Mrs Watts mistook for profound cerebration, but which in reality was connected with his solvency in terms of that important commodity . . . though Starmouth was pretty good peppermint cream country at most hours of the day and night.

'Was he a good mixer?' he asked absently.

'Oh, he got on with everyone, though I wouldn't say he made friends. But he got on with them. They all liked our Max.'

'Was he regular in his habits?' Gently yielded up his cup for a second fill from the hotel-plate teapot.

'I dare say he was . . . as people go when they're on holiday.'

'Tidy . . . a good lodger?'

'Oh yes . . . most of the time.' A frown hovered over the steely eyes as she handed Gently the freshly-filled cup. 'He left his room in a bit of a mess when he went out that last time, but probably he was in a hurry . . . you haven't always time to clear up after you.'

'A mess . . .!' Gently hesitated in the act of plying his plastic-knobbed spoon. 'What sort of a mess?'

'Well, if you ask *me*, Inspector, he'd lost something and was trying to find it quickly, that's what it looked like. The wardrobe was open, the drawers pulled out of the dressing-table – right out, some of them – and if he hadn't up-ended his suitcase on to the floor then he'd given a good imitation of it. And the bed, too, I should say he'd had that apart, not to mention turning up a corner of the carpet. It was a proper mess, you can take it from me!'

Gently drew a long breath. 'But of course,' he said expressionlessly, 'of course you cleared it all up again, Mrs Watts?'

'I did, Inspector,' the regal matron assured him, 'I can't stand untidiness in my house, no matter from whom.'

'Ahh!' sighed Gently, 'I needn't have asked that one, need I . . .?'

The room faced back with a solitary and not-very-large sash window overlooking a small backyard. It was a typical lodging-house 'single', about eight by ten, not much more than a cupboard in which had to be packed the bed, wardrobe, dressing-table, chair and the tiny fitted wash-basin which tried to substantiate the terms Mrs Watts charged for such accommodation. The walls were papered in an irritable grained brown friezed with orange and green, the floor had a strip of carpet which echoed these colours. The bed and other furniture were of flimsy stained wood, late thirties in vintage, and the light-shade was a contraption of orange-sprayed glass with a golden tassel for the flies to perch on. In essence it bore a generic resemblance to the parlour downstairs, thought Gently. There was the same over-crowding and full-bodied vulgarity. It was only the cash index that varied so considerably.

Beside the bed stood an expensive looking suitcase, a rather jazzy affair styled in some sort of plastic with towelling stripes. Copping bent down to pick it up, but Gently laid a sudden hand on his arm. 'Watch it . . . I want this place printed,' he said.

'Printed?' Copping stared in surprise. 'There can't be much left to print after all this clearing-up . . .'

Gently shrugged. 'If there is, I want it.'

'But what does it matter – we've got three witnesses at least to identify him?'

'It isn't only him that interests us . . .'

81

He moved to the window, leaving Copping still staring.

The window was part open at the top. Immediately below it were the red pantiles roofing the outside offices, at the end of which could be seen part of a corrugated steel water-butt. The yard itself was no more than twenty yards long by ten wide. It was separated from its neighbours and the alley on which it backed by grimy brick walls. In the far corner a sad laburnum trembled, in the centre rotted a part-buried Anderson shelter, while close at hand there roosted three dust-bins, one of them with its lid at a rakish angle . . .

Gently produced a not-perfectly-clean handkerchief and closed the window. 'Look,' he said to Copping, pointing to the catch.

Copping looked intelligently. 'It's broken,' he said.

Gently nodded and waited.

'Done from the outside – forced up with a chisel or something . . .'

Gently nodded again.

'Hell's bells – the room's been *burgled!*' exclaimed Copping, suddenly catching on. 'It wasn't the boyo who left it upside-down – it was somebody else – somebody looking for something he left behind here!'

'Which is why I'm printing the place . . .' murmured Gently helpfully.

'It's plain as a pikestaff – I can see the whole thing! He sneaked in up the alley – got in through that broken gate down there – climbed on to the roof by the water-butt and the down-pipe – forced up the catch!'

'Hold it,' interrupted Gently. 'Dutt, step up here a moment.'

Dutt, who had been lingering respectfully in the passage, came quickly to the window. Gently spoke to him without turning his head.

'Over there – where the coping's knocked off the wall . . . don't make it too obvious you're looking.'

'I can see him, sir,' muttered Dutt, 'if he'd just turn his loaf a fraction . . .'

'But who is it!' interrupted Copping, shoving in, 'is it someone you know—?'

'Back!' rapped Gently, 'keep away till Dutt has had a good look . . . there, you've scared him . . . he's off like a hare!'

Dutt raised himself from the stooping position he had taken up. 'It was him, sir,' he asserted positively, 'I saw the scar as he turned to run . . . you can't mistake a face like that.'

'I saw it too, Dutt, right down his cheek.'

'He must have copped a fair packet somewhere . . .'

'Also he has a strange interest in what goes on . . .'

'But who is he?' yapped Copping again, 'what's it all about, this I-spy stuff?'

Gently smiled at some spot that was miles behind Copping's head. 'It's just a little thing between Dutt and me,' he said, 'don't let it bother you . . . it's all over now. Suppose we do what you wanted and take a look in the suitcase?'

They retired from the window and a disgruntled Copping demonstrated how to open a suitcase before it had been printed. It was a charmingly well-filled suitcase. It contained an abundance of shirts and socks and underwear, besides some hairbrushes and toilet accessories which the tidy Mrs Watts had garnered from wash-bowl and dressing-table. And the contents were determined to be helpful. There were makers' labels attached to some of the clothes, names and patent numbers stamped on other items . . . even the suitcase itself had a guarantee label tied to the lining with blue silk. Gently had never seen such a helpful lot of evidence . . .

'It's American,' declared Copping brightly, 'look at this one – "Senfgurken Inc., NY" – and that razor – the toothbrush, even. It's all Yank stuff, right through.'

'And all brand new,' mused Gently.

'He must have bought it for the trip and he can't have been over here long. Or maybe he's a service-man on leave and fixed himself up at his P.X. Anyway, we know where to start looking. If his embassy doesn't know about him, the US Army will.'

'I wonder . . .' Gently breathed.

'Eh?' stared Copping.

'Of course, he said he was an American . . .'

Copping's stare became indignant. 'Who else but a Yank could get hold of this stuff? And who would want to fake up some American luggage, here in Starmouth? What's the point?'

Gently shrugged and dug up the last of his peppermint creams. 'That's what I'd like to know,' he said.

'He's a serviceman got in some bad company, you take my word. It's happened before in Starmouth . . . he's a deserter, that's my bet.'

Gently shook his head. 'It doesn't fit in. There's nothing American about Max except his clothes, and even they seem too good to be true. No . . . everything about him is wrong. He just won't add up into a good American.'

'He might add up into a bad one,' quipped Copping, but Gently didn't seem to be listening.

'The suit – his dark suit! What happened to that?'

'His dark suit?' echoed Copping.

'The one he wore on Sunday. Look in the wardrobe, Dutt. It may still be hanging there.'

Obediently Dutt pulled out his handkerchief and unlatched the wardrobe door. Sure enough a dark suit hung there, a shouldery close-waisted number in discreet midnight blue. Dutt turned back a lapel to show the tailor's label. It was of one Klingelschwitz, operating in Baltimore.

'Still American,' commented Copping, a shade triumphant.

'Go through the pockets,' ordered Gently dully.

Dutt went through them. There wasn't even any fluff. But as he was re-folding the trousers something small and bright fell from one of the turn-ups, a little disc of metal. Copping swooped on it and held it up.

'His lucky charm. He ought to have had it with him on Tuesday.'

'A circle with a line through it!' exclaimed Dutt, 'there's something familiar about that, sir – I've seen it before somewhere.'

'So have I.' A gleam came into Gently's eye. 'I saw it last night on the ring of a Mr Louis Hooker. I wonder if Louey has ever been to America . . .?'

CHAPTER SIX

THE SUPER WAS out when they arrived back at headquarters – rather to Gently's disappointment, because he would like to have bounced some of his findings on that sceptical man's desk. But the super was out: he had received a hot tip about his forgery scare, said the desk sergeant, and had departed with Bryce and two uniform men at a high rate of knots.

'He's got a warped sense of value,' pouted Gently to Copping. 'In some places it's homicide that gets top rating . . .'

'You're forgetting he handed that baby on to you,' grinned Copping, 'he's got an alibi now.'

'I still think a little bit of audience reaction is called for.'

They went into the canteen, where Copping did the honours. It was rather a dull place. The walls were distempered in a dingy neutral tint, the inadequate windows both at one end, the paint worn on lino-top tables and the bentwood chairs looking as though they had been rescued from a jumble sale.

'They've talked about refitting it for years,' Copping apologized, 'but somehow the finance committee never quite gets round to it . . . the food's all right, though. We made a stink about that a couple of months back.'

Gently examined a plate of sausages and beans apathetically. 'You have to make a stink at intervals if you want to keep them up to scratch . . .'

'Yes, but you should have seen what it was like before then!'

Gently shrugged and embarked on his sausages.

'We get in touch with the US authorities now?' inquired Copping, after a silence broken only by the incidental noises made by ingesting policemen.

'Nmp.' Gently pursued an errant bean round the rim of his plate.

'The military's got good records . . . they could tell us straight away.'

'Never mind. Some other time.'

'They'd know in town . . .'

'I know, but never mind.' Gently swallowed the tail-end of a sausage and grounded his knife and fork. 'Your print king,' he said, running his tongue round his lips, 'what's his name?'

'Dack's your man. Sergeant.'

'He's reliable . . . really?'

'You trained him, so he'd better be.'

Gently nodded and added a mouthful of strong tea to the sausages. 'Get him on the job. I can't spare Dutt just now. See that he does everything that might give something . . . *inside* drawers as well as out . . . and then in the yard, at the *back* of that down-pipe . . . he'll probably have to dismantle it. Don't wait for me. If you get results, rush some copies to town and check your own files.'

A smile spread over Copping's heavy features. 'What about Mrs W's new lodger?'

'Nothing about Mrs W's new lodger . . . he can sleep under the pier for all I care. When you've finished in there, seal it up and leave a uniform man in charge.'

'I don't pity the poor swine . . .! Where can I get you?'

'Oh . . . I'll look in later, or maybe ring.'

'You've got something else?'

'Could be,' returned Gently evasively, 'and then again, it couldn't.'

He drank some more tea while Copping indulged in speculative ratiocinations. 'It'd be easy to give the US military a ring . . . just to be sure.'

'No,' said Gently, kindly but firmly, 'we'll leave them to concentrate on Western Defence or whatever else it is they do in these parts . . .'

The Front had become its old gay self again by evening. Everybody hadn't arrived yet – there were still momentary appearances of towering coaches hailing from Coventry, Leicester, Wolves and Brum, dusty from long journeying, their passengers lolling and weary – but enough had already arrived, enough had checked in at their lodgings, deployed their belongings, washed, changed, tea'd, and now sallied forth, cash in hand – they really spent with a will on the Saturday night. Remote from it all, the sea looked cold. Nobody wanted the sea on that day of the week. It was there, it was the alleged attraction, but that was all . . . and in the setting sun it looked cold and hard.

More interesting was the local Evening and the two Londons. They proclaimed the wisdom of having chosen this week for the holiday instead of last week. Last week, of course, the body had been found and the Yard called in, but it was pretty obvious from the way things were going that it would be this week when the mystery was solved, the arrest made . . . BODY IDENTIFIED BY LANDLADY ran the local – Lodger Said to Have Worn False Beard: Missing Suitcase – and there was a photograph showing Gently's back and Copping posed at the top of the steps. The Londons didn't get it early enough to feature. They had to be content with a stop-press and no pics. But they did their best. They whooped it up joyfully. IT WAS ROGER THE LODGER – AND HIS WHISKERS WERE PHONEY, one was captioned, BODY ON THE BEACH – WHY SHAVE IT? asked the other. Yes . . . things were moving. It was obviously the right week to be in Starmouth, quite apart from the races.

'Can't help feeling we've been mucked about, sir,' observed Dutt, as the two of them turned the corner at the end of Duke Street, 'all these new people . . . thahsands of them . . . and we know for a start they haven't got nothink to do with it.'

Gently belched . . . those damned sausages! 'It's the ones who've gone that worry me,' he muttered.

'And then again, there's him we're going to pinch . . . could be any one of them, sir. This bloke coming along here, now, the one with the tasselled hat . . . I wouldn't put it past him.'

Gently clicked his tongue. 'You can't go on that sort of thing, Dutt.'

'I know, sir, but you can't help thinking about it. This isn't like the usual job – as a rule there's one or two to have a go at. But this time there's not a soul, not a blinking sausage' – Gently winced at this unkind reference – 'not a solitary bloke anywheres who you can lay your hand to your heart about. I mean, even that bloke with the scar, sir. What have we got on him, apart from him acting suspicious? I dare say he's up to something he wouldn't like us to know about, but honest now, what connection is that with the deceased? We've often put up pigeons like him on a job.'

Gently sighed, but the sigh was interrupted by a belch. 'This is why we get on so well together, Dutt,' he said bitterly, 'your cockney common sense is the best foil in the world for my forensic intuition . . .'

'Well, there you are, sir. I don't want to look on the black side . . .'

'Of course not, Dutt.'

'But you've got to admit it's still a bit speculative, sir.'

'Highly speculative, Dutt . . . which is why we're keeping firmly on the tail of any pigeons we put up.'

'Yessir. Of course, sir.'

'Including your man with a scar.'

'I wasn't presuming to criticize, sir . . .'

'No, Dutt, please don't . . . at least, not after I've been eating dogs in that damned canteen up there . . .!'

'I'm sorry, sir . . . they was perishing awful dogs.'

They came to a side street running along blankly under the shadow of a Babylonian cinema, a brick vault of Edwardian foundation and contemporary frontage.

'This is me, sir,' said Dutt, halting, 'I can work my way round and come out on the far side of Botolph Street.'

'There's cover there . . . you don't have to lean on a lamp-post?'

'There's a builder's yard with a gate I can get behind.'

'We don't want our pigeon frightened . . . if he's there. I'll give you twenty minutes to get set.'

'That'll be about it, sir.'

'And if he gives any trouble put cuffs on him. My forensic intuition suggests you'll be justified . . .'

Dutt turned off down the side street and Gently, with a dyspeptic grimace, crossed the carriageway and joined the noisy crowd jostling along the promenade. Everything was in full swing again, the lights, the canned music, the windmill sails, the crashing and spanging of the shooting saloon . . . a sort of fey madness, it seemed, a rash of inferno at the verge of the brooding ocean. He turned his back on it and leaned looking out at the cold water.

Dutt was right, of course. There was precious little connection. You could say Frenchy for certain, and that was all . . . and what did Frenchy add up to, even if you could prove it? A friendly foreigner dressed like a Yank and generous with his pound notes . . . he was natural meat for Frenchy. And of course she would lie. Of course she would dig up an alibi. Quite apart from anything else it was bad business for your last boyfriend to wind up a corpse on the beach.

And after Frenchy it was all surmise. There was nobody else who tied in at all, or not in a way that looked impressive when you wrote a report. He had wandered into town, this enigmatical foreigner, he had taken lodgings, he had found a cafe to his taste and a prostitute to his taste; and then he had been, in a short space of time, kidnapped, tortured, murdered and introduced into the sea, his room ransacked and plundered of something of value. There was a ruthlessness about that . . . it bore the stamp of organization. But there was no other handle. The organization persisted in a strict anonymity.

So he was left with his intuition, thought Gently, his intuition that made pictures and tried to fill them in, to make them focus, to eliminate their distressing areas of blankness. One didn't know, one simply felt. With the facts firmly grasped in the right hand one groped in the dark with the left . . . and if you were a good detective, you were lucky. Mere intellect was simply not enough.

He swallowed and grimaced again. If ever he ate another sausage . . .!

There was an air of restraint in the bar of 'The Feathers', as though everybody had been put on their best behaviour. It wasn't too full, either, considering it was Saturday night. The sporty type sat drinking whisky on a high stool, and one or two other less-than-salubrious characters whom Gently remembered from the previous night were scattered about the nearby tables. But there wasn't any Jeff and Bonce, and there wasn't any Frenchy . . . in fact, Gently noticed, there weren't any women in the bar at all, not of any kind.

He went across to the counter and settled himself on a stool, one from the sporty type.

Artie and the latter exchanged a leer, but there was no comment made.

'The usual?' inquired Artie, with a slight sneer in his voice.

Gently quizzed his ferrety features. 'You wouldn't have any milk, by any chance?'

'*Milk!*' Artie almost snorted the word. 'There's a milk-bar just down the road!'

'I'm serious . . . I want some milk.'

Artie eyed him balefully for a moment, then shrugged his shoulders and snatched a glass from under the counter. 'Boss's orders,' he sneered, 'got to treat policemen like gentlemen.' He ducked under the counter and disappeared through the adjacent door.

The sporty type tipped up the remains of his whisky. 'If you're looking for your girly, you won't find her here, guv,' he observed spiritously. 'Louey's had a purge – no women, no kids, and nothing out of line from no one . . . getting quite pally towards the coppers is Big Louey.'

Gently lifted his eyebrows. 'It's not a bad thing to be in most lines of business . . . what's yours?'

'What's mine?' The sporty type affected jocularity. 'Ho-ho! I'll keep on drinking what I'm drinking, and thank you very much!'

'I mean your business,' said Gently evenly.

'Oh, me business . . . I was going to say it was the first time a copper ever asked me . . . well, there you are! I'm what you might call a Turf Consultant.'

'You mean a tipster?'

'Now guv, when we're trying to add dignity to the profession . . .'

'And you make a living at it?'

'A bit of that and a bit of working with Louey. You don't run a bookie's business on your own.'

'Well, you seem to do all right at it.'

The sporty type squirmed a little, but was relieved of the necessity of making a reply by the return of Artie with the glass of milk. He slammed it down perilously in front of Gently.

'It's on the house . . . with Louey's compliments.'

Gently nodded and drank it slowly. He really needed that milk. Its soothing coolness flooded into his digestive chaos like a summons to order, nature's answer to a canteen sausage. He drained the last drop and regarded the filmy glass with a dreamy eye. There were just a few things in life . . .

'Louey got company?' he asked Artie.

'Nobody who's worried by policemen.'

'Tut, tut, Artie! I'm sure Louey wouldn't approve of that attitude . . . I was just wondering if he could spare me a few minutes.'

'Why ask?' retorted Artie, 'just walk right in like every other cop.'

Gently shook his head. 'You've got the wrong impression, Artie . . . you must have been rude to a policeman when you were a little boy.' He slid off the stool and went over to the door. Then he paused, hand on the knob. 'I suppose you didn't have sausages for tea, Artie?'

★ ★ ★

Louey's office was a comfortable room which exhibited a good deal of taste and some quiet expense. The walls were papered in two colours, maroon and grey, the floor was completely carpeted in grey to match and the pebble-grained glass windows, being on grey walls, had maroon curtains relieved by hand-blocked designs in dark blue. The furniture was in keeping. It was of discreet contemporary design showing Scandinavian influence. On the walls hung two coloured prints of race-horses after Toulouse-Lautrec, and under one of the windows stood a jardinière of cream wrought-iron containing a pleasant assortment of indoor plants. There was a short passage separating the office from the bar: it had the effect of reducing the canned crooners in the arcade to a distant, refined murmur.

Louey sat sprawled in a chair by his desk when Gently entered. He was nursing a cat on his knees, a black-and-white tom with a blue ribbon round its neck and a purr like an unoccupied buzzsaw. On another chair was seated the parrot-faced man, still garbed in his dubious evening-dress and still armed with his yard of gold-plated cigarette-holder. Louey greeted Gently with a smile from which his gold tooth shone.

'Pleased to see you, Inspector. I was wondering if you would honour us tonight.'

'Indeed? Then I won't be interrupting any business.'

Louey laughed his comfortable laugh and chivvied the tom with a huge hand. 'No business tonight . . . it's been a bad day for the punters. Not a favourite came home at Wolverhampton. A bad day, eh, Peachey?'

The parrot-faced man mumbled a nervous affirmative. He seemed equally apprehensive of both Gently and Louey. His small pale eyes wandered from one to the other, and he sat in his chair as though it were a penance to him.

'Peachey's my clerk,' explained Louey, seeming to linger on the words, 'he's a good boy . . . very useful . . . aren't you, Peachey? *Very* useful! But sit down, Inspector, make yourself at home . . . as a matter of fact, we've just been talking about you.'

'Really?'

Louey smiled auriferously. 'The evening papers . . . probably exaggerated . . . still, we feel you deserve congratulations. The inspector has got a long way in twenty-four hours, hasn't he, Peachey – eh?'

Gently selected a chair upholstered in blue candy-stripe and swung it round, back to front. Then he seated himself heavily. Louey continued to smile.

'Will you have a drink . . .? Some more milk, if you prefer it?'

'No, thank you. I'll just smoke.'

Louey swept up a silver box from the desk and inclined his gigantic frame towards Gently.

'Try one of these . . . Russian. It's a taste I've acquired.'

'Thanks, but I smoke a pipe.'

'You watch your health, Inspector.'

Such a polite and obliging Louey, thought Gently, as he stuffed his pipe-bowl. Who would have expected such polish from the Goliath who had bawled out the bar last night? There seemed to be two of him . . . one for out there and one for in here, a Jekyll and Hyde Louey. He glanced around the room. Certainly it wasn't furnished by a moron . . .

'You like my office?' Louey leaned forward again with a lighter.

'It's not the usual sort of bookmaker's office.'

The gold tooth appeared. 'Perhaps I'm not the usual sort of bookmaker . . . eh? But most of my business is done in the outer office. I keep this one for myself and my friends.'

His eyes met Gently's, frank, steady, even the sinister effect of the fleck in the pupil seeming softened and modified. We are equals, they were trying to say, you are a man like myself: I recognize you. When we talk together there is no need for subterfuge . . .

'So you don't know that prostitute, Frenchy?' demanded Gently roughly – so roughly, in fact, that Peachey dropped his cigarette brandisher. But the grey eyes remained fixed unwaveringly upon his own.

'I'm afraid not, Inspector . . . apart from warning her to leave the bar once or twice.'

'Does *he* know her?' Gently motioned towards Peachey with his head. Louey turned slowly towards his trembling clerk.

'Go on . . . tell the inspector.'

'I've s-spoken to her once or twice . . .!' Peachey had a whining, high-pitched voice, oddly reminiscent of Nits.

'Nothing else but that?'

'N-no . . . honest I haven't! Just in the bar . . . a joke . . .'

'You've never seen her with this fellow?' Gently whipped out one of the doctored photographs and shoved it under Peachey's nose. The unhappy clerk shot back a foot in his chair.

'Tell him,' rumbled Louey, 'don't waste the inspector's time.'

'No . . . n-never . . . I never seen him at all!'

'Then you know who he is?' snapped Gently.

'I tell you I never seen him!'

'Yet you recognize the photograph?'

'I never . . . I tell you!'

Louey broke in with his comfortable laugh and reached out a great hand to tilt the photograph in his direction.

'I think he can guess, Inspector . . . it isn't difficult, with all this talk of beards in the evening papers.'

'I'm asking Peachey!' Gently snatched the photograph out of Louey's fingers. 'You recognized him – didn't you? You didn't have to stop to work it out!'

'It's like Louey says!' burst out Peachey in desperation, 'I read about it in the papers . . . just like he says!'

Gently eased back in his candy-striped seat and laid the photograph on the corner of the desk. Louey studied it with interest, leaning his massive bald head a little to one side.

'They've touched it up neatly . . . the beard looks quite convincing.'

Gently felt for his matches but said nothing.

'No doubt he's a foreigner,' mused Louey, 'what part of the world would you say he came from . . . Inspector?'

Gently shrugged and struck a match.

'Of course, he could be a first-generation American . . . eh?'

Gently puffed a negative stream of smoke.

'Perhaps not. I've a feeling I'm wrong.'

Gently reached out to drop his match in an ashtray.

'Maybe Central European is nearer . . . or further east. Behind the Curtain, even?' Louey's eyes drifted slowly back to Gently, strong, assured.

'The Balkans?' suggested Gently quietly.

The grey eyes smiled approval. 'That would be my guess, too. Or perhaps we could be more definite . . . after all, the cast of feature is very distinctive. Shall we say Bulgarian?'

Gently nodded his mandarin nod.

'And – I think – a cultivated man . . . possibly Sofia?'

'As you say . . . possibly.'

Still smiling, Louey fondled the purring tom which continued to loll on his knees. It stretched itself and yawned contentedly. Then it flexed its claws with an exaggerated expression of unconcern, whisked its tail and tucked its head under one of its paws.

'Rain,' said Louey, 'it'll make the going soft . . . eh, Peachey?'

Peachey was sitting with his mouth open and giving an imitation of someone expecting an atomic bomb to explode.

'Then there's the other one . . .' murmured Gently, absently blowing a smoke-ring. 'You were saying, Inspector?'

'The man with the scar, doesn't he strike you as belonging to the same racial group?'

There was a pause broken only by the muted skirl of electronic jazz. Louey's fingers paused halfway along the tom's back. Even Gently's smoke-ring seemed to pause and hover, exactly between the three of them.

'Do I . . . know him, Inspector?' queried Louey in a finely-blended tone of frustrated helpfulness.

'You should do. He was here last night.'

'Last night? You mean here in the bar?'

'I mean here in the office – this one or the outer one.'

There was a further pause while Louey shook his head perplexedly. 'I don't know . . . it's rather puzzling. I'm afraid I'm not acquainted with a man with a scar – it's a conspicuous scar, I suppose, something that stands out?'

'Very conspicuous.'

'And he was here in the office?'

'He left at nine thirty-one.'

'Someone saw him leave?'

'Exactly.'

Louey looked hopelessly blank. 'If I knew his name, Inspector . . .'

'I intended to ask you for it.'

Louey sighed regretfully and reached out for the silver cigarette-box. 'He couldn't have been in here . . . I was here myself the whole evening. And as for the other office—' he hesitated in the act of selecting a primrose-coloured cigarette – 'Peachey!'

Peachey jerked as though yanked by a wire.

'*You* were in the other office at half past nine . . . Peachey!'

'B-but boss—!'

100

'Now no excuses – you were working there till ten – you didn't leave the place except to fetch me something from the bar. He was getting out accounts, Inspector . . . we do a good deal of postal work.'

'But *boss*!' interrupted the anguished Peachey.

Louey pinned him with an unanswerable eye. 'Who was it, Peachey – who was the man with the scar? The inspector isn't asking these questions out of idle curiosity, you know . . .'

Poor Peachey gaped and gasped like a hooked cod.

'But wait a minute!' boomed Louey, 'half past nine – that must have been about the time I sent you for my whisky. Inspector' – his eye dropped Peachey as a terrier drops a rat – 'you were in the bar yourself just then, I believe. Did you notice Peachey come out, by any chance?'

Gently nodded reluctantly.

'Of course! Perhaps you can tell us at what time?'

'About half past nine . . . more or less.'

'Half past nine! Then it seems that Peachey *wasn't* in the office when this man of yours was alleged to have left. Is that what you wanted to tell me, Peachey – is it?'

Peachey gulped apoplectically. 'That's right, boss! I wasn't there to s-see nobody!'

'And nobody looked in before that . . . none of our regulars about their accounts?'

'No, boss – no one at all!'

Louey extended a gigantic hand towards Gently. 'Sorry, Inspector . . . it doesn't look as though we can help much . . . does it?'

'No,' admitted Gently expressionlessly, 'it doesn't, does it?'

'Of course, this man may have looked in while the office was unoccupied.'

Gently shook his head. 'Let's not bother about that one, shall we?'

The grey eyes smiled approval again and Peachey sagged down into his chair, breathing heavily. Louey lit his cigarette, slowly, thoughtfully.

'You know, I've given this business a certain amount of thought, Inspector . . . one can't be indifferent, with the Press making so much of it . . . and there are certain points which seem to stand out.'

Gently hoisted an inquiring eyebrow, but said nothing.

'I admit in advance that I'm the merest amateur . . . naturally! But it's just possible that being outside it, away from the . . . tactical problems? . . . I'm in a more favourable position to study the strategy.'

'Go on,' grunted Gently.

Louey inhaled deeply and raised his head to blow smoke above Gently's face.

'There's this man . . . what is he doing here? A complete stranger – nobody knows him – the police don't know him (at least, I presume they don't?) – turning up one day at a popular English seaside resort – and disguised. What would bring him here? His motive is past guessing at. Why should anybody kill him when he got here? The motive is just as obscure.'

'Robbery,' suggested Gently, puffing some Navy Cut into a haze of Russian.

'Robbery?' The gold tooth showed lazily for a moment. 'You're forgetting, Inspector, he was reported to have been killed in cold blood. His hands were tied. Does that seem like robbery?'

'It seems like more than one person being involved.'

'Exactly . . . and that's my point! It wasn't the crime of an individual. All the facts are against it. The more you juggle with them, the more emphatic they become. It was an organized killing, an act carried out by a group of some description . . . who knows?'

The grey eyes slid up and fastened on Gently's, holding him, commanding him.

'A political killing, Inspector. The execution of a traitor . . . that's my reading of the situation. Your man was a fugitive. He chose Starmouth for his haven. But the organization he had betrayed found him out and exacted justice . . . doesn't that seem to fit what we know?'

Gently blew an exquisite ring.

'I think it does . . . better than any other interpretation. I hope I'm wrong – for your sake, Inspector. I believe these political killings are planned with a care which makes detection onerous and arrests unlikely. But the odds seem to lie that way . . . at least to my amateur way of thinking.'

The smile strayed back into the magnetic eyes and Louey part snuffed, part sucked a tremendous inhalation of smoke.

'I'd like you to know I appreciate your difficulties,' he concluded, spilling smoke as he talked. 'My admiration for your abilities won't be lessened, Inspector . . . what can be done by the police in these cases I am sure you will do.'

Gently nodded towards a peak in Darien. Then he reached for the photograph, pulled out his pen and drew on the matt surface a clumsy circle divided by a line. Without looking he handed it to Louey. The big man took it and stared at it.

'Is this something I should know about?' he inquired softly.

Gently lofted a careless shoulder. 'You were wearing it on your ring last night.'

'*My* ring?' Louey extended his hand to display his solitaire.

'The one you were wearing last night.'

Louey hesitated a split second and then laughed. 'No, Inspector, you are mistaken . . . this is the only ring I wear. Tell him, Peachey, tell him . . . I wear this diamond to impress the clients . . . eh?'

The miserable Peachey contrived to nod.

'They like to do business with a man of substance . . . it's paid for itself over and over again.'

Gently turned towards him. There was a glint of excitement in the masterful, smiling eyes.

'So you see, you were mistaken, Inspector . . . you do see that, don't you?'

'Yes,' murmured Gently, 'I see it very plainly indeed.'

He didn't have far to go outside before he was joined by Dutt. The sergeant's cockney visage had a glum expression which told Gently all there was to know . . .

'No pigeon, Dutt . . . the dovecote was empty.'

'That's right, sir. Not a flipping feather.'

'I got the impression it might be. Everyone was so

pleased to see me. A pity, Dutt. I get more and more interested in that laddie.'

'We could put out a portrait parley, sir. He shouldn't be difficult to pick up.'

'I wonder, Dutt. My feeling is that he's a bit of a traveller . . . it's the docks and airports that'll need an eye kept on them. On the other hand . . .'

'Yessir?'

'If he's the bird I think him, it's a matter of some curiosity why he's hung around here so long already.'

'You mean you know who he is, sir?'

'I wouldn't put my hand to my heart, Dutt. I'm of a suspicious character, like all good policemen. And then again . . . it doesn't do to overestimate. There's one thing, though: I want a sound sure ruling on the origin of that circle with a line through it.'

'You mean that little charm, sir?' queried Dutt, brightening.

'I do indeed, Dutt – that little charm.'

'Well, sir, I can tell you that right off the cuff . . . it came to me as I was standing there watching, sir. I knew I'd seen it before, like I said when we found it.'

'Go on, man . . . stop beating about the bush!'

'It's the sign of the TSK Party, sir – I come across it when I was attached to the Special.'

Gently halted under the blaze of one of the multi-coloured standards that afforested the Front. 'And what,' he inquired, 'do we know about TSK Parties, Dutt?'

'Not a darn sight, sir,' replied Dutt, 'not if you put it like that. It's a sort of Bolshie outfit – they reckoned it picked up where the old Bolshie boys left off. They didn't even know wevver Joe was backing it or not – sort of freelance it was, if you get me. That Navy sabotage business was TSK. We had some US Federal men attached to us – they've had a lot of trouble with them in the States.'

'The States!' echoed Gently, 'It's always the States. Have you noticed, Dutt, how the American eagle keeps worrying us as we go about our quiet Central Office occasions?'

CHAPTER SEVEN

THE FLAP WAS still on at headquarters, in fact it had stepped up considerably during Gently's absence. There were lights on where they were usually off at such an hour, cars parked that ought to have been garaged and policemen due off duty, still buzzing around like (as Dutt rather coarsely described it) 'blue-arsed flies'. Gently, going down the corridor, was nearly bowled over by an impetuous Copping clutching a file.

'We've picked up the boyo who passed that note!' exclaimed the Borough Police maestro, sorting himself out. 'He's a skipper from up north – he's lousy with them – and what a yarn he's spun! They must think we're cracked, trying to pull gags like that. But the super'll give him a going over he won't forget in a hurry!'

Gently sniffed a little peevishly. 'Don't think I'm frivolous . . . I'm still trying to keep my mind on the crime before the last. Did your man get some prints?'

'Oh, the prints! He got a couple of sets that didn't tally with anything we've got.'

'A couple?'

'That's right . . . one lot on the suitcase and one on the window-frame. They turned up in other places, too, but those were the best impressions.'

'He compared them with Mrs W's and the rest, of course?'

'We know a little bit about the job . . .!'

'And you've sent them to town?'

'Right away, as per instructions.'

Gently fished out his wallet and extracted from it the doctored photograph. 'I want this printed now . . . is your man still around? He'll find mine on it amongst some others, but he needn't bother about them . . .'

Dutt was despatched with the photograph and Gently accompanied Copping to the super's office. That austere abode, always impressive, was now fairly crackling with forensic atmosphere. The super sat behind his desk as stiff as a ramrod. At a discreet distance a sergeant was ensconced at a table, taking down some details. At the same table sat a constable with a shorthand book and three pencils. On the door was a second constable, uneasily at ease. The focus of all this talent, a fresh-complexioned middle-aged man, had been arranged on a chair in the geometrical centre of the office: he sat there with a nervous awkwardness, like a member of an audience suddenly hoicked up on to the stage.

The super nodded to Gently as the latter entered and motioned him to take a seat. 'You'll excuse me, Inspector . . . I'm rather busy. I'd like a conference with you later, if you don't mind waiting.'

Gently inclined his head and sat down at the less congested end of the office. Copping delivered the file and appended himself to the end of the super's desk.

'Dalhoosie Road,' spelled out the sergeant. 'McKinky & Mucklebrowse Ltd, Potleekie Street, Frazerburgh. I think that's the lot, sir. It checks with the ship's papers.'

The super stiffened himself a few more degrees. 'Now, McParsons . . . I want you to listen very carefully to what I have to say. I'm charging you with being in possession and uttering a counterfeit United States banknote, and also with being in possession of four similar notes. Do you wish to say anything in answer to this charge? You are not obliged to say anything unless you wish to do so, but whatever you say will be taken down in writing and may be used in evidence.'

McParsons screwed up his weather-beaten face. 'But I tellt yer the whorl *lot*, sir – I gi'ed ye all the evidence to prove I'm an honest man . . . what more do yer want noo?'

'It isn't evidence,' snapped the super, 'we didn't take it down and we're prepared to forget it. Think carefully, McParsons. You're in trouble, quite a lot of trouble, and the tale you told me down at the docks won't impress a jury – I can assure you of that. My advice to you is to forget it. The truth will help you a lot more, especially if it enables us to arrest the counterfeiters.'

'But losh, man, it *was* the truth! I canna make up tales out of my heid.'

'Stop!' interrupted the super sharply. 'All you say now is evidence.'

'Then Gordamighty, let it be so – I'll noo complain

o' ye puitin fause words into my mouth. It's jist the way I tellt it, nae more and nae less, so yer may as well scratch it doon on yer paper — it's all the evidence Andy McParsons can gi' ye.'

The super drilled at the same Andy McParsons for ten acetylene-edged seconds before replying . . . quite a feat, thought Gently, who was a connoisseur of superlatives. Then he snapped off a 'Right!' which seemed to suggest every bit of ten years and opened the file Copping had brought. The pages rustled accusingly.

'Starmouth Branch of the City & Provincial Bank . . . US banknote of one hundred dollar denomination, etc, etc . . . paid in by Joseph William Hackett, licensee of the "Ocean Sun" . . . see preceding report. Hackett on being questioned deposed that he changed the note for a seaman, a stranger to him . . . sparely built man, about five feet ten, aged about fifty, dressed in navy-blue suit and cap, fresh complexion etc . . . Scots accent. Detective Sergeant Haynes questioned Andrew Carnegie McParsons, Skipper of the steam-drifter *Harvest Sea*, at the yard of Wylie-Marine, where the said steam-drifter was undergoing a refit . . . denied all knowledge, etc—'

Gently coughed loudly and the super broke off to throw him a sharp stare. 'You had something to say, Inspector?'

'The name of the yard,' murmured Gently apologetically, 'could you repeat it, please?'

'Wylie-Marine, Inspector.'

'Thank you. I thought it sounded familiar.'

The super snorted and returned to his recitation.

'Afternoon of the fifteenth Hackett reported having seen aforementioned seaman in the neighbourhood of the yard of Wylie-Marine . . . proceeded to the same yard . . . Hackett picked out McParsons . . . McParsons admitted changing the note and was taken into custody . . . four similar notes of one hundred dollar denomination found in McParsons's possession.'

The super paused again and smoothed out the nicely typed report sheet.

'*Now*,' he said bitingly, 'we come to your story, McParsons.'

'But ye've had it a'ready,' replied the disconsolate skipper, 'hoo often maun I tell it to yer?'

'What you told us before you were charged will not be used as evidence. If you want to make a statement, now is the time.'

'Och, aye . . . ye're all for doing it by the buik, I ken that. Well, jist pit doon I had the notes fra ain Amurrican body . . . I see fine yer dinna believe a word of it.'

The super signalled to the shorthand constable. 'Begin at the beginning, McParsons. If this story of yours is to go on record we want the whole of it.'

McParsons sighed feelingly to himself. 'Aweel . . . ye'll have your way, there's noo doot. It was on the Tuesday then, the Tuesday last but one . . . we'd been in Hull a week, y'ken, wi' the boiler puffin' oot steam fra every crook an cranny . . . the engineer had puit in his report lang since, but auld Mucklebrowse is awfu' canny aboot runnin' up bills for repair . . . then awa' comes a wire to the agent tellin' us to puit out for

111

Wylie's, me ainsell to stay wi' the ship and the crew to take train back to Frazer. Sae we jist tuik aboard ain or twa necessaries and hung waitin' there for the evenin' tide. Noo the crew bodies was all ashore takin' their wee drap for the trip and Andy McParsons had jist come awa' fra the agent's, when along happens this Amurrican I tellt ye of . . . "Captain," says he (and morst respectful, the de'il take him!), "is that your ain ship lyin' there with steam up?" "It is," says I, "sae long as the rivets stick in the boiler." "Then ye're aboot goin' to sea," says he. "Aye," says I, "jist as soon as the laddies get back, which'll noo be a great while." "And you'll be goin' a long trip?" says he, gi'en a luik ower his shoulder. "Jist drappin' down the coast," says I, "we'll be sittin' tight in Starmouth before breakfast-time."

'Noo ye maun believe this, Supereentendent, or ye maun not – it's a' ain to the truth – but I hadna been gabbin' five minutes with this smooth-spaken cheil when he was jawin' me into stowin' him awa' in the *Harvest Sea*. "But wit's the trouble?" says I, "is it the police ye have stuck on yer sternsides?" "Naethin' of that, I swear," says he, "it's a private matter, an like to be the dearth of me if I canna get clear of this dock wi'out walkin' back off it. I'll pay ye," says he, "it's noo a question of money – but for the luve of the A'mighty let's gae doon into the cabin," and the puir loon luikit sae anxious I hadna the heart tae refuse.

'Weel, the short and the lang o't was we struck a bargain – twa hundred dollars and nae questions asked. I couldna take less, says I, since the crew maun be squared on tap, and in ony case it was a wee bit inconvenient tae get it in dollar notes, and sich big ains at that. "Och, but the crew mauna ken!" says he, "ain body's ower muckle – I canna bide more." "Then I doot the deal's off," says I, "for de'il a bit can ye be stowed awa' in sich a corckle-shell as this wi'out the crew being privy, not," says I, "unless we pop yer into a herring-bunker, where ye'll be wantin' a stomach lined wi' galvanized sheet to say the least o't." "Let it be sae," says he, "I've sleepit in places as bad or worrse." "Mon," says I, "if ye've nae been jowed around in a herring-bunker on the North Sea ye havena lived up till noo, sae dinna gae boastin'. Take yer ease in the cabin, where yell nose a' the fish ye'll be wantin' if there's a wee swell ootbye."

'But listen he wouldna, sae it was agreed he should ship in a bunker – though had I kent then whit I ken noo it'd been into the dorck wi' him, and nae mair argument – and he paid up his twa hundred dollars . . . not mentioning some wee discount business on three ither notes (I'd ta'n a bodle o' cash fra the agent and it rubbed against the grain tae say nay, ye understand). "Keep an eye lifted for strangers," says he, as I clappit him doon under the hatch, "dinna let a soul aboard ither than the crew bodies." "Dinna fash yersel," says I, "I ken fine how to earn twa hundred dollars."

'Weel, there ye have it, Supereentendent. We drappit doon here owernight and fetchit up at Wylie's before the toon was astir. I paid aff the crew bodies and saw them awa' to the station, then I lifted the hatch and huiked out the cargo. He wasna in the best o' shape, ye ken – it gi'es me a deal o' consolation thinkin' o't – but I gar him ha' a wash, whilk he did, and a swig at the borttle, whilk he didna, and betwixt doin' the ain and not doin' t'ither he was sune on his legs agin and marchin' off doon the quay. And that's the spae, evidence or testament of Andy Carnegie McParsons, the truth of whilk is kenned by him on the ain part and his creator in pairpetuity, whatever doots may occur in the more limited minds of his accusers.'

Saying which he folded his arms independently and returned the super some measure of that worthy's police-issue stare.

'And you expect to have this colourful account believed?' fired the latter corrosively.

'Och, noo! It's naethin' but the naked truth,' returned the Scot ironically, 'I dinna expec' the police to believe sich simple things.'

'I see nothing simple about it, McParsons. It has all the marks of being deliberately contrived. First this hypothetical American meets you just as you're about to put to sea – and when you're alone. Then, for reasons the most vague, he elects to spend a night on the North Sea immured in a herring-bunker rather than show himself to the crew. And finally he takes his leave when, once more, there are no witnesses. It's pretty thin, McParsons. It'll be cut to ribbons in court. If I were you I'd stop trying to shield whoever it is behind this racket and try to be helpful – we shall get them in the long run, you can depend on that.'

'Then for Gord's sake get them, Supereentendent, and dinna waste any mair time! Ye're noo the ain half sae anxious aboot it as I am sittin' here.'

'So you're sticking to your story?'

'Aye – onless ye can puit me up tae some lees whilk will suit yer better.'

The super glanced down at the file with something which might have been a low sigh. 'Very well,' he said dangerously, 'if you insist on having it that way . . . describe the man!'

'The Amurrican body?'

'Precisely, McParsons.'

'Weel, I doot I'm noo a policeman to be forever noticin' the crinks and crankles o' folk . . .'

The super snorted. 'Don't strain your imagination.'

'I willna, Supereentendent . . . it's me memory I'm jowin' the noo.'

'For instance . . . was he clean-shaven?' mumbled Gently, apparently studying his stubby fingernails. The Scot turned quickly towards him.

'Noo yer mention it, he wasna – he had a beard fra the temples doon.'

'He would have, wouldn't he?' demanded the super derisively.

'And his suit . . . Scots tweed?' suggested Gently.

'Na, man, it was ain o' they Yanky-doodle jobs, a' tap and noo bottom.'

'Dark?'

'Na . . . aboot the colour o' pipe-ash.'

'He was a youngish man?'

'Ower forty, ain or twa.'

'And he spoke with an educated accent?'

'Noo this cheil – he was Amurrican by adoption, ye ken . . . he spoke a fair smatterin' o' Sassenach, but he hadna it fra his mither.'

Gently felt once more in his breast-pocket for one of his doctored prints.

'Had he a beard like this one?'

McParsons rose excitedly to his feet. 'But yon's the man – the verra spittin' image! Sae ye kent him – ye kent him a' the while – it's jist a try-on, a' this chargin' and fulin' – ye've got yer hands on him a' the while!'

Gently's gaze strayed mildly to the thunderstruck super. 'I'd like to get Hull on the wire . . . it may be a longish call.' He turned back to McParsons. 'You wouldn't remember what ships docked at Hull on that Tuesday . . . from the continent, say?'

'Fra the Continent? Och aye! There was that Porlish ship they made a' the fuss aboot aince – we ganged roon to ha' a luik at her. But concairnin' the body on yon photygraph—!'

'Thank you, Skipper,' murmured Gently distantly, 'the body on the photograph is undoubtedly your next port of call.'

They were obliging, the Hull City Police, without being able to do much more than fill in a few details. They knocked up numerous people (including constables) from the first and important hours of their slumber. No, they had no record of a man of Max's description. No, their life was not being blighted by an irruption of counterfeit hundred-dollar notes. Yes, the Polish liner *Ortory* had broken her Danzig-New York run at Hull on the Tuesday week last. She had docked at noon and sailed again at 19.30 hours: she had discharged seventy-five crates of Russian canned salmon and picked up a Finnish trade delegation on its way to

Washington. Yes, they would get on to the dock police if Gently would hang on for a while.

'So he was a Pole, was he?' brooded the super, sniffing meanly at the Navy Cut contaminating the aseptic night air of his office.

Gently shook his head. 'A Bulgar from Sofia.'

'You know that for a fact?'

'Not really . . . but I'm prepared to accept it as a working hypothesis.'

'How do you mean?'

'Just a hunch. I don't think someone I know could bear to tell a lie about it . . . provided he wasn't implicating himself.'

'And who is this someone?'

'Oh, it's a bit vague at the moment . . .' returned Gently evasively.

The super grunted and toyed with a retractable ball-point which seemed to be a novelty with him. 'So he was a member of this TSK . . . they were sending him to the States guyed up like a Yank and loaded with counterfeit . . . is that the angle?'

Gently nodded through his smoke.

'What was he supposed to do when he got there?'

'Oh . . . they'd have put him ashore quietly before the ship docked.'

'And then?'

Gently shrugged. 'Sabotage seems to be their line . . . he was probably going over to organize it.'

'He must have been well up in the party,' mused the super, 'it was a position of trust . . . what do you suppose went wrong?'

117

'That's something we're not likely to know.'

'A double-cross inside the party, maybe.'

'You're probably safe in saying that . . .'

There was a dulled, small-hour silence broken only by a scratching in the uncoupled phone and a sizzle from Gently's pipe. From the nearby harbour came the mournfully alert toot of a siren, twice repeated.

'Of course you'll get on to the Special,' muttered the super drowsily.

'Dutt's getting them for me . . . he was attached to them a time back.'

'They may know something . . . then there's the US Federal . . . could be something they're looking for.' The super jerked himself to attention. 'Look here . . . there's something that puzzles me. If this fellow was so worried about his health, why didn't he seek political asylum when he skipped the *Ortory*? That would have been his obvious move. There was no need for all this chasing around and stowing-away aboard fishing-boats.'

Gently gave himself a little shake. 'There's the missing suitcase . . . if it were stuffed with hundred-dollar bills it seems a fairish reason for keeping things private.'

'But they were counterfeit!'

'He may not have known that.'

'You mean his party sent him off on this mission without telling him?'

'It would seem to square with what we know about the methods of these parties . . .'

The super nodded sapiently. 'But the person who swiped that suitcase must have known they were phoney, because he hasn't been passing them.'

'You can't bank on that either . . . the TSK weren't planning to spend them in Starmouth. What puzzles me is the way that bedroom was frisked. You don't have to tear a bedroom apart to find a suitcase . . .'

They were interrupted by the entry of a constable with a tray from the canteen. It bore a plate of corned-beef sandwiches and two mugs of hot coffee. Gently gladly grounded his pipe in favour of the more substantial fare – there was an almost psychic quality about corned-beef sandwiches and hot coffee at that hour of the morning. He chewed and swilled largely, and the super kept in strict step with him.

'May have hidden the stuff about the room,' mumbled the super, flipping a crumb from his moustache.

'Then why was he always carting the suitcase about with him? Everyone's agreed about that.'

'Could have been a blind.'

'Why should he bother? . . . the stuff would be safer by him.'

'He seems to have left it behind in the last instance, at all events,' grunted the super beefily.

'There may have been a purely incidental reason for that . . .'

Dutt came in, looking peeked and heavy-eyed. 'Special is going into it, sir,' he said laconically. 'I gave them a p.p. as good as I could remember and all the information we've got to date.'

'What did they say?' asked Gently, shoving him a charitable sandwich.

'Nothink, sir. They never does.'

'Did they confirm the identity of the charm?'

'Only after I'd got on to 'em, sir, and told them it was hanging up the case. You never knew such a lot for keeping their traps shut.'

Gently drank the last of his coffee and looked sadly into the empty mug before returning it to the tray. 'Maybe they don't know much . . . maybe they aren't going to until the day-shift turns up. Did Sergeant Dack get any results with that photograph?'

'Yessir. A lot of beautiful prints.'

'Any on record?'

'He thought there was, sir – would've sworn blind about one lot. He said they matched up with the prints of a con man who specialized in flogging licences to manufacture Starmouth Rock.'

'And did they, Dutt?'

'No, sir. They was yours.'

Gently shook his head modestly. 'You compared them with the ones out of the bedroom?'

'Yessir. No resemblance.'

'And sent a set off to town?'

'Automatic, sir.'

'Have another sandwich, Dutt.'

'Thank you, sir . . . this night work makes you peckish.'

The telephone scratched its gritty throat and began to emit adenoidal language. Gently picked it up and murmured kindly to it. The dock police had been roused and briefed. They had pulled in, or rather out, the two men who had been on duty at the pier where the *Ortory* had docked on the day in question. No. 1 was applied to the line and upon invitation gave an efficient description of what occurred.

'And no civilian disembarked from the time she docked to the time you went off duty at five?' queried Gently encouragingly.

'Only one, sir, and he came down with three or four of the ship's officers . . . they seemed to be inspecting the cases of salmon which had been unloaded.'

'The salmon? Would that have been unloaded by the ship's crew?'

'Yes, sir, it was in this instance.'

'Down a separate gangway?'

'That's right, sir.'

'And loaded on to trucks?'

'No, sir, not directly. They built it up on a pile on the pier and it wasn't till the evening when it was taken away.'

('That's it!' whispered the super, listening on an extension, 'he bribed the sailors to get him off . . . they built a hollow pile for him to hide in.')

'This civilian who came to inspect the cases . . . when did he come ashore?'

'Just before I was relieved, sir.'

'What do you mean by "inspected"?'

'Well, sir, they appeared to be counting them . . . they got one or two off the top to see how many were underneath.'

'You noticed nothing unusual take place?'

'No, sir. They just did their check and then stood about talking and looking about them for a minute or two. After that they strolled up the pier to the office and went inside.'

'The civilian too?'

'Yes, sir, the civilian and the officers.'

'Can you describe the civilian?'

'Middle-aged, about five-nine, medium-build, dark, dark-eyed, slanting brows, long, straight nose, small mouth, rather harsh voice.'

'Distinguishing marks?'

'I thought he had a scar on one side of his face, sir, but I only caught a glimpse of it as he came down the gangway. The rest of the time it was turned away from me.'

'Ah!' breathed Gently and propped himself up at a better functional angle with the super's desk. 'Now . . . this is important . . . did the civilian return on board with the officers?'

'I don't know, sir. My relief came just then and I went off duty. He's in the office now, sir, if you'd like to speak to him.'

There were some confused ringing sounds at the other end and No. 2 took over. Gently repeated his question.

'Well, sir . . . I regret to say I didn't notice.'

'Didn't notice? Didn't the other fellow tell you there was a civilian ashore?'

'Oh yes, sir, he did. But soon after I got on the pier there was a row amongst some of the Polish seamen and it sort of took my mind off the others.'

'What sort of a row was that?'

'I don't know what it was about, sir. Half a dozen of them came ashore and started shifting some of the cases that had been unloaded. Then all of a sudden a row broke out and a couple of them started a fight. I went up and separated them, but they kept on shouting at each other and making as though they'd let fly again, so I had to stand by and keep an eye on them. In the end one of their officers came up and sent them on board again.'

'And during that little diversion the party in the pier office slipped aboard?'

'I suppose they must have done, sir . . . they weren't there when I checked up later.'

'So if the civilian stayed ashore you wouldn't have noticed?'

'I'm afraid not, sir . . . I'm very sorry . . .'

('Cunning lot of bastards!' interjected the super with reluctant admiration, 'you can see they're professionals!')

Gently took in a few more inches of desktop. 'Give me the other bloke again,' he said. The other bloke was given him. 'What else was going on at the pier while the *Ortory* was there?'

'What sort of thing, sir?'

'Any loading or unloading going on?'

'There was a Swedish vessel unloading timber on the other side, sir.'

'And that meant a bit of traffic up and down the pier?'

'Quite a bit, sir. They were trucking some of it.'

'Was it going past the pile of cases from the *Ortory?*'

'Yes, sir, just behind it. Some of the trucks parked there to wait their turn.'

Gently nodded towards the slow-mantling dawn. 'And the Finnish Delegation?' he asked, 'what time did that embark?'

'Just after lunch, sir . . . might have been half past two.'

They sat drinking a final mug of coffee with the electric light growing thin and fey under its regulation shade. The super was looking sleepily pleased with himself, as though he felt he had a good case to go before the ratepayers, both in forgery and homicide. After all, nobody could hang Special Branch business round his neck . . . concern he might show, when secret agents bumped each other off on Starmouth Sands, but he was only nominally responsible . . .

'I suppose the bloke who did it is miles away by now,' he murmured into his coffee. 'If he shows the same ingenuity getting out of this country as he did getting into it . . .'

Gently shrugged slightly, but he didn't seem to be listening.

'And even if they get him I don't suppose we can make a murder rap stick . . .'

There was a tap on the door and the duty sergeant entered.

'Excuse me, sir,' he said to the super, 'but PC Timms has just turned in this here. It was given to him by the publican of the "Southend Smack". He changed it for a Teddy boy in his bar last night, but later on somebody tells him about some duff ones going about, so he's handed it in to be on the safe side.'

The super extended a nerveless hand. The duty sergeant placed therein a certain bill or note. And from an unexpected backyard at no great distance a cock crowed.

CHAPTER EIGHT

SUNDAY SUN FALLING steadily on the platinum beaches, on the lazy combers, on the strangely subdued streets. On the well-spaced, comely mansions of High Town. On the quaint, huddled rookeries of the Grids. On the highly-polished bonnet of a police Wolseley as it halted on the crisp gravel of Christopher Wylie's retired drive. On the more sober bonnet of PC Atkins as he knocked on the door of No. 17 Kittle Witches Grid.

'I knew he won't come to no good, that kid of Baines's,' said a frowsy matron to the newspaperman as they watched a goggle-eyed Bonce being marched away. 'I said so as soon as I saw him in that fancy get-up of his. Did you ever see such frights as they look? And then for him to be mixing with that young Wylie . . . I said it would be his ruination.'

'Going about the town at all hours and taking up with all sorts,' said the cook at Wylie's, relinquishing her vantage-point at the larder window, 'they should've let *me* had the handling of Master Jeff – I'd have let him mix with riff-raff like the Baineses, *I* would!'

'I dunno,' returned the kitchen-maid dreamily, 'I rather *liked* him in that silly suit of his.'

The cook snorted. 'Well, you can see where it's got him now, my girl!'

In the ill-lit parlour of No. 17 John George Baines, dock labourer, sat in his shirt-sleeves staring sullenly at the *News of the World*. His wife, a bold-faced woman, was slapping together the breakfast plates at a table covered with oil-cloth and two juvenile Baineses were scuffling and screaming on the floor.

'It wouldn't have happened,' snapped Mrs Baines for the twentieth time, 'it wouldn't have happened, not if you'd kept a proper hand on him . . .!'

'Oh, shut your mouth, woman . . . it's your fault if it's anyone's.'

'You've never give him a good hiding in your life!'

'And who was it encouraged him with that bloody suit – trying to be up to His Nibs . . .?'

More silent was the breakfast-room in High Town. No sound fell upon the ears of Christopher Wylie, except the sobbing of his wife Cora. He stood with his back to her, staring out of the expensive oriel window, staring at his cypress and monkey-puzzle trees, his impeccable gravel drive.

'I'll get on to the chief constable,' he muttered at last, 'we'll get it straightened out, Cora . . . there can't be anything in it.'

'Oh, Chris . . . I'm so frightened . . . so frightened!'

'It's all a mistake . . . we'll get it straightened out. The lad's due for his service in October . . .'

Up the long High Street marched PC Atkins, the

Sunday-silent High Street with its newspaper-men, milkmen and a few early-stirring visitors in holiday attire. Beside him slouched Bonce, looking neither to right nor left. Behind him frisked Nits, a chattering, excited Nits. Halfway along the High Street PC Atkins paused to address the ragged idiot. 'You run along home, m'lad, and stop making a nuisance of yourself . . . off with you now, off with you!' Nits backed away apprehensively while the constable's eyes were on him, but as soon as the march recommenced he was dancing along in the rear again . . .

The sunshine had renewed Gently's feeling of nostalgia. They had all been sunny days, on that holiday of long ago. He remembered getting sunburned and his nose peeling, and the peculiarly pungent lotion they had put on his arms to stop them blistering (though of course they did blister), and, by association the suave smell of the oiled-paper sunshades which had been fashionable about then.

'We had rooms somewhere about where we've got them now,' he confided to a bleary-eyed Dutt as they set out for headquarters. 'They used to do you awfully well in those days . . . I can remember having chops at breakfast.'

'Don't know as I should think so much of that, sir,' admitted Dutt honestly.

'Nonsense! You've been having these degenerate meals of bacon-and-egg too long.'

'I should think a chop sits a bit heavy on your stomach first thing, sir.'

'It's true I was only a boy, Dutt . . . all the same, I think I could still face one.' He plodded along silently for a space, a little frown gathered on his brow. 'We seemed to be younger in those days, Dutt . . .'

'*Younger*, sir?' inquired Dutt in surprise.

'Yes, Dutt . . . younger.'

'Well, sir, I s'pose we was – in those days!'

But there was no smile on the face of his superior as they turned up the steps at headquarters.

The landlord of the Southend Smack was waiting patiently in the office which the super had assigned to Gently, and Copping, who had got to bed earlier than most, and was consequently his old spry self, officiously performed the introduction.

'You think you can remember the youth who changed the note?' inquired Gently dryly.

'Ho yes, sir – don't you worry about that!' replied the landlord, a red-faced beery individual called Biggers.

'You've seen him before, then?'

'Ah, I have – once or twice.'

'You know his name?'

'No. No, sir. But he's been in the bar once or twice, I can tell you that.'

'It didn't occur to you that he might be a little young to be served in a bar?'

'W'no, sir . . . I mean . . . there you are!' Biggers faltered uneasily, beginning to catch on that he wasn't Gently's blue-eyed boy. 'He *looked* old enough, sir . . . couldn't be far off. You can't ask all of them to pull out their birth-certificates.'

'Was he on his own?'

'Ho yes, sir!'

'Does he always come into your bar on his own?'

'Y–yes, sir, as far as I remember.'

'How do you mean, as far as you remember?'

'Well, sir . . . I wouldn't like to swear he never had no one with him.'

'A woman, perhaps.'

'No, sir – no women!'

'Another youngster dressed like himself?'

'Yes, sir, that's it!'

'Dressed exactly like himself?'

'Yes, sir, exactly!'

'And younger – about a year?'

'Yes, sir . . . I mean . . .!' Biggers trailed away, realizing the trap into which he had been unceremoniously precipitated. Gently eyed him with contempt.

'This hundred–dollar bill . . . didn't it seem odd to you that a young fellow should have one in his possession?'

'Oh, I dunno, sir . . . what with the Yanks about and all . . .'

'And how should he have acquired it from an American?'

'Well, sir, they're master men for playing dice.'

'You thought he'd won it gambling?'

'I never really thought . . . that's the truth!'

'Good,' retorted Gently freezingly, 'I'm glad it's the truth, Biggers. The truth is what we are primarily interested in . . . let's try sticking to it, shall we? How much did you give him for it?'

'I . . . I give him its value.'

'How much?'

'Why, all it was worth to me . . .'

'*How much?*'

Biggers halted sulkily. 'I give him a tenner . . . now turn round and tell me it wasn't enough, when it was a dud note in the first place!'

Gently turned his back on the sweating publican. 'Is the parade lined up?' he asked Copping.

'They're in the yard – just give me a moment.'

It was a scrupulously fair parade. Copping had wanted to impress Gently by his handling of it, and after witnessing the momentary appearance of the mailed hand lurking beneath the chief inspector's velvet glove he was glad that he had so wanted. There was something almost deceitful about Gently, he thought . . .

Biggers took his time in going down the line, as though wishing to display his helpful care and attention. He paused before several law-abiding youths before making his final selection. He also paused before Bonce, whose wild-eyed guilt proclaimed itself to high heaven, but the pause was a brief one and might even have been involuntary . . . Having done his conscientious best, he carried his findings to Gently.

'That's him . . . fifth from the far end . . . kid in the brown suit.'

Gently nodded briefly. 'And this one . . . the carroty-headed boy?'

'No, sir. Don't know him. Never seen him before!'

'Positive?'

'Ho yes, sir . . . I never forgets a face.'

The same mailed hand which Copping had so judiciously observed fell lightly on Bigger's arm and the astonished publican found himself whirled a matter of three yards in a direction not of his choosing.

'Now see here, Biggers, you've come forward voluntarily and given us some useful information, but there's not much doubt that you're sailing a bit too close to the wind. From now on there'll be an eye on you, so watch your step. Don't change any more money, American or otherwise, and if any of your customers looks a day under fifty – ask for his birth certificate. Is that clear?'

'Y–yes, sir!'

'Quite clear?'

Biggers gulped assent.

'Then get away out of here . . . we've finished with you – for the moment!'

A blue-bottle buzzed in a sunny pane of the office window, a casual, preoccupied buzzing which focussed and concentrated in itself a vision of all fine Sundays from time immemorial. Copping lifted the bottom of the window and let it out. It fizzed skywards in a fine frenzy of indignant release, wavered, scented a canteen dustbin and toppled down again from the height of its Homeric disdain. Copping left the window half-open.

'One at a time?' he asked.

'Yes. Shove the Baines boy into a room by himself where he can do a little quiet thinking.'

Copping nodded and went out. Gently seated himself in awful state behind the bleak steel desk with its virgin blotter, jotting-pad and desk-set. He slid open a drawer. It contained a well-thumbed copy of Moriarty's *Police*

Law and some paper-clips. The drawer on the other side contained nothing but ink-stains and punch confetti.

'I wonder who the super turfed out to make room for us?' he mused to Dutt.

Copping returned, prodding Jeff before him. The Teddy boy looked a good deal less exotic in his quieter lounge-suit, but there was still plenty of swagger about him. He stared round him with a sullen defiance, his thin-lipped mouth set tight and trapped.

'Sit down,' said Gently, indicating a chair placed in front but a little to the side of the desk. Jeff sat as though he were conferring a favour. Copping took the chair on the other side and Dutt hovered respectfully in the background.

'Your full name and address?'

'You know that already—'

'Answer the inspector!' snapped Copping.

Jeff glared at him and clenched his hands. 'Jeffery Wylie, Manor House, High Town.'

'Your full name, please.'

'Jeffery . . . Algernon.'

Gently wrote it down on his jotter.

'Now, Wylie . . . you had better understand that you are here on a very serious matter, perhaps more serious than you at first supposed. You have been identified as possessing and uttering counterfeit United States currency – wait a minute!' he exclaimed, as Jeff tried to interrupt, 'You'll have plenty of opportunity to have your say – you've been identified as handling this money and we happen to know the source from which it emanated. Now what I have to say to you is this: you may be able to explain satisfactorily how you came to be in possession of that note, in which case there will be no charge made against you. But you are not obliged to give an explanation and you are not advised to if you think it may implicate you in a graver charge. At the same time, if you take the latter course I shall automatically charge you and you will be held in custody on that charge while further investigations are made. Is the situation quite plain to you?'

Jeff shuffled his feet. 'I can see you're out to get me, one way or the other . . .'

'We're not out to "get" anyone, Wylie, if they happen to be innocent. I'm simply warning you of where you stand. And I'd like to add to that some advice if you help us you'll be helping yourself. But it's up to you entirely. Nobody here is going to use third-degree methods.'

The Teddy boy sniffed derisively and stuck his hands into his pockets. 'I know how you get people to say what you want . . . I've heard what goes on.'

'Then you'd better forget what you've heard and consider your own position.'

'A fat lot of good that'll do me . . .'

'It'll do you more good than trying to be clever with policemen.'

'You say yourself I don't have to tell you anything.'

There was a silence during which Copping, to judge from his expression, was meditating a modified use of the third-degree methods which Gently had disowned.

'It's only his word against mine . . .' began Jeff at last.

Gently cocked an eyebrow. 'Whose word?'

'His – the pub-keeper's.'

'And who told you he was a publican?'

Jeff flushed. 'Isn't that what he looked like?'

'He may have looked like a publican or he may have looked like a barman. What made you think he was one and not the other?'

'I just said the first thing that came into my head, that's what I did!'

Gently nodded a mandarin nod but said nothing.

'He could have been wrong,' continued Jeff, encouraged, 'he might've just picked on me because he couldn't remember and thought you'd jump on him if he didn't find someone. He can't prove it was me.'

'I dare say other people were present . . .'

'There were only two of them and—' Jeff stopped abruptly, glowering.

'And they were busy playing dominoes or something?' suggested Gently helpfully.

Jeff dug deeper into his pockets. 'I won't say any more – you're trying to trap me, that's what it is! You're trying to get me to say things I don't mean . . .!'

'Suppose,' said Gently, beginning to draw pencil-strokes on his pad, 'suppose we go back to the beginning and try a different tack?'

'There isn't any tack to try – it wasn't me and nobody can prove it was.'

'Then you didn't change a dollar bill . . .'

'I never had a hundred-dollar bill in my life.' Gently's pencil paused. 'What size bill?'

Jeff bit his lip and was silent.

134

'He doesn't even know how to lie . . .' observed Copping disgustedly.

Gently finished off his stroke-pattern with aggravating deliberation. Then he felt in his pocket for the spare photograph and regarded it indifferently for a few moments. Finally he leaned across the desk and shoved it at Jeff.

'Here . . . take a look at this.'

Jeff unpocketed a hand to take it, but Gently was being so clumsy that he knocked it out of the Teddy boy's hand and on to the floor. Sullenly Jeff reached down and scrabbled under his chair for it.

'Was he the man who gave you the note?'

'I told you I never had one.'

'Have you ever seen this man before?'

'I saw his picture on the screen at the Marina, only it didn't have a beard.'

'But you've never seen the man?'

'No.'

Gently retrieved the photograph carefully from fingers that trembled and beckoned to Dutt.

'Take this along to the print department and see if they've got an enlargement, Dutt . . .'

'Print department, sir?' queried Dutt in surprise.

Gently nodded meaningly. 'And check it with the original, Dutt . . . it might bring out some interesting points.'

'Yessir. I get you, sir.' Dutt took the photograph gingerly by the extreme margins and went out with it. Gently picked up his pencil again and began laying out a fresh stroke-pattern. Through the open window could be heard, faint and far-off, Copping's blue-bottle or one of its mates improving the shining hour round the canteen dustbin, while more distantly sounded the hum of excursion traffic coming up the High Street. A perfect day for anything but police business . . .

'You see, Wylie . . . I'll come to the point. The note you are alleged to have had in your possession was one introduced into this country by the man on the photograph. That man, as you are aware, was murdered.'

'I never knew him – it's nothing to do with me!'

'If it's nothing to do with you then it would be a good idea to tell the truth about the note.'

'But I never had any note – it's all a lie . . . I keep telling you.'

Gently shook his head remorselessly. 'All you've told me to date has convinced me of the reverse. Besides, the man who identified you gave a pretty damning description when he handed in the note. That suit of yours is rather distinctive, you know. I don't suppose anybody else in Starmouth wears one excepting Baines . . . and I shall be questioning him in due course.'

'He's seen me before, he could have made it up.'

'He's seen you before? I thought he wasn't supposed to be known to you?'

'He *could* have seen me before . . .'

'And made up the whole story about a complete stranger?' Gently hatched a few of the lines in his pattern.

Copping snorted impatiently. 'You're lying . . . it's too obvious. We know what you got for the note and

136

when we picked you two up this morning you each had five-pound notes on you. What was that – a coincidence?'

'I get pocket-money!' Jeff exclaimed, 'my father isn't a labourer.'

'No, but Baines's father is. Where did *he* get five pounds?'

'He works – he's got a job!'

'That's right – thirty bob a week as an errand boy and pays his mother a pound of it. Do you think we're fools?'

Jeff's breath came fast. 'I tip him a pound now and again . . .'

'And he saves it up?'

'How should I know what he does with it?'

'If you don't, nobody else does. What were you doing at ten to ten last night?'

'I . . . I was on the Front.'

'Alone?'

'I . . .'

'Answer me!' snapped Copping, 'you don't have to think if you're telling the truth. Baines was with you, wasn't he?'

'No! I mean . . .!'

'Yes! Of course he was. Why bother to lie? And you were skint, weren't you? You'd got rid of your precious pocket money and Baines's ten bob with it. All you'd got left was an American note – a note you'd begged, borrowed, stolen and perhaps murdered for—'

'No!'

'—and that was all there was between you and a bleak weekend. So you picked out a quiet-looking pub – one

137

where you knew there wouldn't be many witnesses to the transaction – and slipped in and flogged the note to the publican. He wasn't offering much, was he? Less than a third of what it was worth! But you couldn't stop and argue – it might draw attention – they might ask questions you hadn't got the answers for—'

'It's a lie!' screamed Jeff, as white as a sheet, 'you're making it all up – it's all a lie!'

'Then you can prove you were somewhere else?'

'I was never near that pub!'

'Then what pub were you near?'

'I wasn't near any pub at all!'

'Is the only pub on the Front the one you weren't near?'

'I don't know . . . I didn't notice . . . I didn't go into a pub anywhere last night!'

Gently clicked his tongue. 'It's a pity about that . . . it might have helped you to establish an alibi that doesn't otherwise seem to be forthcoming.'

Copping repeated his snort and seemed, with flaming eyes, about to continue his verbal assault upon the shaking Teddy boy: but at that moment Dutt re-entered.

'Ah!' murmured Gently, 'did you make a comparison, Dutt?'

'Yessir.' The sergeant's eye strayed to Jeff. 'Very like, sir, at a rough check. Sergeant Dack thinks so too, sir. He's going over them proper now.'

Gently nodded and stroked off a square. 'Bring in Baines, Dutt . . . oh, and just a minute . . .'

'Yessir?'

'Take him along to the prints department first, will you?'

Dutt withdrew and Copping looked questioningly at Gently. But Gently was busy with his patterns again.

'Y-you can't go on anything Baines says,' muttered Jeff tremblingly.

'Oh? And why can't we?' barked the ferocious Copping.

'He'll say anything . . . you can make him say what you like.'

'If we can make him tell the truth it'll be the first time we've heard it this morning, my lad. I should button my lip, if I were you.'

Jeff licked dry lips and took the advice. There wasn't an ounce of swagger left in him. He sat sagging back in his chair, his feet at an awkward angle, his hands digging ever deeper into his pockets. Copping got up and went over to the window. The fine weather outside seemed to anger him. He studied it tigerishly for a moment, sniffed at the balmy sea air, then turned to eye the Teddy boy from between half-closed lids.

'A nice day for a picnic,' suggested Gently cautioningly.

'I was going round the links . . . if I'd got away early enough.'

Gently shrugged. 'Something always turns up . . . it's the bright day that brings forth the adder.'

But Copping sniffed and would not be comforted.

Bonce was brought in, as wild-eyed as ever, and scrubbing recently-inked fingers on the seat of his cheap trousers. Jeff pulled himself together a little at the sight of his henchman, as though conscious of a sudden that

139

he was cutting a poor figure. Gently glanced at Dutt, who shook his head.

'Not this one, sir. Nothing like.'

'Are you sure of that?' asked Gently in surprise.

'Positive, sir.'

'Well . . . they're not supposed to lie! Sit down, Baines. You can wash your hands later on.'

Bonce sat down automatically in the chair indicated to him. He had an air of bereftness, as though he had lost all will of his own. His mouth was hanging a little open and his face had a boiled look. His eyes resolutely refused to focus on anything more distant than the blunt tip of his freckled nose.

Gently pondered this woebegone figure without expression.

'Robert Henry Baines of seventeen Kittle Witches Grid?'

Bonce nodded twice as though the question had operated a spring.

Gently cautioned him at some length, though it seemed doubtful if what he was saying penetrated very clearly into Bonce's shocked and bewildered mind.

'I'm going to ask you one question, Baines, and it's entirely up to you whether you answer it or not. You understand me?'

The spring was operated again. Gently paused with his pencil at one corner of his pad.

'I want you to tell me, Baines . . . if you assisted Wylie when, on the night of Tuesday last, he entered a rear bedroom of 52 Blantyre Road and removed from there a suitcase containing United States treasury notes.'

'Don't tell him, Bonce!' screamed Jeff, leaping to his feet, 'don't tell him, you bloody little fool!'

'*Silence*!' thundered Gently in a voice that made even Dutt wince, 'get back in your chair, Wylie!'

'But it's a lie . . . he'll say anything . . .!'

'*Get back in your chair*!'

Copping sent the Teddy boy sprawling into his seat again and held him there struggling and panting.

'Now, Baines . . . have you anything to answer?'

Bonce gaped and gurgled in his throat, his eyes rolling pitiably. Then the spring clicked and his head began to nod. 'I went with him . . . it's true . . . I kept watch in the alley . . .'

'You fool – oh, you bloody little fool!' sobbed Jeff, 'don't you understand it's murder they're after us for – don't you understand it's murder?'

There was a ripping sound as Gently's pencil crossed from one corner of the pad to the other.

The charge was made: burglary on the night of the eleventh. Jeff was in tears as he gave his statement. Of the two of them, it was Bonce who showed the better front. Having shed the intolerable load of conscious guilt he seemed to stiffen up and gain some sort of control of himself, while Jeff, on the other hand, went more and more to pieces. It was from Bonce that Gently received the more coherent picture.

They had been in 'The Feathers' late on the Tuesday evening when the prostitute Frenchy entered. She was well known to them – Jeff claimed to have slept with her and Bonce wasn't sure that Jeff hadn't – and she

141

approached them with the information that a man-friend of hers had left in his bedroom a suitcase containing something of considerable value.

'Was she in the habit of divulging such information?' queried Gently.

Jeff stoutly denied it, but Bonce admitted one or two instances.

'And were you accustomed to act on it?'

Bonce hung his head. 'Once we did . . .'

Frenchy had struck a quick bargain. They would go halves in whatever the loot realized. She gave them the address, explained the situation of the bedroom and guaranteed to keep the man busy for another hour or two at least. When she left they followed her at a discreet distance and saw her meet a man resembling the one in the photograph. He had exchanged a few words with her and then signalled a taxi. The taxi had departed in the direction of the North Shore.

'Where did the taxi pick them up?' asked Gently.

'It was just outside the Marina.'

'What would have been the time?'

Bonce glanced at Jeff. 'About ten, I should think.'

'Would you know the taxi again?'

'N-no, sir, there wan't nothin' special about it.'

'From which direction did it come?'

'From the Pleasure Beach way, sir.'

The owner of the suitcase having been seen on his way, they hastened round to Blantyre Road and identified No. 52. Then they approached it by the back alley and while Bonce kept watch outside, Jeff broke into the rear bedroom.

'Weren't you taking a bit of a risk?' inquired Gently of Jeff. 'The lodger may have been out, but it's pretty certain the landlady wasn't.'

'We could see them down below,' sniffed Jeff, 'they were watching the telly.'

'The television couldn't have had much longer to go by the time you got there.'

'It's the truth, I tell you!'

'All right, all right – just answer my questions! It may have been running late on Tuesday. How long did it take you to do the job?'

'Ten minutes . . . quarter of an hour, perhaps.'

'No longer than that?' Gently glanced at Bonce.

'That's about it, sir.'

'But you had to hunt around for it?'

'Why should I?' sniffed Jeff, 'I knew what I was looking for . . . a blue suitcase with chromium locks. It was standing with the other one near the wardrobe.'

'Did you look in the other one?'

'No . . . I never touched it.'

'Didn't you go through the drawers or anything of that sort?'

'I tell you I didn't touch anything! I just got what I came for and went. Ask him if I aren't telling the truth.'

Bonce corroborate his leader's statement – he had returned with the blue suitcase and nothing else. They had carried it off to a quiet spot in Blantyre Gardens, forced the locks and discovered the astounding contents. Immediately there was a change of plans. Jeff decided they would tell Frenchy that they had been unable to

143

find the suitcase – a proposition she wasn't situated to contradict – while in reality they would keep it hidden until the hue and cry had died down and then dispose of it by slow and cautious degrees. This they did, and for some reason Frenchy accepted their story without much fuss. When the murder became news and they recognized the pictures which were issued as being of Frenchy's man-friend, they had an additional incentive for keeping the stolen notes under cover. Unfortunately, their patience was soon exhausted. A financial crisis at the end of the week had slackened their caution. Surely, they had thought, there could be no harm in cashing just *one* of that inexhaustible pile of notes . . . just one, to see them comfortably through the weekend . . .

Gently sighed at the end of the recital. 'And the rest of them, where are they now?'

Bonce swallowed and glanced again at Jeff. 'They're under the pier.'

'Which pier is that?'

'Albion Pier . . . there's a hole between two girders.'

'You'd better show me . . . Dutt!'

'Yessir?'

'Tell them to bring a car round, will you?' He returned to Bonce. 'That evening . . . in the bar at "The Feathers" . . . were all the usual crowd there?'

Bonce twisted his snub nose perplexedly. 'I – I suppose so, sir.'

'Was Artie serving at the bar?'

'Oh yes, sir.'

'That fellow who wears loud checks and lives on whisky?'

'Yes, sir.'

'Louey?'

'N-no, sir . . . *you* don't often see him in the bar.'

'Peachey?'

'I think he looked in while we were talking to Frenchy . . .'

There was the sound of a car swinging out of the yard and Copping rose to his feet. He looked at Gently questioningly and motioned to the two youths with his head. 'Cuffs on them . . . just to keep on the safe side?'

Gently smiled amongst the nebulae. 'Let's be devils this morning, shall we? Let's take a risk!'

Exceeding Sunday-white lay the Albion Pier under mid-morning sun. Its two square towers, each capped with gold, notched firmly into an azure sky and its peak-roofed pavilion, home of Poppa Pickle's Pierrots, notched equally firmly into a green–and–amethyst sea. Its gates were closed. They were not to open till half past two. The brightly dressed strollers, each infected in some degree by the prevailing Sundayness, were constrained to the languid buying of ice-cream, the indifferent booking of seats or the bored contemplation of Poppa Pickle's Pierrots' pics. They didn't complain. They knew it was their lot. Being English, one was never at a loss for a moral attitude.

Even the arrival of a police car with three obvious plain-clothes men and two obvious wrong-doers didn't seriously upset the moral atmosphere, though it may have intensified it a little.

'Which end?' inquired Gently, shepherding his flock down the steps to the beach.

'This end . . . up here where the pier nearly touches the sand.'

They marched laboriously through soft dry sand, the cynosure for an increasing number of eyes. Dutt led the way, the Teddy boys followed, and Copping and Gently brought up the rear. Under the pier they went, where the sand was cold and grey. A forest of dank and rusty piles enclosed them in an echoing twilight.

'Up there,' snuffled Jeff, indicating a girder which nearly met the sand, 'there's another one joins it behind . . . it's in the gap between them.'

'Get it out,' ordered Gently to Dutt.

The gallant sergeant went down on his stomach and squirmed vigorously till he was under the girder. Then he turned on his back and began feeling in the remote obscurity beyond. He seemed to be prying there for an unconscionable length of time.

'Have you found the hole?' asked Gently, his voice echoing marinely amongst the piles.

'Yessir,' came muffledly from Dutt, 'hole's there, sir . . . it's what's in it I aren't sure about . . . couldn't get hold of me legs and pull me out, sir?'

Copping went to the rescue and a grimy Dutt renewed acquaintance with the light of day. In his arms he bore a bundle, also grimy. 'This is all there was, sir . . . ain't no trace of any suitcase.'

'Open it!' snapped Gently.

Copping broke the string and unwrapped the paper. There lay revealed a crumpled grey suit, a pair of two-colour shoes, shirt, socks, underclothes, suspenders and a blue bow tie.

'Sakes alive!' exclaimed Copping. 'Look at this label – Klingelschwitz – it's the same as in the boyo's suit!'

'And look at this shirt,' added Gently grimly, 'four nicely grouped stab-holes ... same as in the boyo's thorax.'

A sugary thump made them all turn sharply. It was Jeff going out cold on a sand that was even colder.

CHAPTER NINE

I T WAS A hefty lunch for a hot day and Gently followed Dutt's example of shedding his jacket and rolling his sleeves up. There wasn't any frippery about it. Just straight roast beef and Yorkshire pudding, and vegetables followed by hot apple turnover with custard. But either Mrs Davis was a demon cook, or else the Starmouth ozone had really come into its own that day . . . there wasn't much in the way of conversation for quite some time.

'Superintendents!' muttered Gently at last, evaluating the remains of the turnover with sad resignation.

'Never alters,' agreed Dutt sympathetically, cutting an absent-minded slice.

'I can't help coming to the conclusion, Dutt . . .'

'Yessir?'

'. . . if it didn't savour of insubordination . . .'

'Aye, aye!' Dutt winked at his superior over a spoonful of juicy pastry. 'Don't have to say it, sir. I knows well enough what you mean.'

Gently picked up his plate and placed it at some

distance from himself, as though finally to sever connections with that beguiling turnover. 'You make a pinch ... you dig up some evidence ... it does something to them. They're all the same, Dutt.'

'Yessir. Noticed it.'

'They suddenly turn impatient. It's an occupational disease with superintendents. At a certain stage in the proceedings they get the charge-lust. They want to charge someone. And if there's half a case against anybody it's the devil's own job to head a super off and make him be a good boy ...'

'Don't we know it, sir?'

Gently drew a deep breath and pulled out his familiar sandblast. 'Of course, you have to admit it ... there's enough on Baines and Wylie to make the average super sit up and howl blue murder. But at the same time, it only needs the average forensic eye. Baines isn't a liar, for instance, and Wylie's got too scared to lie. No, Dutt, no. Our super is doing himself no good by tearing the bricks apart at the Wylie's. He won't find anything, and he won't improve his standing with anyone.'

Mrs Davis brought in their cuppa, making room for the tray beside Gently. She hesitated on seeing the chief inspector's pipe on the point of being lit and then produced, from nowhere as it seemed, a capacious glass ashtray. Gently nodded a solemn acknowledgement. Mrs Davis beamed at the still-eating Dutt. 'Aren't you going down to the beach now this afternoon, Inspector?'

Gently smiled wanly and unbonneted the teapot.

'Well, sir ... what do *you* make of them clothes

149

turning up like that?' queried Dutt when the tea was poured and Mrs Davis had retired.

'They were planted deliberately, Dutt. By the person who lifted the suitcase.'

'But how did they know where it was, sir?'

'By deduction and observation – just as we find out things.' Gently doused a match and took one or two comfortable pulls. 'Obviously . . . they wanted that suitcase back. Whether they still intended to use the money or not we don't know, but they feel it's important that a large consignment of it shouldn't be lying around loose . . . it would almost inevitably finish up in our hands. So their first move after settling with Max was to recover the suitcase and I can imagine they were a little upset to find it missing when they got to his lodgings . . .'

'Lord luvvus, sir – that other set of prints! I've been puzzling my loaf about them all the morning.'

'Exactly, Dutt . . . the first little slip our friends seem to have made. But I don't suppose they aimed to be around when those prints came to light. It was just a bit of bad luck that the suitcase had vanished into thin air . . .'

'So it was them who ransacked the room, sir.'

'Undoubtedly.'

'On account of he may have hidden the stuff somewhere.'

'It was a possibility they wouldn't overlook.'

Dutt gave a little chuckle. 'You're right, sir . . . their faces must have dropped a mile when they found the cupboard was bare!'

'A good mile, Dutt, and possibly two. It upset all their calculations. It meant they would have to hang around and look for it instead of getting to hell out of the country . . . and hanging around would get to be more and more dangerous as the investigation went on. At first, I imagine, they hadn't a clue about it. They may have visited the bedroom more than once and they were certainly interested to know what we found when we got there . . . and then, of course, they began to think it out and perhaps make some inquiries. They found out, or possibly they knew, that Max had been consorting with Frenchy . . . that was an obvious lead. No doubt they gave her flat a going-over. They might even have questioned her. But there was no suitcase at the flat, and all that Frenchy could tell them – even if she came clean – was of Jeff and Bonce's allegedly fruitless attempt to get the suitcase . . . Anyway, they got on to Jeff and Bonce somehow. It wouldn't have been too difficult if they checked up on Frenchy.'

'And then they kept them under observation, sir?'

'Just as we would have done, Dutt.'

'And last night they found out where the case was hidden – and left the clothes there for a false scent, sir?'

Gently nodded pontifically. 'A false scent for a charge-happy super.'

Dutt swallowed a mouthful of tea and looked a little dubiously at the remaining shoulder of apple turnover. 'Just one thing, sir . . .'

'Yes, Dutt?'

'I don't want to seem critical, sir . . .'

'Don't be modest, Dutt – just come to the point.'

'Well, sir, what I want to say is, how did they know we was ever going to find them clothes, let alone connect them with the Teddy boys?'

Gently nodded again and smiled around his pipe. 'That's what we want to know, isn't it, Dutt. That's going to be the clincher!'

He rose from the table and went over to Mrs Davis's telephone. The phonebook lay beside it. He flicked through it and traced down a column with a clumsy finger.

'Starmouth 75629 . . . this is Chief Inspector Gently.' He tilted the instrument to one side so that Dutt could hear too. 'Biggers? There's something else I want to ask you, Biggers . . . yes, about last night.'

'Ho yes, sir?' came the publican's anxious voice from the other end.

'You told us in your statement that after you had changed the note you heard there were some counterfeit ones going about. I want to know where you obtained that information.'

'Yes, sir! Certainly, sir! It was a bloke in the bar what told me that.'

'A bloke you know?'

'Ho no, sir. Quite a stranger.'

'He was in the bar at the time of the transaction?'

'No, sir, not as I remember. The first time I noticed him there was when the young feller went out.'

'You mean he came in while the transaction was in progress?'

'Must've done, sir, 'cause he soon ups and tells me to watch my step with regard to Yank money. "Wasn't that a hundred-dollar bill?'' he says. "Ah, it was," I says. "Then it's ten to one you've been had," he says, or words to that effect, "there was a sailor got copped with some this afternoon."'

'Oh did he . . .?' Gently exchanged a glance with Dutt.

'Yes, sir . . . God's honest truth!' The voice on the phone sounded panicky. 'I don't have no cause to lie, now do I—!'

'All right, Biggers . . . never mind the trimmings. What else did this man tell you?'

'Well, he told me I could get five years, sir, and that I ought to hand it over to the police . . . naturally, me just having paid ten quid . . .'

'We know about that. Did he say anything else?'

'No, sir . . . not apart from ordering a whisky. It was nearly closing-time.'

'Would you recognize him again?'

'Ho yes, sir! Like I was telling you, I never forget a face.'

'Can you describe him?'

'Well, sir . . . he wasn't English, that I can say.'

'Did you notice a mole on his cheek by any chance?'

'No, sir. No. But he'd got a scar running all down one side . . .'

Gently hung up the instrument and leaned on it ponderingly for a few moments. His eyes were fixed on Mrs Davis's flowered wallpaper, but to a watchful Dutt they seemed to be staring at something a good six feet on the other side of the wall. Then he sighed and straightened his bulky form.

'So there it is, Dutt . . . our clincher. And they even knew about McParsons . . . eh?'

Dutt shook his head ruefully. 'They must have quite an organization, sir . . .'

'An organization!' Gently laughed shortly. 'Well . . . we'd better get our own organization moving, too. Go back to headquarters, Dutt, and tell them to put a man each on the two stations and another on the bus terminus, and to warn the men on the docks to keep their eyes double-skinned. It's an even bet that our scar-faced acquaintance is well clear of Starmouth, but we can't take any risks . . . Then give Special a ring and let them know.'

Dutt nodded intelligently. 'And the clothes, sir . . .?'

'Get them sent to the lab, and the paper and string. Oh, and that cab-driver . . . the one who picked up Max and Frenchy on Tuesday night . . . see if you can get a line on him, Dutt.'

'Yessir. Do my best.'

Gently scratched a match and applied it to his pipe. 'Me, I'm going to pay a little social call in Dulford Street. I think it's time that Frenchy assisted the police by supplying the answers to one or two interesting questions.'

Dulford Street was a shabby thoroughfare adjoining the lower part of the Front. It began as though by accident where some clumsily-placed buildings had left a gap and proceeded narrowly and crookedly until it got lost in a maze of uncomely backstreets. There was a feeling of having-gone-to-seed about it, as though its original inhabitants had given it up in despair and left it to go its own way. From one end to the other it could boast of no fresh paint except the lurid red-and-cream of an odiferous fish and chip shop.

Gently eyed the assemblage moodily and applied to a new bag of peppermint creams for encouragement. Sunday was obviously an off-day in Dulford Street. The signs of life disturbing its charms were few. On the right-hand side was a frowsy little corner-shop with some newspapers in a rack at the door, and at the entry from the Front lurked a furtive and ragged figure . . . Nits, who had been following Gently all the way along the promenade. Gently shrugged his bulky shoulders and pushed open the clanging door of the newspaper shop.

'Chief Inspector Gently . . . I wonder if you can give me some information?'

It was a white-haired old lady with beaming specs and an expression of anxious affability.

'What was it you were wanting?'

'Some information, madam.'

'The newspapers is all outside . . . just take one, sir!'

'I want some information.' Gently raised his voice, but the only effect was to increase the old lady's look of anxiety. He pointed out of the dusty window.

'That apartment over there . . . do you know who lives in it?'

'Oh yes, I do! She isn't nothing to do with me!'

'Is that her permanent address or does she just make use of it?'

'Eh . . . eh?' The old lady peered at him as though she suspected him of having said something rude.

'Is that her permanent address?' began Gently, *fortissimo*, then he shook his head and gave it up. 'Here, how much are these street directories?'

'They're sixpence,' retorted the old lady sharply, 'sixpence – that's what they are!'

Gently put a shilling on her rubber mat and made a noisy exit.

Frenchy's apartment, flat, or whatever other dignity it aspired to was situated above a disused fruiterer's shop. The shop itself had been anciently boarded up, but the degree of paintwork it exhibited matched evenly with that of Frenchy's door and the windows above, leaving no doubt about the contemporaneity of the decoration. Gently tried the door and found it open. It gave directly on to uncarpeted stairs which rose steeply to a narrow landing. At the top were two more doors, one with a transom light which did its best to illumine the shadow of the landing, and at this he knocked with a regular policeman's rhythm.

'Who is id . . .?' came Frenchy's croon.

'It's Chief Inspector Gently. All right if I come in?'

There was a creaking and scuffling, and finally the sound of shuffling footsteps. Then the door opened to display a draggle-haired Frenchy, partly-clad in a green dressing-gown. She glared at Gently.

'What are you after now?'

'I'm after you,' said Gently cheerfully, 'weren't you expecting me to call?'

Her eyes narrowed like the eyes of a cat. 'You've got nothing to pinch me for . . . you bloody well know it! Why can't you leave a girl alone?'

156

Gently tutted. 'This isn't the attitude, Frenchy. You should try to be co-operative, you know – it pays, in your profession.'

'That's none of your business and you ain't got nothing on me!'

Gently shook his head admonishingly and pressed past her into the room. It wasn't an inviting prospect. The furniture consisted of an iron bedstead, a deal table and three cheap bedroom chairs. The floor was covered with unpolished brown lino, the walls with faded paper. At the window, curtains were drawn to keep out the sun, but in spite of this the room was like a large and unventilated oven, an oven, moreover, that possessed a vigorously compounded odour, part dry rot, part cigarette smoke and part Frenchy. Gently fanned himself thoughtfully with his trilby.

'Doesn't seem a very comfortable digging for a trouper like you, Frenchy,' he observed.

'What's it got to do with you?' spat Frenchy, closing the door with a bang.

'And you're travelling light this season.' He indicated a dress and a white two-piece which hung on hangers from a hook in the wall.

'If you're going to pinch a girl for being short of clothes . . .!'

Gently concluded his unhurried survey with the dishevelled bed, some empty beer-bottles and a chamber-pot. 'And then again, my dear, this place is in the wrong direction . . .'

'Whadyermean – wrong direction?'

'It isn't in the direction the taxi took.'

'What taxi – what are you getting at?' Frenchy whisked round fiercely to confront him.

'Why . . . the taxi you and Max took from outside the Marina at about 10 p.m. last Tuesday. It went off towards the North Shore . . . that's in a diametrically opposite direction, isn't it, Frenchy?'

The sudden pallor of the blonde woman's face showed up the dark wells of her eyes like two pools, but she took a furious grip on herself. 'It's a filthy dirty lie . . . I didn't take no taxi! I was in "The Feathers" at ten . . . ask anyone who was there . . . ask Jeff Wylie – it was him who came away with me!' She broke off, breathing hard, crouching as though prepared to ward off a physical blow.

Gently's head wagged a measured negative and he felt in his pocket for some carelessly-folded sheets of the copy-paper. 'It won't do, Frenchy . . . it isn't good enough any longer. I've got a couple of statements here which tell a different story.'

'Then some b—'s been lying!' Frenchy tried to snatch the sheets out of Gently's hand.

'Nobody's been lying and you'll get a chance to read these in a couple of minutes. Now sit down like a good girl.'

Frenchy hovered a moment as though still meditating an attempt on the papers. Then she swore an atrocious oath and dumped herself down on the side of the bed, an action which endangered the decency of her sparsely-clad person. Gently turned one of the chairs back-to-front and seated himself also.

'First, I'd better have your name.'

'What's wrong with Frenchy . . . it suits everyone else round here.'

Gently clicked his tongue. 'Let's not be childish, Frenchy. Why make me bother the boys in Records?'

'Trust a bloody copper! So it's Meek, then. Agnes Meek.'

Gently scribbled it in his notebook. 'And where do you hail from, Agnes?'

'I was born and bred in Maida . . . but don't use that filthy bleeding name!'

'And when did you come up here?'

''Bout Whitsun or just before.'

'And whose idea was it?'

'Mine – who the hell's do you think it was?'

'Now Frenchy! I'm only asking a civil question.'

'And I'm telling you I came up on my own! Don't you think a girl needs a holiday?'

Gently shrugged. 'It's up to you . . . So you've been living at this address since Whitsun?'

'That's right.'

'And nowhere else at all?'

Frenchy swore a presumable negative.

'How did you find it? Who's your landlord?'

'Why not ask your pals up at the station – they're supposed to know every bloody thing going on round here!'

Gently sighed sadly. 'You're not being helpful, Frenchy . . . and I had hoped you were going to be.' He served himself a peppermint cream and chewed it sombrely for a moment. 'Well . . . to come to the business. I'm pinching you for conspiracy to burgle, Frenchy—'

Frenchy screeched and shot up off the bed. 'It's a frame-up, that's what it is, a filthy, stinking—!'

'Shh!' murmured Gently, 'I don't have to warn an old-stager like you.'

'They'd say anything in a jam, dirty little bastards!'

Gently handed over his sheets of copy-paper. 'In effect they said this . . . and there's a certain amount of evidence to back them up.'

Frenchy seized the sheets and went over to the window with them, turning her back on Gently. It didn't take her long to extract the gist of them. There was a moment when she discovered how she had been double-crossed that added three distinct new words to Gently's vocabulary.

'It's a filthy bag of lies!' she burst out at last. 'The – little liars – they're trying to pin it all on me!'

'They seem to have made a job of it, too . . .'

'There isn't a word of truth!'

'But there's some evidence that goes with it . . .'

Frenchy stormed up and down the muggy room with perspiration beading on her pasty face. 'You know what it is . . . You know why these pigs have said this. It's because I wouldn't go to bed with them . . . that's what they've wanted! They've wanted to be little men, to go to bed with a woman . . . they've been hanging round me ever since I came up here. But I don't go to bed with children . . . nobody can blame me for that! . . . and now they're in trouble they're trying to blame me – somebody it's easy to get in bad with the police!'

'Whoa!' interrupted Gently pacifically, 'it's no use

getting out of breath, my dear. Somebody had to tell them about that suitcase and where to find it . . .'

'It wasn't me! I didn't know nothing about it.'

'Then who did – who else knew about it?'

'How the hell should I know? Perhaps they saw him carting it around and got the idea it was something valuable . . .'

'Who told you he was given to carting it around?'

'Nobody told me—!'

'And how did they know where he lodged – that he was out – that for some reason he'd left it in his room?'

'They could've watched him, couldn't they?'

'They aren't professionals, Frenchy.'

'They're sneaking little swine, that's what they are!'

She flung herself at the bed and disinterred some cigarettes from under the pillow. Gently produced a match and gave her a light, steady brown fingers against her trembling pale ones. She swallowed down the smoke as though it were nectar.

'You know, Frenchy, it isn't burglary you've got to worry about . . . we aren't terribly interested in that. It's the way your customer finished up on the beach the next morning that's the real headache.'

'He wasn't my customer – I never knew him!'

Gently shook his head. 'I've got another witness who saw you with him, quite independent. Do you remember having lunch at the Beachside Cafe?'

'I was never in the place!'

'And now, according to these two statements, you were the last person we know to see Max alive . . .'

A shudder passed through the blonde woman's body

and she had to struggle to keep her hold on the jerking cigarette.

'Weight it up, Frenchy . . . it's a nasty position to be in.'

'But mister,' – her voice was hoarse now – 'it wasn't nothing to do with me – nothing – I'll swear to it!'

Gently shrugged and picked up his hat to fan himself again.

'I didn't have no hand in it . . . honest to God!'

Gently fanned himself impassively.

'I didn't – I *didn't* – I *didn't*!' The voice was a scream now and she threw herself on her knees in a fit of anguish. 'You got to believe me . . . mister . . . you *got* to!'

Gently nodded a single, indefinite nod and went on fanning.

'But *you've got to*, mister!'

Gently paused at the end of a stroke. 'If,' he said, 'you *didn't*, Frenchy, then the best thing you can do is to come clean . . .'

'But I can't, mister!' Her face twisted in indescribable torment.

'You can't?' Gently stared at her bleakly and recommenced his fanning.

'I can't – I *can't*! Don't you understand?'

'I understand there's a murder charge being kept on ice for someone.'

Frenchy moaned and sank in a heap on the floor. 'I didn't do it,' she babbled, 'I didn't do it . . . you got to believe me!'

Gently bent over and picked up the cigarette, which was making an oily mark on the dubious lino. 'Listen,

Frenchy, if it's any consolation to you, I don't think you knocked off Max, and I'm not personally trying to pin it on you. But you're obviously in it up to your neck, and unless you make yourself useful to us you're going to have a pretty rough passage in court. Now what about it . . . suppose we do a deal?'

'I can't, mister – I daren't!'

'We'll give you protection. You've nothing to be afraid of.'

The dyed-blonde hair shook hopelessly. 'They'd get me . . . they always do. They don't never forget, mister.'

'Nonsense,' said Gently stoutly, 'this is England, Frenchy.'

Her haunted eyes looked up at him, hesitating. Then she gave a hysterical little laugh. 'That's what Max thought, too . . . he'd be safe once he got to England!'

They went down the naked stairway, Frenchy clicking her high heels, Gently clumping in the rear. She had put on her white two-piece with its red piping and split skirt, and there was almost a degree of respectability about her make-up. At the bottom she fished a key out of her handbag and locked the street door. Gently took it from her and slipped it into his pocket.

'And to save a little trouble . . .?'

Frenchy sniffed and tossed her head towards the corner shop. 'Mother Goffin over the way . . . and don't let her kid you up she's deaf.'

'I won't,' murmured Gently, 'at least, not twice in one day.'

They proceeded towards the Front, Gently feeling a

trifle self-conscious beside so much window-dressing. At the corner of the street lurked Nits, his bulging eyes fixed upon them. As they drew closer he sidled out to meet them.

'Giddout of the way, you!' snapped Frenchy, angering suddenly. But Nits' attention had focused on Gently.

'You leave her alone – you leave her alone!' he piped, 'she's a good girl, you mustn't take her away!'

'Clear out!' screeched Frenchy, 'I've had enough of you hanging round me!'

Gently put his hand in his pocket for a coin, but as he did so the halfwit came flying at him with flailing arms and legs.

'You shan't take her away – you shan't – I won't let you!'

'Here, here,' said Gently, 'that's no way for a young man to behave—!'

'I'll kill you, I will, I tell you I'll kill you!'

'And I'll bleedin' kill you!' screamed Frenchy, catching Nits such a cuff across the face that he was almost cart-wheeled into the gutter. For a moment he lay there, pop-eyed and gibbering, then he sprang to his feet in a whirl of limbs and darted away down Dulford Street like a bewildered animal.

'Dirty little git!' jeered Frenchy, 'they're all the same – doesn't matter what they are. Men are all one filthy pack together!'

The super wasn't feeling his pluperfect best just then. He'd been butting his head against brick walls all day. He'd disregarded Gently, made an enemy of Christopher Wylie, been torn off a helluva strip by the chief constable, failed to find the merest trace of a suitcase full of hundred-dollar bills and, to cap it all, he was beginning to realize that he'd been wrong anyway. It was this last that really hurt. The rest he was prepared to take in his superintendental stride . . .

'So she won't talk!' he almost snarled, as Gently and he sluiced down canteen tea in the latter's office.

Gently shrugged woodenly. 'You can't really blame her. She's convinced she'd be signing her own death-warrant.'

'Well, if she doesn't sign it I shall – she can bank on that for a start!' yapped the super.

'Oh, I don't know . . .' Gently put down his cup and mopped his forehead with a handkerchief that had been seeing life. 'I've got a couple of men looking for the taxi that picked them up on Tuesday night . . . if we can find that, we shall be getting somewhere.'

'Now look here, Gently!' The super almost choked. 'This woman is the crux of the case. If your guessing is correct she knows everything – where he went to, who picked him up, who was after the money – she may even have been a witness to the murder, for all we know! And all you can tell me is she won't talk. That's all! They've put a scare into her, so she won't talk!'

'It isn't a small size in scares, when you come to think of it.'

'I don't care what size it was!' raved the super. 'I've got a scare up my sleeve, too, quite as big as any of theirs. We'll soon see who's got the biggest!'

Gently looked woodener than ever. 'She's got a perfect right to keep quiet. And you're overestimating

165

your scare. There's nothing you can pin to Frenchy apart from conspiracy to burgle, and she's not such a fool that she doesn't know it.'

'Oh, she isn't, isn't she? We'll soon see about that! I'll make a pass at her with a murder charge that'll put paid to all this nonsense . . .!'

'No.' Gently shook his head. 'I've tried it, anyway. The position is that you *might* get her, but they *certainly* will. They're the ones who are holding a pistol in her back . . . or at least they've made her think so. No . . . Frenchy's our ace in the hole, and for the moment we'll have to leave her there. I've got an impression she'll be a lot more vocal when she sees certain people wearing handcuffs.'

'But how the devil are you going to get handcuffs on them when she won't talk? And the man we want – let's face it, Gently, it's the fellow with the scar who's got high jump written all over him – where will you ever lay hands on him again?'

'He was here last night,' muttered Gently obstinately.

'Last night, last night! But where is he now – today? He isn't just a criminal on the run. He's part of a powerful and ruthless organization, professionals to their fingertips.'

Gently smiled feebly. 'Even organizations are run by human beings . . . they're sometimes quite modest concerns when you get to grips with them. Anyway . . . about Frenchy. I want to ask a favour.'

The super grunted fiercely, as though indicating it wasn't his day for such things.

'I don't want her kept here . . . I'd like her released on bail.'

'On BAIL!!!' erupted the super, his eyes jumping open as though he had been stung.

'Yes ... nothing very heavy. Just a modest little reminder.'

'But good heavens, man – bail! A woman of that character – arrested for a felony – suspected of complicity in murder – and you're asking for bail! What the devil do you think I should put on my report?'

'Just say it was at my request,' murmured Gently soothingly, 'I'll carry the can if she doesn't turn up.'

'But I'm already in bad with the CC over this business—!'

'She'll be in court. You needn't worry about that.'

The super treated Gently to several seconds of his best three-phase stare. 'All right,' he said at last, 'it's your idea, Gently. You can have her. But God help you if she's missing when we go to court. You'll have her tailed, of course?'

'Oh yes ... Dutt's one of the best tails in the business. And I'd like someone to check up on the flat in Dulford Street. The rent is paid to a Mrs Goffin who keeps a newsagent's opposite ... I'm just the wee-ish bit interested to know where it goes after that.'

The telephone rang and the super hooked it wearily to his ear. Gently rose to go, but the super, after a couple of exchanges, motioned for him to wait and grabbed a pencil out of his tray.

'Yes ... yes ... d'you mind spelling it? ... yes ... as in Mau-Mau ... got it ... you'll send his cards ... right ... yes ... thank you!'

He hung up and pushed his desk-pad across for

Gently's inspection. 'There you are – for what it's worth!'

Gently glanced at the pad and back at the super.

'The names of our playmates . . . Special *does* work on a Sunday! Olaf Streifer is Scarface – he's an agent of this precious TSK Party's secret police . . . Maulik, it's called. Special want him in connection with some naval sabotage at Portsmouth two years ago. You seem to have got a set of his prints from somewhere, incidentally . . .'

Gently nodded. 'And this . . . Stratilesceul?'

'Stephan Stratilesceul – the lad on the slab. He wasn't known over here, but the Sûreté had records. They wanted him in connection with a similar business at Toulon . . . the TSK seems to have a lien on naval naughtiness.' He picked up the pad and held it up ironically. 'So now we know – and how much further does it get us?'

Gently hoisted a neutral shoulder. 'It all helps to fill in the picture . . . you can't know too much about a murder.'

CHAPTER TEN

I T HAD BEEN too fine.

The peerless sky which had filled the beaches yesterday had vanished overnight literally in a clap of thunder and its place was filled by low, yellow-grey cloud which drizzled warmly, as though somewhere that wonderful sun was still trying to filter its way through. Perhaps it was wise of nature. There had been havoc enough wrought by one fine Sunday. In the damp streets plastic-caped holidaymakers went about with a wonderful solicitude for their fiery backs and arms . . .

Now it was the cafes that came into their own. The innumerable little boxes clustered cheek by jowl all the way down Duke Street, empty and forlorn while the sun reigned, filled up now to the last tubular steel chair. After all, it wasn't an unpleasant rain . . . one expected it some time during the holiday. And there were worse things to be done than drinking one's coffee, smoking, writing cards and going through the newspapers . . .

Not that it was front-page today, their own especial murder. The super had kindly released the news of the arrest of Jeff and Bonce and the discovery of the grey suit, but in the face of fierce competition from a Cabinet re-shuffle it hadn't made the grade. It had slipped to page five. Strangely unanimous, the editors of the dailies had each come to the conclusion that the Body on the Beach wasn't going to get anywhere, and they were quietly preparing to forget the whole thing.

Like a certain superintendent, thought Gently, resting his elbows on the low wall bounding the promenade . . . though of course, the man had his reasons.

He hitched up his fawn raincoat and produced his pipe. He couldn't help it . . . this sort of weather always made him moody. To wake up and find it raining induced in him a vein of pessimism, both with himself and with society. He just wanted to turn over and go to sleep again and forget all about them . . .

Well . . . if it *would* rain!

He lit the sizzling pipe, tossed the match on to the sand below and turned abruptly away from the melancholy sea.

Opposite him, across the carriage-way, loomed the garish tiled front of the Marina Cinema. A spare, florid-faced man with a wrinkled brow and a shock of tow hair was polishing the chrome handles of the swing-doors. Gently went across to him.

'You're at it early this morning . . .'

The man paused to throw him a sharp look and then went on with his polishing. 'It's got to be done some time, mate.'

'The sea air can't do them a lot of good.'

'Telling me! It plays the bloody hell with them.'

He rubbed away till he came to the top of the handle, Gently watching patiently the while. At last he straightened out and gave his cloth a shaking.

'What are you – a cop, mate?' he asked briefly.

Gently nodded sadly. 'Only I was hoping it didn't show quite so much . . .'

'Huh! I can always smell a cop a mile away.'

'I shouldn't have stood to windward, should I?'

The tow-haired man took a reef in his cloth and advanced to the next door-handle. 'What do you want here, anyway?'

'The usual thing. Some information.'

'And suppose I haven't got any?'

'Suppose,' said Gently smoothly, 'suppose you be a smart little ex-con and keep a civil tongue when you talk to a policeman?'

'An ex-con . . .! What creeping nark told you that?'

Gently smiled at a diagonal frame filled with Lollo-brigida. 'You aren't the only one with a developed sense of smell . . .'

But he didn't get any information from the man. He didn't, or wouldn't, remember anything about people taking taxis on Tuesday night last. Yes, he would have been in the vestibule just before the last house turned out, but he was probably chatting to the cashier or one of the girls . . . no, there wasn't anybody else on late turn that night . . . no, he didn't know Frenchy or anyone like her . . . going straight he was, and he defied anyone to prove different.

Gently left him to his handles and plodded on down the Front, pessimism confirmed in his soul.

'The Feathers' was open, but it seemed rather a waste of electricity on such a customless morning. Its arrow was darting away with customary vigour, albeit it fizzed a little in the rain, but there were few enough strollers to be pricked into the temporary refuge of the arcade: its music drooled hollowly down empty aisles. Gently went up the steps and through the doors. Not a soul was about except the attendant, who was sweeping the floor at the far end. Through the doors of the bar, which were stood open with two chairs, could be seen a figure similarly engaged and a 'closed' notice hung rakishly on a chair-back. Obviously, they weren't expecting a rush of business.

He turned to the nearest machine and dropped a penny in the slot. It was one of the pre-war 'Stock Exchange' type and a pull on the handle yielded a brisk no-dividends. Gently tried again. He'd got quite a pocket-full of coppers. Absently he yanked the lever and watched the colourful passage of Rubber, Textiles, Railways and Gold . . . it seemed hard that such a well furnished wheel should come up no-dividends twice in a row. But it did. It was clever. It sorted out a solitary white from a whole rainbow of coloured, and stuck to it with an obstinate firmness.

A gigantic hand ornamented with a solitaire diamond suddenly covered the handle and its guard.

'You haven't got the knack, Inspector,' purred Louey's voice behind him, 'let an old professional show you how to beat the book!'

Gently stood back without replying and Louey pressed a coin into the slot. Then he caressed the handle with an even, almost casual pressure and the wheel drifted lazily round to a Gold segment. A second coin brought coppers cascading down the shoot.

'You see, Inspector?' Louey's gold tooth shone its message of innocent goodwill. 'It *is a* matter of skill, after all . . .'

Gently shrugged and repossessed himself of his twopence. 'It needs a safe-breaker's touch . . . the way one tickles a combination lock.'

Louey's smile broadened. 'Some of the kids learn how to play them, though it costs them a few weeks' pocket-money. But I don't mind that . . . there are fifty who never learn for every one who does.'

'Sounds like an expensive accomplishment to me.'

'We have to risk our stakes, Inspector, when we're out to win something.'

Louey picked up the rest of the coins from the shoot and paid them back into the machine, one by one. They flicked up no-dividends as surely as a till flicking up no-sales.

'Skill,' purred Louey, 'you can't really call it gambling, Inspector.'

Gently quizzed the huge man's sack-like raincoat and corduroy cap. 'You were just going out?'

'My morning constitutional,' nodded Louey, 'I always take it, summer and winter.'

'Mind if I come too?'

'Delighted, Inspector! I was hoping for the opportunity of another little chat.'

He ushered Gently out, holding the door obsequiously for him. They crossed the carriage-way and turned southwards along the almost deserted Front. The rain, from being a drizzle, had now become quite steady and gusts of sea-breeze made it cut across their faces as they walked. Louey snuffed the air and looked up at the sky.

'It's set in for the day . . . I shall be a richer man by tomorrow night, Inspector. You remember my pussy? I expect you thought he'd got his lines crossed yesterday, but he never makes a mistake. I suppose we shan't have the pleasure of your company at the races tomorrow?'

Gently grunted. 'I follow my business . . . wherever it takes me.'

'Ah yes . . . and I see by the papers that you're making great strides. Well, well! Those two youngsters in their ridiculous suits! It must be a lesson to me to keep a tighter check on the customers in the bar . . .'

Gently flipped the sodden brim of his trilby. 'I still prefer your first theory, the one about a political organization.'

'You do?' Louey seemed pleasantly surprised. 'I thought you must have forgotten that, Inspector . . . my amateur summing-up of the case! But these new facts explode it, I'm afraid. There wouldn't seem to be much connection between Teddy boys and politics.'

'There isn't,' grunted Gently.

'Then surely we must give up my theory . . .?'

'We could if the Teddy boys killed Stratilesceul, but as it is they only pinched his suitcase.'

Three strides went by in silence. 'Stratilesceul?' echoed Louey, 'is that the name of the murdered man?'

'The man who skipped the *Ortory* at Hull and was chased down here by Streifer.'

'Streifer . . .?' This time Gently lost count of the number of strides. 'I'm sorry, Inspector . . . a lot of this hasn't appeared in the papers, or if it has, I've missed it. Was it from Hull that this unfortunate man came?'

'It was.'

'And he was chased by someone?'

'By Streifer. Olaf Streifer. A member of the Maulik, the TSK secret police. It was just like in your theory, Louey . . . the execution of a traitor by an organization he had betrayed.'

The big man shook his head with an air of bewilderment. 'You must excuse me if I seem a little dense . . . I'm not so familiar with the business as yourself, Inspector. Am I to take it that the case is closed and that you have arrested this . . . Streifer?'

Gently didn't seem to have heard. He was poking in his pocket for a peppermint cream.

Louey gave a little laugh. 'I was saying, Inspector . . . has this Streifer been arrested?'

The peppermint cream was found and Gently nibbled it with deaf composure . . . it might have been the rain which was making him so hard of hearing. Louey shook his head again as though realizing that it was necessary to humour a Yard man. After all, he seemed to be saying, it was a privilege thus to be taken into the great man's confidence at all . . .

They strode on towards South Shore. The rain kept driving in from the sea. There were warm sheets of it now, really wetting, and Gently's experienced brogues were beginning to squelch. Even Louey was constrained to do up his top button, though it meant veiling the glories of a pearl tie-pin stuck in a grey silk tie but there weren't many people to see it in any case.

'Of course, it was Streifer we saw coming out of your office on Friday night,' grunted Gently at last, the peppermint cream being fairly disposed of.

'I thought we had disposed of that point, Inspector.' Louey sounded justifiably piqued. 'But it was Streifer all right, and it was your office all right.'

'Well, if you say so . . . but I can't imagine what he was doing there. Naturally we had a little check after you'd told us about it, but as far as we were able to discover nothing had been stolen or disturbed.' Louey turned his huge head towards Gently. 'Do you want my opinion, Inspector?'

Gently shrugged, hunched down in a leaky collar.

'My opinion is that *if* it was Streifer and *if* it was my office, he must have ducked in there to avoid running into your man. Doesn't that sound a reasonable explanation?'

'Very reasonable . . . and why did he duck out again?'

'Obviously he would have heard Peachey coming back.'

'Why wasn't he worried by the risk of meeting Peachey when he ducked in?'

'Oh, come now, Inspector, I can't work out the minute details for you . . .!'

'And how did he know the door was unlocked in the first place?'

'One must use one's imagination. Perhaps he took cover in the doorway, and then tried the handle . . .'

'Why, in fact, would he take cover at all? On Friday

night he wasn't known to us, and neither was my man known to him.'

Louey chuckled softly. 'There you are, Inspector! My naïve amateur deductions don't hold water for a moment, do they? I'm afraid it's as big a mystery as ever . . . I would never have made a policeman.'

'One other thing,' added Gently evenly, 'how did you come to know that it was my man who saw Streifer leave your office?'

Louey's chuckle continued. 'How else could you have known about it? You admit that Streifer meant nothing to you on Friday night, so you could hardly have been making inquiries after him, Inspector . . .'

They had passed by the Wellesley, its wrought-iron fantasia washed and gleaming, and were approaching the weirdly incongruous skyline of the Pleasure Beach. High over all reared the Scenic Railway, a miniature Bass Rock fashioned out of painted canvas and paper mache, and under it, like a brood of Easter chicks under a hen, the gay-painted turrets and roofs of side shows, booths and the other mechanical entertainments. Harsh strains of music through the rain suggested that the Pleasure Beachers, like lesser mortals, were assuming a custom though they had it not.

Louey gestured comfortably towards the gateway. 'Rivals of mine . . . but they don't have a licence! Shall we stroll through?'

Gently nodded drippingly. 'I want to see the place. It's where Streifer dropped the man who was tailing him on Friday.'

'Which shows he knew his job, Inspector. Isn't this where you would come to shake off a tail?'

'I can't say I've had much experience . . .'

They passed under the flaunting portal with its electric jewellery. The close-packed attractions within wore a rueful look, unsupported by the crowds. Larger and more expensive pieces were frankly at a standstill – the Caterpillar had postponed its gallop, the Glee Cars their jaunting – while the smaller roundabouts and rides were operating at a profit margin which was doubtful. Booth attendants stood about in each other's stalls. They were drinking tea and staring around them morosely. The owner of the Ghost Train, for want of something to do, was riding round in his own contraption, but all its promised thrills seemed unable to raise the siege of boredom which had invested his countenance.

'Of course there's Frenchy,' brooded Gently, obstinately undiverted by all these diversions.

'Frenchy?' echoed Louey indifferently, 'is she mixed up with the business too? She took a hint the other night, Inspector. She hasn't been near the bar since then.'

'Stratilesceul was a client of hers . . . she went off to the North Shore with him in a taxi just before he was murdered.'

'Ah, that accounts for a rumour I heard that she had been arrested.'

'You heard such a rumour?'

'We're for ever hearing them in our business.'

'Undoubtedly . . . you are very well placed.'

Gently halted to inspect the front of a sideshow. It was an exhibition of methods of execution through the centuries and was advertised by some particularly lurid illustrations. He seemed to be strangely fascinated.

'And she will have given you some useful information?' suggested Louey, moving on a step impatiently.

'She knows a good deal . . . she'll be a devastating witness.'

'There would be some danger in it for her.'

'Danger? With police protection?'

Louey turned his back on the sideshow and busied himself with lighting a cigarette. 'If this murder was the work of an organization – and you don't seem to be in any doubt about it now – then there would be a very real danger for anyone bearing material witness. Men can be hanged, Inspector, but organizations cannot. And my feeling is that a person of Frenchy's kidney wouldn't risk too much for pure love of our excellent police force.'

Gently stooped to get a closer view of a gentleman who had been given too long a drop, with the usual top-secret result. 'You know Frenchy well?' he asked carelessly.

'I? Not apart from running her out of my bar on several occasions.'

'Dulton . . . Dulsome Street is where she lives.'

'Dulford Street, Inspector.'

'That's right. You've been there?'

'Not visiting Frenchy, if that's what you mean.'

'You're sure of that? Not in the last day or two?'

'Quite positive, Inspector. My tastes have never been that way inclined.'

Gently straightened up slowly. 'Odd,' he said, frowning.

'What's odd about that?'

'These two cigarette ends.' Gently felt in his pocket and produced a crumpled envelope. 'There . . . you see? Your blend of Russian. I found them in an ashtray in Frenchy's bedroom yesterday afternoon.'

Louey poked at them with a gigantic finger and nodded heavily. 'You're right, Inspector . . . it is my blend.'

'I was sure of it . . . I was feeling positive you'd been there.'

The grey eyes rested on his firmly, the flecked pupil seeming curiously larger than its neighbour. 'Isn't it a shame, Inspector,' purred Louey, 'I thought my cigarettes were exclusive. And now, in the commission of your duty, you've proved that someone else in Starmouth smokes them too . . . at least, I take it, it was in the commission of your duty?'

Gently shrugged and shoved the envelope back into his pocket.

The Scenic Railway had its shutters up, though someone was tinkering with one of the trolleys. It wasn't quite so impressive on a nearer view. Its cliffs and crags were so palpably props, its tunnels and bridges so contrived. And the rain made it look sorrier still, a great, hollow, sodden mockery. Gently took refuge in a peppermint cream as they squelched past it. If only he'd thought to bring a more reliable pair of shoes . . .!

'I suppose I don't have to ask you to account for your movements last Tuesday night?' he growled, as they got out on to the promenade again.

'But of course!' Louey chuckled, as though he welcomed the inquiry. 'I was having a little party in the back . . . Peachey, Artie, Tizer and some more of the boys. You ask them, Inspector. They'll all remember my party on Tuesday night.'

'I'm sure they will. And of course it went on till late?'

'Not terribly late. I cleared them out at two.'

'Just late enough, in fact.'

'Well . . . it was late enough for me.'

'And that would be your story – supposing you had to have a story?'

'Certainly, Inspector. Why should I tell any other?'

'There's no knowing what Frenchy may say.'

'She's a woman without character.'

'Or Streifer, for example.'

'Streifer?' Louey hung on to the word, as though expecting an explanation.

'And then there's your car,' continued Gently, ignoring him. 'Was that borrowed or something on the Tuesday night?'

'My car . . .?' This time the inquiring tone had an edge of anxiety.

'You lent it to someone – and they went up to North Shore?'

'I don't understand, Inspector. My car would have been in its lock-up in Botolph Street.'

'Even though it was seen somewhere else?'

'That would hardly be possible . . .'

'Then you didn't lend it to anyone?'

'No. It was never out of the garage.'

'So the people who saw it at North Shore would be liars?'

'They were certainly under a misapprehension . . .'

Gently flicked briskly at his over-worked trilby. 'You'll have got rid of the ring, of course . . . that was too much of a coincidence.'

The big features relaxed and there was a glimpse of gold. 'If you don't mind me saying it, Inspector, I think we had better consider that ring to have been an illusion.'

'I'm not subject to illusions, Louey.'

'But just once, perhaps, in a long career?'

'Not even once, and certainly not prophetically. I didn't know the TSK or its secret sign existed when I saw your ring, but I knew where I'd seen it before when it turned up a second time.'

'A trick of the memory, perhaps.'

'The police aren't much subject to them.'

'Well, shall we say rather dubious evidence?'

In a court of law it would be for the jury to decide.'

Louey laughed his low, caressing laugh. 'How we talk, Inspector . . . how we do. But I like these examples of your official approach to a problem. It's comforting to feel that the guardians of our law and order work so efficiently and so intelligently. As I said on a former occasion, I could only wish you had more promising material to deal with in the present instance.'

'I'll make do,' grunted Gently, 'it doesn't seem to be running out on me at the moment.'

Louey shook his head with a sort of playful sympathy. 'I respect your attitude . . . it's the attitude one would expect and look for in such a man as yourself. But honestly, Inspector, when one takes stock of the situation . . . for instance, this Streifer. What can you do about him? You can connect him with the murdered man in a dozen ways, you can show he was the most likely one to have done it – but what's all that worth when you haven't got a scrap of proof that he did it? I don't have to remind you of our careful court procedure. In some countries Streifer would be executed out-of-hand on a tenth of the evidence . . . and perhaps you'll allow, without too much injustice. But here you have to convince your jury. Here you are obliged to go to fanatical lengths to show proof and double proof. And you don't seem to have it, Inspector. You are faced with a planned execution, the details of which have been efficiently erased. I've no doubt that a jury would convict Streifer of something – there must be several lesser charges you could bring – but as a betting man, Inspector, I'm willing to give you ten to one they never convict him of murdering Stratilesceul.'

Louey took a farewell puff at his cigarette and seemed about to toss it away. Then he changed his mind and with a gilded smile handed it to Gently.

'Another one for your collection!'

Gently nodded and extinguished it carefully.

'The previous remarks,' continued Louey, watching him, 'supposing you have in fact arrested Streifer . . .?'

Gently tucked away the sodden end without replying. Louey nodded as though that were sufficient answer.

'And I don't think you will, Inspector . . . I don't really think you will. If he was, as you say, a member of the . . . what was it? A secret police? I imagine he will know his way out of a country . . . don't you? Especially with the assistance we must assume he will get from his organization over here.'

Gently stuck his hands in his pockets and plodded on. He seemed completely immersed in something taking place over the pale sea-horizon.

'It's wrong of me,' mused Louey, 'I shouldn't say it . . . but I can't help feeling a little sympathy for the man.'

'Sympathy? For a cold-blooded murderer?'

'Not a murderer, Inspector . . . an executioner, I think you must call him.'

'Stratilesceul's hands were tied – do you sympathize with that?'

'You're forgetting, Inspector, we also tie a man's hands for execution. If killing is the order, one may as well kill efficiently.'

'But we don't torture, Louey. Stratilesceul was burned with cigarettes.'

'Our torture is mental, Inspector . . . it lasts longer, and it isn't done for useful ends, such as eliciting information. No . . . I'm sorry. You must permit me to feel some sympathy for Streifer. He did what he did in the service of an ideal, rightly or wrongly . . . you really mustn't equate him with even the common hangman.'

Gently's shoulders hunched ever higher. 'He was paid, wasn't he . . . just like the common hangman?'

'Naturally, a labourer is worthy of his hire. But the pay wasn't his motive, you know. It wouldn't be an adequate incentive to such risk and responsibility. Your hangman is a mere assassin . . . you hand him his thirty pieces of silver and say Murder; we have bound your victim. And he murders, Inspector. He has your full protection. His crime is written up to humanity and he departs to spend the blood-money. Is this the way of the man you want to hang? Is this the way of any of the men you hang?'

'At least we kill only the killers . . .'

'Is that better than killing for an ideal?'

'It is an ideal – to protect people on their lawful occasions.'

'If only it protected them, Inspector . . . if only it did! But your ideal is a pathetic fallacy, I'm afraid. Of course it's wrong to say this . . . I understand your position. Your duty is to catch a criminal and judgment is elsewhere. But I want you to understand me when I say I feel a little sympathy with Streifer . . . we can talk together, Inspector. You are a man of intelligence.'

They had come to the end of the town, a straggle of houses on one hand, wasteground and the beach on the other. Louey paused as they came abreast with a decaying pill-box.

'This is as far as I go, fair weather or foul.'

Gently nodded woodenly and gave his trilby a further flick. Then he turned to face the two grey eyes which rested on him confidently, almost affectionately.

'I'm glad you made the point . . .' The eyes were interrogative. '. . . about my duty. It *is* to catch the criminal.'

Louey's enormous head tilted backwards and for-wards almost imperceptibly.

'And since I'm in betting company, Louey, I'll take you at the odds. Wasn't it ten to one you quoted?'

'At ten to one . . . and Louey always pays.'

'I'll have a pound on. You can open my account.'

The grey eyes flashed and the big man burst into laughter.

'You're on, Inspector . . . the first policeman I ever had on my books!'

Gently quizzed him expressionlessly from the depths of his comfortless collar. 'Let's hope you're lucky,' he said, 'let's hope I'm not the last.'

The lonely phone-box had a tilt in it, due to the subsidence of its sandy foundation. But it was dry inside and Gently took time off to light his pipe before getting down to business. He gave headquarters' number.

'Get me Inspector Copping.'

Copping arrived in fairly prompt switchboard time.

'Gently here . . . are we still entertaining Frenchy?'

'Entertaining's the word!' came Copping's disgusted voice. 'She's been yelling her head off since they brought her back . . . says she wants a lawyer and that we're holding her under false pretences.'

Gently grinned in a cloud of pipe-smoke. 'She's got her bail . . . what more does she want?'

'The cash, apparently . . . you seem to have pinched her at the end of the month.'

'Well . . . keep her nice and cosy. Has anything else come in?'

'Not a darned thing.'

'Have the lab made anything of that paper?'

'They say it's manufactured in Bristol and used for packing mattresses. I've got a man going round the stores trying to match it.'

'No prints worth having?'

'Nothing anybody's heard of.'

'You haven't traced that taxi?'

'Not so's you'd notice it.'

Gently clicked his tongue. 'It's a wet Monday all right, isn't it? Is Dutt anywhere handy?'

'He's hanging about waiting for someone to bail Frenchy.'

'I want him for a job . . . one of your own men will have to watch our Frenchy.'

The phone at the other end was laid down and Gently whiled away the odd moments watching two raindrops making tracks down the ebony panel in the back of the box. Then Dutt's chirpy accents saluted him from the receiver.

'Yessir? You was wanting me?'

'Yes, Dutt . . . I want you to do a little scouting in your old pitch in Botolph Street. There's a lock-up garage there where Louey keeps his car. You might find out if anyone noticed the car being used on Tuesday night . . .'

'Yessir. I think I knows the very garage you're talking about.'

'Stout fellow, Dutt. And don't forget your mac.'

'No, sir! Don't you worry!'

Gently eyed the rain-swept vista outside his box with a jaundiced stare. 'And while we're at it, Dutt, get them to send a car to pick me up at South Shore . . . I've had all the constitutional my constitution will stand for one wet day!'

CHAPTER ELEVEN

THERE WAS A hiatus in the proceedings and the super, excellent man, had scented it out with his keen, service-minded nostrils. Gently had come to a standstill. His case was bogging down. He had pushed it up the hill with his bulky shoulder until he was in hailing distance of the top and now, with the deceptive vision of arrests and charges dead ahead, he was stuck fast as though he had run into an invisible barrier. It was a sad sight, but not an unexpected one. The super had had a strong intuition all along that this was how it would wind up. Because he knew something about secret agents, did the super. He had come across them before in his long career and he could tell Gently, if Gently was harbouring any illusions, just how slippery these birds inevitably were . . .

'You see, they *plan* their murders . . . that's the vital difference between them and the ordinary homicide. They know what we'll do and they take damn' good care to protect themselves.'

Gently looked up from a large-scale map and smiled

with an irony which the super was unable to appreciate. 'In fact we're . . . "faced with a planned execution, the details of which have been efficiently erased".'

'Precisely.' The super cast him a suspicious glance. 'We may as well face it, Gently. We're not infallible. We make use of our skill and technique to the best of our ability, but the people on the other side start with an enormous advantage and if they use it intelligently then we're batting on a pretty sticky wicket.'

'I know, I've heard it once before today. We haven't got Streifer, we can't prove he did it and' – he rustled the map on his desk – 'we don't even know where it was done.'

'Well – those are the facts, Gently, and you'd better add that we've exhausted most of the chances of improving on them. Oh, I don't want to be discouraging, and I'm certainly not disparaging all the sound work you've put in getting this case into perspective, but you are scraping the bottom of the barrel now and getting precious little for it – and every hour that passes makes it less and less likely that we shall lay hands on Streifer. This isn't his first job here, you must remember. The Special have been after him before without finding hide nor hair of him and there's no reason to expect they'll be luckier this time.'

'You think I should write my report?'

The super's grizzled brows knitted in a frown. 'I'm not saying that, Gently. I'll leave you to be the judge of when you can no longer usefully continue the investigation. The point I'm making is that we should look at the thing realistically. For instance, those men of mine at the stations and the bus terminus.'

'You can have them back now,' Gently shrugged.

'And the two men you put on the taxis . . . they've checked and re-checked every hackney-carriage driver in town.'

Gently looked obstinate. 'That taxi must be somewhere.'

'You say it must – but your only evidence is Wylie's and Baines's statements. I wouldn't be inclined to give it too much weight if I were you.'

'They'd no reason to lie.'

'They'd every reason to lie. They wanted to make it seem that Frenchy was the principal . . . it could just be that she's as innocent as she says she is.'

Gently shook his head impatiently. 'Baines wasn't lying. The statements agree except where Wylie is trying to whitewash himself.'

'The fact remains that no taxi driver in town remembers the incident and nobody's got records of such a journey. Of course it's just possible that it was a taxi licensed at Norchester or Lewiston that picked them up . . . you know the distances, you can judge how likely it would be.'

'I'm sorry . . . but that taxi has got to be found.'

'Then what do you suggest – a general check-up of all the taxis in a fifty-mile radius?'

'It may come to that, though first I would like your men to re-check their re-check . . . it's surprising how repetition sometimes jogs people's memories.'

The super gave Gently what from meaner men would have been classed as a dirty look.

'Very well . . . you know your job. But remember

that I've got plenty of routine work going begging when you're through with the bottom of the barrel . . .!'

It was a good exit line and the super duly acted upon it. Gently folded up his map with a sigh and stowed it in the drawer with the Moriarty. He didn't blame the super. He would have felt exactly the same in the great man's shoes. Police routine didn't stop because a couple of Yard men were trying to hatch a murder charge . . . it just became more difficult. And when the murder charge didn't look like hatching anyway, well then the Yard men started to become a nuisance about the place. The trouble was that the super hadn't got an incentive any more. He was reasonably happy with the way things had panned out. His corpse was no longer an unsolved mystery, he had pinched a small handful of auxiliaries in the case and if the principal had made tracks for a far country it wasn't through any dereliction of the super's duty . . . All that really concerned the super now was the propitiation of Christopher Wylie and the making of his peace with the chief constable.

Gently sighed again and unhooked his clammy raincoat. There were times when being a Central Office man wasn't all it was cracked up to be.

Accoutred for the fray, he went along to the canteen for a preliminary cup of tea. It was a quiet time there. He had the gloomy room all to himself. Behind the scenes could be heard the chink and clatter of washing-up in progress, but the only other excitement the place afforded was the distant view of someone working on a car under a tilt. Gently sauntered to the window to watch the operation while he sipped. There was something soothing about watching other people grapple with their troubles.

And then, perhaps inspired by the tea, a dreamy expression crept into his eye. He drew closer to the window. He pulled back one of the blue cotton curtains. At one stage he was even pressing his nose against the pane.

Finally he put down his cup half-finished and let himself out into the yard by the side-door.

It was an elderly car of the high-built and spacious days, and the elderly man who worked on it, though not high built, was spacious also. The dungareed rear end of him which protruded from the bonnet was particularly spacious, and so too was the language which rose in a muttered stream from somewhere in the interior. Gently hooked his fingers in the climb-proof wire fence which surrounded HQ property and conducted a leisurely survey.

'Having a spot of bother?' he inquired affably.

The stream of language faltered and a red, moon-like face disengaged itself from the oily deeps.

'Bother! Can't you hear I'm a-havin' some bother?'

'Well . . . it sounded like a big end gone, to say the least.'

The spacious one heaved himself upright and shored his bulk against the off-side mudguard. 'Jenny!' he observed feelingly, 'that's the bloomin' trouble – Jenny!'

'There's a woman in the case?' queried Gently, who wasn't mechanically minded.

'Woman? Naow – the Jenny! Stuck away there at the bottom till it's nearly draggin' on the ground – an' they must know it's goin' to give trouble – Jennies *allus* give trouble!'

He waved an adjustable at Gently as though daring him to contradict, but Gently's interest had slipped to some crude white lettering just visible on the uptilted bonnet. It read: 'Henry Artichoke, Hire Car, 76 High Street.'

'This your car?' he asked casually.

''Course it's my car – who's did you think it was?' Mr Artichoke gave the vehicle a glance of mingled affection and exasperation. 'Good now as half your modern tin-lizzies – only thas like me, getting old . . .'

Gently nodded understandingly. 'And how's business with you these days?'

'Business? Well – I don't complain. Though I aren't saying it's like it was in the old days—!'

'Too many charas and coach-trips.'

'An' all these new-fangled cars about . . . still, don't run away with the idea that I'm complainin'.'

'Were you doing much last week?'

'I was out on a trip or two – can't do without me altogether, you know.'

'Last Tuesday, for instance. Did you have a trip that day?'

Mr Artichoke ruminated a moment and dashed away a raindrop which had leaked on to his oily cheek. 'Tuesday . . . that was the day old Hullah was buried. Yes. Yes. I had a couple of trips on the Tuesday . . . in the mornin' I took Sid Shorter over to see his missus at the nursing home. Then last thing they had me out to fetch an old party and her things from Norchester – that's it!'

'What time would that have been?'

'Well, I hadn't got really set down at the "Hoss-shoes" . . . that couldn't have been much after seven.'

'Then you went to Norchester to pick her up?'

'Her'n her things – you'd be surprised what the old gal fetched away with her!'

'Made you late, I dare say . . .'

'Late enough so's I didn't get into the "Hoss-shoes" again . . .'

'It was after ten by the time you'd got her unpacked?'

'As near to it as makes no difference . . . parrot she'd got too – damn' nearly had my finger as I was carting it in!'

'And where did you take her . . . what was her new address?'

'Oh, she was goin' to live with the Parson of St Nicholas.'

'Is that the big church?'

'No – that's St John's. St Nicholas is the one down in Lighthouse Road.'

'You mean down at South Shore?'

'That's right . . . the one with a herrin' stuck up for a weather-vane.'

Gently relinquished his grip on the wire fence and dived his hand into a pocket that rustled. 'The Front – was it very busy when you came back that night?'

'Huh! Usual lot of rowdies – kids, the best part on'm.'

A peppermint cream came to light and lay poised on a stubby thumb. 'Did you have any luck . . . like picking up an odd fare?'

Mr Artichoke raised two round eyes grown suddenly suspicious. 'Here!' he exclaimed, 'come to think of it, I

194

don't like the side of the fence you're standing on – I don't like it at all!'

'It's the honest side, Mr Artichoke . . .'

'That's as may be – I don't think I like it!'

The peppermint cream went into Gently's mouth and was chewed upon thoughtfully. Mr Artichoke watched the operation indignantly, his broad face flushing a deeper shade of red. One would have thought there was something almost indecent about eating a peppermint cream.

'Now look, Mr Artichoke, I think you're in a position to help me in a rather important matter. I know you haven't got a hackney-carriage licence and that it was an offence for you to pick up a fare in the street, but if you picked up the people I think you did, then between you and me there won't be any charges . . . is that quite plain?'

Mr Artichoke nodded non-committally, but kept his mouth tight shut.

'Well then . . . did you or didn't you?'

Mr Artichoke shrugged his heavy shoulders and stared at the adjustable in his hand. 'That depends a bit on who them people was, don't it?' he remarked tentatively.

'I want you to tell me that.'

'But how am I goin' to know if they're the ones I shan't get pinched over?'

Gently returned the shrug. 'I've got a very bad memory except for criminal offences.'

Mr Artichoke brooded some more on the adjustable. 'Just suppose there were two of them – a male and a female. Is that somewhere about the mark?'

195

'It's right on the target.'

'And suppose this female was a blonde female – one of them there that work up this way during the season . . . am I still going the right way?'

Gently nodded with deliberate slowness.

'And suppose this bloke was a foreigner with a beard, dressed a bit flashy, and answering to the name of Max – and suppose they wanted taking to a house on the cliff which as far as I know has been empty for the last five years. Would I still be heading straight?'

There was the briefest of wavers in Gently's nodding and a smile little short of angelic crept over his face. 'Mr Artichoke . . . you've just answered the sixty-four dollar question, whether you know it or not.'

'Eh?' queried Mr Artichoke.

'The sixty-four dollar question,' repeated Gently. 'Now just stop here. Don't move. Don't go away. I'm going to have a short chat with the superintendent about his man-power problem and after that we'll make a little trip to North Shore together . . . who knows? We may even be lucky enough to find a tenant in that house on the cliff . . .'

Copping made one of the party and Bryce, at Gently's request, was added to the strength. Copping became highly indignant when he heard about Mr Artichoke's activities.

'And after all the ratepayers' money that's been spent trying to find the cabby! What's the use of issuing these licences if a lot of pirates come along and gum up our investigations for us?'

Gently clicked his tongue. 'He was only turning a slightly dishonest penny.'

'We might never have caught up with him . . . you admit it was pure accident.'

'Luck,' said Gently, 'you have to cultivate it in the Central Office . . .'

Copping snorted. 'We shouldn't have needed luck. Routine will catch a criminal if everyone is being completely honest . . .!'

Under Mr Artichoke's directions they proceeded north along the main Norchester road. The dreary suburbs passed by, the expensive splendours of High Town and finally the long, level, white-railed expanse of the race-course, its empty stands lifted gloomily against the rain-pale sea.

'Steady!' warned Mr Artichoke, made uneasy by the driver's reckless and newfangled technique, 'we're turning off here – if you can pull up this side of Barston!'

The driver slowed down to a dangerous thirty.

'There!' exclaimed Mr Artichoke, 'Up that little loke. There's only one house up there, so I shan't have made a mistake.'

'It's "Windy Tops"' muttered Copping, 'it belongs to one of the Thorners of Norchester.'

Gently glanced at him questioningly.

'We had some trouble with them a few years back. The Borough Engineer scheduled it as being unsafe because of cliff erosion and they made a case of it. He won the case, but there hasn't been a cliff-fall in that area from that day to this. Just mention "Windy Tops" if you want to get him in the raw.'

'It's been empty all the time?'

'Naturally. Nobody's allowed to live in it. The B.E. is just living for the day when it goes over the top.'

The narrow road skirted the northern end of the racecourse, crossed the railway line and turned abruptly left. Here the ground rose suddenly to form the first of a line of crumbling gravel cliffs and perched at the top, looking in no-wise conscious of its danger, was a small but well-architected modern house.

'Looks safe enough,' Gently murmured.

'Probably is,' grunted Copping, 'but the B.E. got rapped on the knuckles about a row of cottages that went over . . . he hasn't taken any chances since then.'

The road came to an end at a spacious turning place and the gate to 'Windy Tops'. Bryce was sent round to the back while Gently and Copping advanced on the front. The garden had run to seed and there was grass growing out of the crazy paving, but the house itself seemed in a fair state of preservation and Gently found himself sympathizing with the Thorners in their reluctance to abandon the place. He stooped to inspect the crazy paving.

'Someone's been up here recently all right.'

The grass had been bruised by trampling feet. But Copping was already trying the front-door handle and apparently expressing surprise at finding it locked against him. He ran an eagle eye over the front of the house and thus discovered a partly-open window which Gently had noticed as they got out of the car.

'Easy!' called Gently, 'there may be some interesting prints about.'

Copping whisked up the sash and dumped himself over the low sill. Gently followed him at a more dignified pace. It was a large room and had probably been the lounge, but it was quite empty except for some ashes of burnt paper in the grate. Copping swooped on them, sniffing like a well-trained hound.

'They're fresh!' he exclaimed, 'they haven't been there longer than a few days.'

Gently nodded and applied a speculative finger to the light switch. Pale radiance shone from an unshaded bulb.

'Every modern con . . . and I think I can hear a cistern hissing somewhere.'

'He's been living here!'

'Undoubtedly . . .'

'He might be here now!'

'There's just the remotest chance . . .'

The efficient Copping needed no more. He invaded the house like an unleashed jumping-cracker, pouncing from room to room, poking in cupboards, surprising the backs of doors and generally making life hectic for anything in the shape of a secret agent.

'He slept up here!' came his muffled cry from above-stairs, 'There's a mattress and some blankets . . . cigarette-ash . . . empty matchbox!'

Gently shook his head sadly and went to unlock the kitchen door. The cupboard was bare, he knew it intuitively. There had been that chance, that one chance, that Streifer had decided to lie low until the heat was off, but he had sensed it evaporating the moment he had set foot in this so-silent house. He called to Bryce.

'Any signs of life out there?'

'No sir, nobody – not even on the beach.'

'What about the garage?'

'The door's on the latch – there's nothing in there except a pair of old tyres.'

'Well, come in and give Inspector Copping a hand upstairs. You'll have to get into the loft somehow.'

Bryce came in without much enthusiasm and went up to join his superior. Gently remained below in the kitchen. There were plenty of signs there of recent occupation. On the draining-board stood a plastic cup and plate with a knife and fork, all dirty. A hot-plate was plugged in at the electric switch-point, upon it a tin kettle and nearby an aluminium teapot. In a wall-safe were a tin of condensed milk, tea, sugar, a couple of rolls . . . stale of course, but no staler than Saturday's rolls usually are on Monday afternoon . . . butter and an unopened tin of anchovies. By the wall leaned two cheap folding-stools. Under the sink stood a rusty distemper-tin containing refuse. And there were several newspapers, including Sunday's, and a pile of brown paper. Gently unfolded a *Sunday Express*. It had had a cutting taken from it. He unfolded three others. Each had cuttings taken from them.

'He's hopped it all right.' Copping came in, dusty and aggrieved. 'Bryce is up in the loft now, but he'd have hardly got up there without someone to give him a bunk . . . there's nothing to stand on. I'm afraid we're just too late . . . they always seem one jump ahead, these bastards!'

Gently pointed to the pile of brown paper. 'What do you make of that?'

Copping stared intelligently. 'Looks as though he bought a geyser or something.'

'Was that mattress upstairs a new one?'

'Brand new – and so were the blankets.'

'And what does that suggest to us . . . knowing what we do?'

There was a pause and then the divine spark fell. 'By glory – it's the same paper that was used to wrap the clothes!' Gently nodded approvingly. 'Used to wrap mattresses – and there's the new mattress and you can *see* it's the same paper – it's got that crimp in it, just the same!'

'And it's had a piece torn off it . . . just about the same size.'

Copping's heavy features flushed with excitement. 'We've got him, then – we can tie him in! We've got proof now, good, hard, producible proof – the sort of thing juries love – material proof!'

'Just one thing, though,' murmured Gently.

'Proof!' boomed Copping, 'what more do we need?'

'We need something we haven't got right at this moment and that's the initial proof that Streifer was ever in the house at all.'

Copping faltered in his raptures. 'But good lord . . . it *must* have been him!'

Gently shook an indulgent head. 'Remember that jury and keep your hands to yourself. Don't touch the paper, the taps, the dishes or anything else that's lying about. I suppose it's too late to worry about the doorknobs. As soon as Bryce is through having fun in the loft he'd better light out for your print man. It isn't likely that Streifer was too careful here . . . he expected to be far otherwheres when and if we ever identified the place.'

'And how right he was – how dead bloody right!'

Gently hunched his shoulders soberly. 'He's a man like you and me. People don't become magicians when they join a secret police.'

'It's enough to make you think so, the way this bloke keeps himself lost.'

A dishevelled and wash-prone Bryce was dispatched in the car and Gently, having completed his tour of the house, went out to inspect the grounds. They had nothing relevant to disclose. The tumpy wilderness which had been a lawn, the nettled and willow-herbed flower-beds, these looked as though a full five years had elapsed since a foot had trodden there, or a hand had been raised in their defence. Gently went round to the Achilles heel, the seaward side. Not more than five yards of stony land separated the house from its inevitable tumble to the beach.

'Can't last another winter,' observed Copping knowingly, 'should have gone in the January gales. It was sheer cussedness that made it hang on . . . there were falls everywhere except here.'

Gently approached timidly to the treacherous edge. Seventy feet below the wet sand looked dark and solid. North, south, the sullen lines of slanted combers fretted wearily, told their perpetual lie of harmlessness and non-aggression. Down by the racecourse a lonely path wore its way to the beach.

'That's it,' muttered Gently, 'they carted him down

there. How far would you say we were above the Front?'

Copping did some calculations. 'Two miles, about . . . might be a trifle less.'

'It just about tallies . . . I was reckoning on two miles. They dumped him in down there in the ebb, expecting the current to pick him up and carry him right down south. It was just rank bad luck that he finished up on their doorstep again . . .'

'You're positive it was done in the house?'

'Quite positive . . . I can see the whole picture now.'

'There weren't any signs of it – no blood-stains or anything.'

Gently smiled grimly. 'Professionals, Copping. He wasn't hacked about. Didn't you notice how little blood there was on the clothes?'

'And if they'd used violence it wouldn't have shown much, not in an empty house.'

'But they didn't use any . . . they didn't have to. He was delivered right into their hands, unarmed and unsuspecting. My guess is that the first thing he knew about it was an automatic dug into his ribs . . . you don't argue with a thing like that in the first instance. By the time he'd weighed the situation up his hands were tied and he hadn't any option. It's a classic case, Copping. Only our Delilahs come a bit coarser these days.'

'Delilahs!' Copping gave a laugh. 'He must have wanted his brains tested to take up with a mare like Frenchy.'

There was a sound of two cars pulling up and they returned to the front of the house. To their surprise it was the super who came stalking up the crazy-paving. The great man had a taut look, as though primed with high enterprise, and having stalked to the end of the crazy-paving he halted smartly, straddled his legs and quizzed Gently with a sideways look in which were blended both jealousy and admiration.

'All right!' he rapped, 'you're a happy man, Gently. You know your job, and I'm just a blasted ex-infantry officer who's got shoved into a rural police force!'

Gently bowed modestly, as though disclaiming praise from such high places. The super snorted and directed his gaze at a 'Windy Tops' chimney.

'So they got him!' he jerked from the corner of his mouth, 'laid for him on information – Special and the Limehouse lot – picked him up going aboard a Polish tramp. Nearly shot two men and laid out a third. They're bringing him up now and a big-shot from Special along with them.'

There was a gratifying silence.

'You mean . . . *Streifer*?' gasped Copping.

The super withered him with an acetylene flicker of his eye. 'We're not after Malenkov – nor Senator McCarthy! And just to temper the general glee I may as well add that Special are not the teeniest weeniest bit interested in our lousy little homicide. They couldn't care less. What they're coming for is the whole TSK Party handed to them on a platter and if we can't produce it then they aim to make life irksome in these parts – you understand?'

Gently nodded his mandarin nod. 'I've worked with Special . . .'

'Then you know what's coming – and it'll be here just after tea! So get your facts marshalled, Gently. There's a top-level conference staring you in the face. Amongst other things I've had to pull the CC off a theatre party he's had planned for the last six weeks . . . that's one nasty-minded person who's going to be there, for a start!'

CHAPTER TWELVE

ASSUREDLY THERE WAS was an array of formidable talent lined up in the super's office on that grey August evening. It required the impression of seating accommodation from several other departments and it was sad to see so many men of such lustre crammed together like constables at a compulsory lecture. As far as sheer superiority of rank was concerned, the home team had a clear advantage. They were led by the Chief Constable of Northshire, Sir Daynes Broke, CBE, ably supported by his Assistant CC, Colonel Shotover Grout, DSO, MC, with the redoubtable flanks of Superintendent Symms and Inspector Copping. But rank, of course, wasn't everything. There was a matter of quality also, and in this respect, to judge from their attitude, the visiting team felt themselves to have the edge. They were four in number, a sort of Special commando unit. Their ranks comprised Detective Sergeants Drill and Nickman, as dour a pair of bloodhounds as ever signed reports; their lieutenant was Chief Inspector Lasher, a man who had earned the hearty dislike of a select list of international organizations. But it was their No. 1 who really set the seal on the outfit. You could feel his presence through six-inch armour plate. He was a comparatively small man with a large squarish head and blue eyes that glowed hypnotically, as though lit by the perpetual and unfaltering generation of his brain. His name was Chief Superintendent Gish and the date of his retirement had been set aside by the entire world of espionage as one for public holiday and heartfelt rejoicing.

Between these two mighty factions Gently, the lonely representative of the Central Office, felt somewhat in the character of a light skirmisher. He'd got a nuisance value, they would probably concede him that, but otherwise he was merely there as a point of reference. So he squeezed himself into a seat behind Detective Sergeant Nickman, and contented himself with issuing entirely unauthorized smoke-rings.

Chief Superintendent Gish said: 'I want to impress on everybody concerned the urgency and importance of our mission down here. We have sent you a certain amount of information already to assist you in the homicide investigation . . . we've got your man for you and I take it you have prepared a case against him. If you haven't, it doesn't matter because we can put him away ourselves on a certain charge of sabotage. The importance and urgency of this business lies elsewhere and it's that I want to talk about.'

He paused, not so much for comment as to drive home his conviction that comment was superfluous. Gently puffed a sly ring over Detective Sergeant

Nickman's right ear. There was a general silence on all fronts.

'Very well, gentlemen,' continued Superintendent Gish, his floor confirmed. 'Now it must certainly have occurred to you, though possibly you have been unable to trace it, that Streifer has received assistance in what he did here. The circumstances of the crime as they are known to me leave no doubt about that. They are typical of the organized killing, the sort that we of the Special Branch are all too familiar with. Now that in itself is an important and urgent matter, but it becomes doubly so in the light of what I am about to tell you.

'The TSK Party came into existence shortly after the war. Officially it has no connection with the authorities on the other side of the Curtain, but I don't have to tell you that it wouldn't have thrived so long as it has done without connivance, and probably assistance, from the gentlemen over the way. It contains a strong Trotskyite element, which no doubt accounts for the nomenclature, but it pursues its aims not by assassination – though it isn't above it – but by extraordinarily well-executed sabotage.

'We first came across it in Yugoslavia. Later on it turned up in Czechoslovakia, Western Germany, France and the Suez Canal Zone. Three years ago the FBI were considerably shaken up to find it active and flourishing in the States – not just one or two agents but a complete organization, with some very dangerous contacts inside two atomic research stations. Fortunately they got on to them in time and pretty well stamped them out, though if this little affair is anything to go by the TSK still have a foot-hold over there. In the suitcase

Streifer was carrying there were $1,000,000 in counter-feit bills.

'Over here our first brush with them occurred at about the same time. They suborned a couple of atomic research physicists and when the balloon went up, I regret to say that they succeeded in getting one of them out of the country. After that we had the sabotage trouble down at Portsmouth in which Streifer was identified as the agent. There was nothing else then for some time. But about a year ago, as you may remember, a rash of naval sabotage broke out from Scapa down to Plymouth and it didn't take us long to discover that the TSK were back, this time in some strength. In fact, gentlemen, they had built an organization over here, an organization similar, though perhaps not so extensive, as the one they had built in the States.

'I need hardly mention that we have left no stone unturned to get at grips with this organization. Chief Inspector Lasher and myself were assigned to the task and we have pursued every opening and lead with the not inconsiderable resources at our command. We have had some success. We have arrested and deported or imprisoned a round half-dozen of agents. But we have never been able to locate the centre, the headquarters of the organization – there are never any lines back to it. The men we arrested wouldn't talk, and the impression I received after personal interrogation was that they didn't know anyway.

'Of course, we've had theories about it. We decided early on that it was probably on the east coast. Here there's some little traffic with the other side –

cargo-boats trade in and out of the ports, fishing-boats operate off-shore, liners like the *Ortory* touch in on some pretext or another. It seemed logical to give the east coast preference. And knowing the sort of people we were up against, we didn't necessarily expect to find it in an obvious centre such as Newcastle or Hull. We felt it was much more likely to turn up in a smaller place, an innocent-seeming place . . . a holiday resort like Starmouth, gentlemen, with its perpetual comings and goings, its absorption with visitors, its easy-going port and fleet of fishing vessels . . .'

Chief Superintendent Gish dwelt fondly on his theory, as though he enjoyed its sweet reasonableness. But he had got the opposition in a raw spot. There were underground growlings from Colonel Shotover Grout, an aggressive cough from Superintendent Symms and finally the home team found its voice in an exclamation by its illustrious leader:

'But good God, man, there's nothing like that in Starmouth!'

'Indeed, Sir Daynes?' Chief Superintendent Gish looked bored.

'No, sir. Quite impossible! The Borough Police Force is one of the most efficient in the country, including the Metropolitan, and the crime figures for this town, sir, bear comparison with those of any similar town anywhere. We harbour no criminal organizations in Starmouth, political or otherwise. Starmouth is by way of being a model of a respectable popular resort.'

'Here, here!' grumbled Colonel Shotover Grout chestily. 'You are mistaken, sir, gravely mistaken.'

'I'm not prepared to say,' added Sir Daynes generously, 'that Starmouth is completely free from undesirable activity. There are features – ahem! – moral features which we would gladly see removed. But that is an evil common to this sort of town, sir, and under the present limitations forced upon the police of this country we have not the power to stamp it out, though we keep it rigidly in check. Apart from this I may safely say that Starmouth is an unusually orderly and well-policed town. I assure you that nothing of the sort you describe could establish itself here without our knowledge.'

'Quite impossible, sir!' rumbled the colonel, 'you don't know Starmouth.'

Chief Superintendent Gish let play his hypnotic blue eyes from Sir Daynes to the colonel, and back again to Sir Daynes. 'And yet you wake up one morning to find a TSK agent and saboteur lying stabbed on your beach,' he commented steelily.

'It was hardly in our province to have prevented it!' came back Sir Daynes. 'If agents and saboteurs are permitted such easy entry into this country, then responsibility for their misdeeds must lie elsewhere than with the Starmouth Borough Police.'

'I agree, Sir Daynes. My point is that the Starmouth Borough Police knew nothing of their presence until a dead body turned up.'

'And the Special Branch, sir, knew nothing of their presence until informed by the Starmouth Borough Police.'

'With some Central Office assistance.'

'Invoked in the common round of our duty.'

There was a silence-at-arms, each mighty antagonist feeling he had struck an equal blow. Chief Superintendent Gish appeared to be putting the super's desk calendar into a trance. Sir Daynes Broke was giving his best performance of an affronted nobleman. Gently, after waiting politely for the launching of some fresh assault, improved the situation by relighting his pipe and involving Detective Sergeant Nickman in a humanizing haze of Navy Cut.

'You'll have to admit,' continued Chief Superintendent Gish at length, 'that Streifer received assistance in killing Stratilesceul.'

'I admit nothing of the sort,' countered Sir Daynes warily.

'What other interpretation can be put on the facts? Is there any doubt that his hands were tied?'

'One man can tie another's hands, Superintendent.'

'He can if the other will submit to it.'

'Streifer had a gun when he was arrested. Why should he not have threatened Stratilesceul into submission?'

'Have you ever tried tying the hands of a man you are threatening with a gun, Sir Daynes?'

'He could have bludgeoned him.'

'There were no head injuries.'

'Or drugs, perhaps.'

'Where would he obtain such drugs at short notice, supposing he could have induced Stratilesceul to take them? No, Sir Daynes, it won't do. Streifer wasn't on his own. He found help here, in this town, and help for the like of Streifer can only come from one source.'

'That source, sir, need not be in Starmouth. You have offered no certain grounds for your assumption that it is in Starmouth. Since TSK agents proliferate to such an amazing extent in this country I see no reason why Streifer, having followed Stratilesceul to Starmouth, should not have summoned one of them to his assistance. He had time enough. The murder was not committed till almost a week after Stratilesceul arrived.'

'It is possible, Sir Daynes, but that is all one can say for it.'

'As possible as your own hypothesis, and a good deal more probable.'

'I beg to differ. If I thought otherwise I should not be here.'

'Then, sir, there is little doubt that you have made a fruitless journey.'

'We will defer judgment until we see the results, Sir Daynes. I do not propose to be deflected from my object.'

At this point an interruption became a diplomatic necessity and it was fortunate that Colonel Shotover Grout, who had been preparing himself with a great deal of throat work, chose the slight pause which ensued for his cue.

'I suppose we can have the fella in – question him – see what he has to say himself about the business?'

They both turned to regard the colonel with unanimous unamiability.

'I mean he's the one who knows – can't get away from that.'

Chief Superintendent Gish gestured. 'Of course he

has been questioned. The results were as anticipated. You'll get nothing out of Streifer.'

'But simply as a formality, y'know—'

'This type of man never talks.'

A light of battle gleamed in Sir Daynes's eye. 'Symms!' he exclaimed, 'be good enough to have our prisoner brought in, will you?'

Superintendent Symms hesitated a moment, catching the Special Branch chief's petrifying glance.

'What are you waiting for, man?' rapped Sir Daynes, 'didn't you hear what I said?'

'I can assure you,' interrupted Chief Superintendent Gish, well below zero, 'that Streifer has been thoroughly and scientifically interrogated without the least success—'

'Superintendent Gish,' cut in Sir Daynes, 'I feel obliged to point out that Streifer is required by this authority to answer a charge of murder and that however high the Special Branch may privately rate sabotage, in the official calendar it is homicide which takes pride of place. Streifer has been brought here primarily to answer such a charge and I propose to make it forthwith. I suppose' – a sudden note of unease crept into his voice – 'I suppose a case has now been made out on which a charge can be based, Symms?'

The super looked at Copping, and Copping looked at Gently. Gently nodded and puffed some smoke at Detective Sergeant Nickman's long-suffering ear.

'Very well, then – have him brought in, Symms!'

Streifer was produced in handcuffs, presumably on the strength of his record – he certainly looked subdued enough, being prodded into the crowded office. He was a man of forty or forty-two, dark hair, dark eyes, slanting brows, a long, straight nose and a small thin-lipped mouth. He wore a well-cut suit of dark grey and had an air of refinement, almost of delicacy, about him. The only thing suggesting something else was the long, crooked scar which stretched lividly down his right cheek, beginning under the temple and trailing away at the angle of the jaw.

Colonel Shotover Grout gave a premonitory rumble. 'Cuffs, sir – take it they're absolutely necessary?'

Chief Superintendent Gish spared him a look of hypnotic pity.

'Remove them,' ordered Sir Daynes crisply. 'There would appear to be sufficient men with police training present to render the step unperilous.'

The cuffs were removed. A chair was drafted in. With a shorthand constable at his elbow Sir Daynes levelled a model charge and caution at the silent Streifer, inasmuch as he had, on the twelfth instant, with malice aforethought, stabbed to death one Stephan Stratiles-ceul, alias Max.

The baby being passed to Streifer, he simply shook his head.

'You don't wish to make a statement?'

'No.' His voice was harsh but not unpleasant.

'You realize the invariable penalty annexed to a conviction of homicide in this country?'

'I am not . . . unacquainted.'

'It is a capital offence.'

'Ah yes – England hangs.'

'Yet you still do not wish to say anything in your own defence?'

Streifer shrugged his elegant shoulders. 'Have you proof of this thing?'

'We have a very good case.'

'Enough to drop me into your pit?'

'To convict you – yes.'

'Then what should I say? Have you a confession for me to sign?'

The chief constable frowned. 'We don't do things that way. You may anticipate perfectly fair proceedings in this country. We have a case against you, but you are perfectly free to defend yourself. What you say will be equally considered with what we say in the court in which you will be tried.'

'Then I shall plead that I am innocent. What more will be necessary?'

'It will be necessary to prove it – as we shall seek to prove our contentions.'

Streifer smiled ironically and cast a deliberate glance round the assembled company. 'What pains you take! In my country we are more economical. But let me hear these contentions of yours. I have no doubt that your scrupulous system permits it.'

Sir Daynes signalled to the super, who once more communicated with Gently by the medium of Copping. Gently, however, having produced a crumpled sheet of paper, elected to pass it back to the seat of authority. The super straightened it out hastily and began to read.

'We can show that the accused, Olaf Streifer, is a member of a revolutionary party known as the TSK and that he is a member of the Maulik or secret police appertaining to that party and that previous to the present instance he has illicitly entered this country for the purpose of forwarding the aims of that party by criminal process.

'We can show that the murdered man, Stephan Stratilesceul, was also a member of the TSK party, and that he was similarly engaged in forwarding its aims.

'We can show that, on Tuesday, 5 August, Stephan Stratilesceul entered this country as a fugitive from the Polish liner *Ortory*, which liner was at that time breaking at Hull a voyage from Danzig to New York, and that he was pursued ashore by Streifer, and that he escaped in the trawler *Harvest Sea*, which brought him to Starmouth where he was landed on the morning of Wednesday, 6 August.

'We can show that Streifer also arrived in Starmouth, date unknown, and that he took up quarters in a deserted house known as "Windy Tops", and that he traced Stratilesceul to lodgings he had taken at 52 Blantyre Road.

'We can show that on Tuesday, 12 August, at or about 22.00 hours, Stratilesceul proceeded in a hired car to "Windy Tops" in the company of a prostitute named Agnes Meek, alias Frenchy, and that he was not again seen alive.

'We can show that his naked body, bearing four stab-wounds of which two would have been instantly fatal, as well as burns made before death, suggesting that he had been subject to torture, was washed ashore between the Albion and Wellesley Piers some time before 05.10 hours on Wednesday, 13 August, and that the time of death was estimated as being five or six hours previous, and that in the state of the tides and the offshore current then prevailing a body introduced into the sea near "Windy Tops" at or about 24.00 hours Tuesday would, with great probability, be washed ashore at the time and place at which Stratilesceul's body was washed ashore.

'We can show that following Stratilesceul's murder, burglary was committed by Streifer at 52 Blantyre Road in the hope of recovering a suitcase containing a quantity of counterfeit United States Treasury notes, but that his purpose was frustrated by a previous burglary committed by Jeffery Algernon Wylie and Robert Henry Baines on information received from Agnes Meek.

'We can show that Streifer eventually traced the suitcase to its hiding-place under the Albion Pier, that he recovered it, that he substituted for it a brown paper package containing the clothes worn by the deceased at the time of his death, and that he caused the attention of the police to be drawn to the part played by Wylie and Baines, presumably in order to mislead the investigations.' (Here the super seemed smitten by a troublesome cough and the chief constable sniffed rather pointedly.)

'We can show, finally, that the piece of brown paper used to wrap the clothes of the deceased is identical in composition with a sheet of brown paper discovered at "Windy Tops", this sheet forming part of the packing of a mattress acquired for his own use by Streifer, also discovered at "Windy Tops", and that the torn edges of the one piece match exactly the torn edges of the other piece.'

The super halted and laid down his sheet of paper.

'Excellent!' chimed in the colonel, aside. 'First-class case – magnificent phrasing!'

Chief Superintendent Gish turned his head sideways, as though he felt it unnecessary to turn it any further. 'What a pity,' he said to Gently behind, 'what a pity you couldn't have made it water-tight.'

Gently issued a quiet ring at Detective Sergeant Nickman's plastic collar-stud.

'When you've done so well . . . not to be able to show that Streifer was in Starmouth at the time of the murder.'

'What's that?' barked Sir Daynes, 'Not here at the time of the murder? I fail to follow you, sir, I completely fail to follow you!'

'Oh, I dare say you'll get a conviction.' The chief superintendent came back off his half-turn. 'The rest of it's so strong that it's almost bound to carry the day. But as I said, it's a pity that you have to admit a phrase like "date unknown" against the important event of Streifer's arrival in Starmouth . . . his defence are bound to be time-wasting and oratorical about it.'

Sir Daynes stared murder, and the chief superintendent stared it back.

'Is this a fact?' snapped the former at Gently. 'We have just heard it read,' chipped in the chief super scathingly.

Gently raised a calculating eyebrow. 'How long,' he mused, 'how long would you say it would take a man –

even supposing he was a confirmed anchovy addict – to eat five average-size tins of anchovies?'

'Anchovies!' exploded Sir Daynes, 'what the devil have anchovies got to do with it, man?'

Gently shook his head. 'I was going to ask Streifer that, if he had been feeling more communicative. But there were five empty tins in his waste-bucket at "Windy Tops" and I find it difficult to believe that he consumed one whole tin each tea-time for five days together . . .'

'It isn't proof,' whipped in the chief super, razor-sharp.

'No, it isn't proof . . . just a curious example of devotion to anchovies. On the whole,' added Gently mildly, 'I was rather glad to find that a gentleman named Perkins, an employee at Starmouth Super Furnishings, was able to remember selling the mattress to a person resembling Streifer as early as Wednesday, 6 August . . .'

The dust died down and Sir Daynes, full of beans, returned to the problem of the reluctant Streifer.

'You have heard the case against you. I think it is plain that it requires a better answer than mere silence. In your own interest, Streifer, I advise you to be as helpful as you can.'

'In my own interest?' Streifer gave a little laugh. 'You are very kind people – very kind indeed! But what interest have I left when I am faced with this so-excellent case?'

'You will not find the police ungrateful for any assistance you may be able to give them.'

'Their gratitude would be touching. No doubt I

should remember it with pleasure as I stood on your gallows.'

'If you are innocent you can do no better than tell the whole truth. You are probably aware of other charges which will be preferred if you are acquitted on this one and I can say, on certain authority, that those charges will be dropped if you give us the assistance which we know to be in your power.'

'And that would be the names of my associates in this country?'

'Their names and all the information you possess about them.'

'To turn traitor, in fact?'

'To assist the ends of justice.'

Streifer laughed again and fixed his coal-black eyes on Sir Daynes. 'Tell me,' he said, 'on this certain authority of yours – would it not be possible to forget Stratilesceul altogether if I gave this information?'

Sir Daynes jiffled impatiently, but the question pinned him down. 'No,' he admitted at last, 'that charge is irrevocable, Streifer.'

'But you could perhaps buy off the judge, or ensure that these quaint jurymen of yours returned a certain verdict?'

'Quite impossible!' rapped Sir Daynes, 'understand once and for all that such courses are not followed in this country.'

'And even if they were – even if I could be sure – even if you were to hand me a free pardon signed and sealed by your Queen herself – I would not betray the humblest comrade who marches with me towards the final liberation of mankind. That is my answer to you, the policemen. That is the only statement I wish to make. If you are just, as you claim you are just, you will take it down in writing and read it at my trial. But I have nothing more to say, excepting that.'

The silence which followed was slightly embarrassed. Sir Daynes seemed to freeze in his stern official look. Colonel Shotover Grout made rumbling noises, as though he thought the whole thing in very bad taste, and Superintendent Symms sniffed repeatedly in his superintendental way. It was the Special Branch Chief who spoke.

'You see, Sir Daynes? This is the sort of thing we are up against at every turn . . . you may find criminals difficult to deal with, but believe me they are child's play compared with fanatics.'

'I cannot believe he will continue in this – this obstinacy,' returned Sir Daynes, though his non-plussed tone of voice belied him, 'his life is at stake, sir. Men will attempt their defence in however desperate a situation they find themselves.'

'Not once they have become inoculated with creeds of this description,' sneered the chief super. 'They become intoxicated, Sir Daynes. They become tipsy with the most dangerous brand of aggrandizing delusion – political idealism. It means nothing for them to kill, and a triumph for them to die. We know these people. You had better let us handle them.'

Sir Daynes shook his head bewilderedly. 'I must admit that it is something new in my experience . . . I feel somewhat at a loss.' He glanced at the colonel. 'What is your opinion, sir?'

'Preposterous!' grumbled the colonel half-heartedly, 'unstable, sir . . . foreigners . . . unstable.'

'Then, Sir Daynes, I take it you will make no further opposition to my investigations in this town.'

Sir Daynes pursed his lips. 'If you think it is necessary it is my duty to give you every assistance.'

The chief super nodded in the comfortable consciousness of prevailed merit. 'In effect I shall be taking over the present investigations at the point where your men and Chief Inspector Gently have left off. I shall want a full report from everyone engaged on the case and in addition I intend to conduct personal interrogations to bring to light points which may not hitherto have seemed important. Inspector Gently,' – his head turned sideways again – 'I have full authority to release you and your assistant from your duties here. Later on I should like to have a private chat with you and tomorrow you will be free to return to town.'

Gently nodded his mandarin nod and slowly removed his pipe from his mouth. 'I'd like to make a point . . . if it isn't interrupting the proceedings too much.'

The chief super's head remained sideways in indication of his supreme patience.

'One or two side-issues have cropped up in the course of my minor activities . . . I would have liked another day or two to tie them up.'

'Unnecessary, Inspector Gently. They will certainly be taken care of.'

'They concern,' proceeded Gently absently, 'the organization you are interested in disbanding.'

There was a silence in the crowded room. Nine pairs

of eyes focussed with one accord on the man from the Central Office.

'Of course . . . it's not for me to suggest the line of further investigation . . . I don't want to deflect the Special Branch from what it conceives to be its duty. But if they care to hold their horses for just a day or two, I feel I may be able to save them a certain amount of frustration.'

'Come to the point, man!' yapped Chief Superintendent Gish, proving for all time that his neck was fully mobile. 'What is it you're trying to say?'

'I'm trying to say,' replied Gently leisurely, 'that I'm fully aware of the identity and whereabouts of the TSK leader in this country and you could arrest him this evening . . . if you thought it would do you any good.'

CHAPTER THIRTEEN

THEY THOUGHT IT would do them some good for quite a long time together, did the chief super, Sir Daynes and Colonel Shotover Grout. In the first flush of enthusiasm they were for leaping into a Black Maria and descending upon Big Louey with drawn automatics and a full complement of iron-mongery. It took time and a certain amount of cold water to correct their transports. Gently was obliged to apply the latter in generous doses.

'We've got nothing on him . . . nothing whatever . . . we couldn't even take his licence away.'

'But good God, sir!' gabbled Sir Daynes, 'that ring – it's positive evidence – when he denied possession he practically declared his culpability!'

'We should never find it . . . he's a clever man.'

'And being able to tell you Stratilesceul's nationality when even Central Records didn't know him – it's damning, sir, absolutely damning!'

'Just his word against mine . . . or intelligent guess-ing.'

'We'd better throw a cordon round the place and raid it,' snarled the chief super, 'he'll have records – names and addresses – there'll be a short-wave transmitter somewhere.'

Gently shook his head very firmly. 'Not in Louey's place. He's far too fly. If they were ever there – which I doubt – they came out directly this Stratilesceul business got muddled.'

'But how shall we know for sure if we don't raid it?'

'We know for sure now. He would never have behaved so confidently if he'd got anything to hide.'

'There'll be something to give him away.'

'I wouldn't like to bet on it.'

'And we can't just sit around waiting for him to disappear and set up somewhere else.'

'He'll do that all the quicker if he knows you're out gunning for him.'

'I say pull him in!' erupted the colonel from his thoracic deeps. 'Confront him with the other fella – make them see the game is up!'

'I'm afraid it wouldn't have that effect, colonel . . . they're very old hands at this particular game.'

'But damn it, sir, we must do something!'

'Yes!' struck in Sir Daynes irritably, 'you're very good at telling us what we *can't* do, Gently, now suppose for a change you tell us what we *can* do?'

Gently sighed and felt about in his pockets for a peppermint cream that wasn't there.

'There's just one saving grace about this business, as far as I can see . . . and it's up to us to play it for all it's worth. In your previous dealings with the TSK' – he

226

inclined his head deferentially towards the chief super –
'I think you have had to do solely with agents of the
party. Is that correct?'

The chief super scowled what was presumably an
affirmative.

'They were men like Streifer – men with an ideal –
men who would sooner go to the gallows than give the
least particle of information about the party. Now in the
present instance there is a significant difference. We
have here a person involved – deeply involved – who
isn't a party member, who has no burning desire to
liberate mankind, and who is only being prevented from
giving evidence by mortal fear for her personal safety.
That person is the prostitute Frenchy. She knows
enough, I'm reasonably certain, to put Louey into the
dock beside Streifer . . . perhaps somebody else too. But
she's been got at. She doesn't dare testify. She's seen
how Stratilesceul finished up, and no doubt she's been
told that whoever she gives away, there'll always be
someone left to take care of her.

'But there she is – somebody who can do our job
for us. If we can only find a way to coax her to talk
we shall have Louey and possibly his associates in the
palm of our hand. Unfortunately it runs in a circle . . .
we've got to pull in Louey and company before she'll
talk, and before she talks we can't pull in Louey and
company . . .'

'In fact it doesn't seem to be getting us very far, does
it?' interrupted the chief super jealously.

Gently sucked a moment on his unlit pipe. 'What
puzzles me is how they got her to help them in the first

place,' he mused. 'I've never been able to see that quite clearly . . .'

'If they're terrorizing her now they could have terrorized her before.'

'I don't think so . . . not Frenchy. She isn't one to terrorize easily. I imagine Louey would need a corpse at his back before he could get much change out of her and the job she had to do would be better done in the spirit of co-operation than in the spirit of coercion.'

'Well then – she was paid.'

'But she didn't have any money.'

'Of course not!' snapped the chief super, 'her boy-friend would have had it.'

'She doesn't admit to any boyfriend, not even to get herself bailed.'

The chief super drew a deep and ugly breath. 'It isn't *getting* us anywhere!' he bawled. 'Does it matter two hoots how they got her to do it? The fact is that she did do it, and precious little help it looks like being to us!'

Gently shook his head in respectful admonishment. 'It means there's a link somewhere . . . something we don't know about. There's a link between Louey and Frenchy, and as a result of that link Frenchy was prepared to act the decoy, without pressure and probably without payment . . .'

'Perhaps this Louey fella's the boyfriend himself,' suggested the colonel.

'He's too clever . . . and women aren't his weakness. No. It's something else.'

'I really can't see that it's important, Gently,' weighed in Sir Daynes.

'It isn't!' barked the chief super, 'we simply sit here wasting our time while the chief inspector amuses himself by . . .'

He broke off as a tap came at the door. It was Sergeant Dutt's homely visage that appeared.

'Begging your pardon, sir . . .'

'Yes? What is it?'

'It's something for Chief Inspector Gently, sir . . . he wanted to know directly a certain party left the premises.'

'Well, cough it up – don't stand there like a dummy!'

Dutt transferred his stolid gaze to his superior. 'It's Frenchy, sir . . .'

'Frenchy!' Gently rose slowly to his feet.

'I just arrived back, sir, and they tell me she was bailed aht half an hour ago.'

A faraway look stole into Gently's eye. 'And who was it, Dutt . . . did you get the name?'

'Yessir. It was a Mr Peach, sir.'

The faraway look lengthened till it embraced some islands of the distant Hebrides. 'Peachey!' murmured Gently, 'my old friend Peachey! I always had a feeling we should find him sewn into the lining of this case . . . somewhere!'

It rained still, as though it had never thought of stopping that side of Michaelmas. The picture-houses, theatres and pavilions were packed solid with moist audiences, the cafes had never had such a day, the lessees of dance-halls and amusement arcades were indulging in dreams of a late-autumn holiday at Cannes or Capri . . .

Only the beach was having a bad time of it. Only the beach was dark and deserted and desolate to behold. Soft, unnoticed, another flood-tide crept upwards towards the hectic Front. It washed round the piles under the piers, looked up at its auld enemy, the cliffs, and made to list a few more degrees a certain post which some policemen had set up in the shingle.

But there was nobody there to see it, except a crouching halfwit. The rest of Starmouth kept tryst with their bright lights. Rain it might and rain it did, but the electric rash burned on, the music wailed, the rifles spanged, the audiences laughed and the great Till of Starmouth rang its steady chorus.

Artie in the bar was getting quite irritable with his customers, and he could afford to be. They didn't want away once they were there. And it was a gay crowd that night, on the eve of the races. Several old faces had turned up which had been missing for quite a while . . . it was just like it had been before that b. Inspector Gently set foot in the place, as the sporty individual observed. Even Louey seemed in a festive mood. He had been out twice in the course of the evening and each time it had been drinks all round. It was communicative, that mood of Louey's. For better or worse it affected the company in the bar. But now the clouds which had momentarily gathered about the gigantic brow had faded away, the sunshine had returned, the bar was its old happy self again . . .

Or it was till nine-thirty. Nine-thirty-three and a half, to be precise. At that exact moment a bulky figure in a fawn raincoat and a despairing trilby pushed through the swing-doors and looking neither to right nor left, shouldered its way across to the door opposite and disappeared again.

It was done so quickly that it might have been an optical illusion. Ferrety-face Artie had to shake his head to convince himself he wasn't seeing things. The sporty individual, halfway down his eighth Scotch, screwed up his eyes in a search for assurance that he was stone-cold sober.

'That bloke just now . . . it was him, washn't it?'

Artie nodded absently and moved down towards the door, as though hopeful of hearing something above the din outside.

'But whatsh he doing here . . . I thought Louey said it was OK?'

Artie waved him down with his hand and got still closer to the door. The whole bar held its breath in a sort of hushed watchfulness. In the comparative calm a tincased version of 'Cherry Pink' seemed to vibrate the plastic-topped tables with its singeing vehemence.

'I don't undershtand . . .' burbled the sporty individual, 'something's going on, Artie . . . I don't undershtand.'

Artie didn't either, but there wasn't very long to wait. At nine-thirty-seven, or a trifle before, the door reopened with a suddenness that nearly pinned Artie to the wall. Out waddled Peachey, red in the face. Out marched the bulky figure, his hand tucked affectionately under Peachey's arm. Again no time was wasted. Again no looks were cast to right or to left. The brief procession headed forthrightly through the swing-doors and vanished like a dream, though in this case one part

231

of the dream was left standing in the doorway by the bar. It was Big Louey. And his gold tooth wasn't showing at all . . .

Outside Dutt was waiting in a police car. Peachey was bundled in and Gently gave an address to the driver which didn't sound like Headquarters. A short drive brought them to a dark and empty street where but few lamps shone islands of radiance on the gleaming pavement. Dutt alighted and stood by the door.

'Get out,' ordered Gently to Peachey.

Peachey gulped and gave a frightened look up and down the street.

'This isn't the police station! I d–demand to be taken to the police station!'

'Get out!' snapped Gently and Peachey scuttled forth like a startled rabbit. Gently followed him and after tossing a word to the driver, slammed the door resoundingly behind them. He indicated the house by which they had stopped.

'In there.'

'B–but I've g–got rights . . . you c–can't do this!'

Gently poked a steely finger into his plump back and Peachey forgot about his rights with great suddenness.

There was nothing alarming about the house, however. The door opened on a well-lit and comfortable-looking hall containing a hat-stand and an aspidistra on a side-table and the room into which Peachey was marshalled bore all the appurtenances of respectable boarding-house practice. Gently took off his hat and raincoat and hung them familiarly on the hat-stand.

'See if Mrs Davis has got the tea on, will you?' he said to Dutt, 'and ask her if she's got some biscuits . . . I like those shortbread ones we had the other night.'

Dutt departed and Gently joined Peachey in the lounge. Gently seemed in no hurry to begin business. An electric fire was glowing in the fireplace and, standing with his back to it, he slowly filled and lit his seasoned briar. Peachey watched every move with pathetic attention. Twice he seemed about to recall his flouted rights, but each time, catching Gently's mild eye, he thought better of it. The horrid ordeal ended when Dutt re-appeared bearing the tea tray. There were three cups and Peachey was even indulged with two lumps of sugar.

'And now . . .' mused Gently, seating himself with his teacup, 'now we can have our little chat in peace and comfort . . . can't we, Peachey?'

'You haven't g-got no right!' broke out the parrot-faced one unhopefully.

Gently clicked his tongue. 'No right, Peachey? Why, we're treating you like an old friend – bringing you to our nice cosy lodgings, instead of that bare old police station! Now sit yourself down on one of Mrs Davis's best chairs, and try to be a bright lad . . . you need to be a bright lad, don't you, Peachey?'

Peachey blinked and swallowed, then lowered himself into a chair. Gently drank a large mouthful of tea and set his cup down near the electric fire.

'You're here for a reason, Peachey. Two reasons, as a matter of fact. The unimportant reason is because there's a pack of wolves down at Headquarters who would just

233

love to tear a little boy like you into small pieces. The important reason is that I want to talk to you off the record – no charges, no taking it down, nothing being used in evidence. Anything you tell me here is in confidence and it won't appear again till you're ready to give it in a sworn statement . . . you get the idea?'

Peachey's close-set eyes seemed to get closer together than ever. 'I-I'm not going to m-make a statement . . . I don't know nothing to make one about!'

Gently shook his head paternally. 'Don't say that, Peachey. You don't know how useful that statement's going to be. At a rough guess I should say it would make eighteen months' difference to you, besides a slimming course with the pick and shovel. You wouldn't be too handy with a pick and shovel, would you, Peachey?'

'I don't know what you're t-talking about!' Peachey gulped, his cup and saucer beginning to chatter.

'Come, come, Peachey! You're amongst friends. There's no need to be bashful. Almost any time now we're going to run you in for living on immoral earnings and I'm sure you know what that means. If you go before a beak, it'll be six months in one of our more comfortable establishments; if you go up with an indictment, it'll be two years with the pick-and-shovel boys.'

'B-but it isn't true!'

'We've got the goods, Peachey.'

'I'm a b-bookmaker's clerk – you know I am!'

'Six witnesses, Peachey, and two of them your neighbours in Sidlow Street.'

'It's a f-frame, I tell you!'

'And three past convictions, all neatly filed at Central Records . . . no, Peachey. You're due for a holiday. And just between us you'll be lucky if it stops there, won't you?'

The parrot-faced one put down his cup, which he was no longer in a condition to support. He made a pitiful effort to get out a cigarette, but the packet fell from his hands and its contents distributed about the floor. Dutt helped him pick them up. They got him lighted at the second attempt.

'As I was saying,' resumed Gently meditatively, 'you'll be lucky, won't you? You'll need all the goodwill that's going if you're not going to be roped in for complicity in the murder of Stephan Stratilesceul . . . did you know his name? At "Windy Tops"?'

He paused for artistic effect and Peachey shrank down in his chair several degrees.

'Of course, it may be that in making a statement you would incriminate yourself . . . there's always that to be thought about. We shall quite understand your keeping silent if you were in fact an accomplice . . .'

The goad was irresistible. Peachey squirmed as though it had galled him physically. 'I didn't know – I swear – it wasn't nothing to do with me!'

'Nothing to do with you? How can you, Peachey! When it was Frenchy who got him out to "Windy Tops" in the first place.'

'I tell you I didn't know . . . they didn't say n-nothing!'

'You mean they didn't tell you they were going to kill him?'

Peachey sucked hard on a cigarette which was coming to pieces between his lips.

'You might as well come clean, Peachey. It's off the record.'

Peachey gulped and sucked, but he had dried up again.

Gently sighed. 'Let me see if I can reconstruct it. They had a conference, didn't they? Streifer had traced Stratilesceul to his lodgings in Blantyre Road, but he was rather at a loss to know how to deal with him. It wasn't just a question of killing the man and recovering the money. Streifer could handle that well enough on his own. No – what was important about Stratilesceul was certain information he could give . . . with a little persuasion, perhaps . . . about other untrustworthy members of the TSK Party. Am I right?'

The cigarette was definitely a spent force, but Peachey kept on working at it.

'That was the problem, then – to get Stratilesceul in a place where he could be duly persuaded, and afterwards, as a mere formality, put to death. It wasn't an easy problem to solve. Stratilesceul wasn't laying himself open to being kidnapped. As far as he knew, he had shaken off the pursuit, but he was still taking precautions – like lodging in a crowded boarding-house and sticking to the frequented parts of the town. I dare say there were several plans made. The length of time it took to do the job suggests it. But they all fell through for that very simple reason – they could never get him where they could lay their hands on him.

'So we come to the final conference – Louey, Streifer and Little Peachey . . . because you were in on it, weren't you, Peachey? And Louey sits on a striped chair behind that very nice desk of his, thinking, thinking. At last he says to Streifer: "You're familiar with Stratilesceul's confidential record?" – And Streifer nods with that quiet little laugh of his. "Is there nothing in it that might serve our turn?" – Streifer shrugs and says: "He's fond of women." "Women!" says Louey, showing some gold, "any particular sort of women, or just women in general?" "Blonde women," says Streifer, "nice big blondes."

'At that Louey really smiles. "We've got the very thing . . . haven't we, Peachey?" he says, "a nice big blonde who'll do just what we ask her! Why, I dare say that if we play it right we can get friend Stephan delivered to the very door . . ." And what did Little Peachey say to that? He said: "Yes, Louey, of course, Louey, anything you say goes with me, Louey—"'

'I didn't know!' shrieked the tormented Peachey, 'they never said anything about killing him in front of me!'

'You didn't guess?' rapped Gently. 'You thought it was just going to be a social evening?'

'They said he'd hidden the money, that's all. They said they wanted to get him to find out what he'd done with it!'

'So you're entirely innocent – and Frenchy's entirely innocent?'

'She didn't know neither!'

'Just a couple of little lambs! And where were you when Frenchy was doing her dirty work?'

'I don't know – I was in the bar!'

'You were in the bar – then you didn't get Louey's car out of the garage?'

'No!'

'Then two witnesses we've got are liars?'

'I wasn't near the garage!'

'And you didn't pick up the reception committee and take them to "Windy Tops"?'

'. . . I was in the bar!'

'And you didn't wait there with them to give a hand tying up Stratilesceul?'

'I didn't – I didn't! When they'd got him in there they sent me back with Frenchy . . . we never knew nothing . . . nothing at all.'

'So it was just one big surprise when you saw it in the papers.' Gently reached down for his cup of tea and tossed it off fiercely. 'And when you found out, what did you do?'

'I didn't do nothing!' floundered Peachey, his little eyes roving from side to side as though in desperate search for escape.

'Nothing. Nothing! You knew the murderers – you'd been tricked into helping them – unless you spoke up quick you were in it along with them – and yet you did nothing. Is that your tale for the jury?'

'I ain't going before a jury!'

'Oh yes you are, Peachey, somewhere along the line.'

'But you said it wasn't evidence!'

'It will be when you've sworn it.'

'I ain't going to swear it – never – no one can make me.'

'They won't have to, Peachey. You'll do all the

swearing that's necessary when you go up on a murder rap.'

'But I never did it – you know I never did it!'

'I shall feel a lot more certain when I've got a statement on paper with your signature underneath.'

Peachey shrivelled up in the chair like a punctured balloon. 'I ain't going to swear,' he whispered, 'I ain't – I ain't!'

'Then it's two years' hard at the very least.'

'I ain't going to swear, not though it was twenty.'

Gently shrugged his bulky shoulders and handed his cup to Dutt, who silently refilled it. Gently drank some and gnawed a shortbread biscuit. 'Of course, you know we've got Streifer,' he muttered casually amongst the crumbs.

'Str–Streifer?' Peachey unshrivelled a little.

Gently nodded and bit another piece.

'But Streifer is g-gone . . .!'

'We took the trouble to bring him back again . . . your grapevine can't be as good as it was.'

Peachey's small eyes fixed on the pattern of Mrs Davis's best carpet, but he made no other contribution for the moment.

'He's safe and sound,' continued Gently, 'you don't have to worry about *him* any longer. And if a certain little bird would sing his song we could put Louey in with him. Louey in jail,' he added helpfully, 'would be just as harmless as the average mortal.'

The pattern still had Peachey fascinated.

'And with a little further assistance, Peachey – all confidential, you understand, no names published, no questions asked about how a certain individual came by his information – we could arrest and imprison or expel quite a fairish bag of unfriendly-minded persons. In fact, we could make this country a healthy place for little Peacheys to come back to after a six-month vacation . . . couldn't we?'

For a moment the small eyes lifted from the carpet and rested just below Gently's chin. Then they sank again, sullenly, and the dry lips bit together.

'Ah well!' sighed Gently, 'we do our best, don't we? We always do our best!' He appropriated another biscuit and crammed it into his mouth. 'Take him home, Dutt . . . take him to his flat in Sidlow Street. I don't suppose he wants to see Louey again tonight.'

Dutt took a step forward and Peachey looked up suddenly, his mouth dropping open.

'B-but aren't you going to p-pinch me . . .?'

Gently shook his head and swallowed some tea.

'B-but you've got a charge – y-you said you had!'

'Can't bother with it just now, Peachey. The local lads will see to it some time.'

'B-but it's true – you've got some witnesses!'

'You just comalongofme like the chief inspector says,' said Dutt, hoisting the parrot-faced one to his feet, 'he's done with you now . . . you're even getting a nice ride home. You don't want us to lock you up, do you?'

If Peachey's expression was anything to go by he did want that very thing, but neither Gently nor Dutt seemed willing to oblige. He was stood firmly in the hall while Dutt was putting on his raincoat and Gently, still ravaging amongst the biscuits, appeared to be forgetting the existence of both of them. But as Dutt reached for his hat, Gently sauntered to the lounge door.

'By the way, Peachey . . .'

Peachey blinked at him hopefully.

'If you were running a short-wave transmitter it would be useful to have a nice high aerial, wouldn't it?'

'T-transmitter . . .?'

'That's right. For sending little gossip-notes to the Continent.'

'But I don't know nothing about it!'

Gently tut-tutted and felt for a scrap of paper. 'Here we are . . . hot from Central Records. They released you from a stretch in '42 to go into the Services; you were trained as a radio-mechanic at Compton Bassett; radar course at Hereford in '44; demobilized as a Sergeant-Radar-mechanic in '46. Quite a distinguished career, Peachey . . . and of course you'd know all about building and working a simple transmitter, wouldn't you?'

Peachey gulped and tried to get some moisture on to his lips.

'And about that aerial? There aren't so many high places in Starmouth. There's the monument, but that's a bit too bare and obvious. And there's the observation tower, but that would be even worse. No . . . what you'd want would be something unobtrusive . . . something where a little private wiring wouldn't notice very much, where perhaps there was an off-season when you could do the job without interruptions. That's what you'd want, isn't it, Peachey?'

'I forgot all that . . . I don't remember nothing about radio!'

Gently shook his head consolingly. 'Never mind, Peachey. I dare say you will. It'll come back to you with a rush one day. Oh, and just one other thing.'

Peachey sucked in breath.

'Tell Louey I'll be in tomorrow some time to settle up a bet, will you? He'll know what I mean . . . just tell him that.'

Dutt hustled him out and the door closed behind them. Gently hesitated a moment till he heard the car pull away, then he returned swiftly to the lounge, uncoupled the phone, dialled a number crisply.

'Chief Inspector Gently . . . oh, hullo, Louey! I thought it was only fair to ring you up . . .'

He smiled pleasantly to himself at the note of tenseness in the voice at the other end.

'Yes, of course you have to know . . . with the races tomorrow too . . . naturally you'll be stuck if we pinch your head boy. But there's nothing to worry about, Louey . . . no, we came to an agreement. I've just sent him home now, as free as a bird. He's a sensible chap, Louey . . . knows when it's time to do a deal. We all have to play along with the police sometimes . . . eh? Yes . . . yes . . . Sidlow Street . . . yes. I'm glad it's eased your mind, Louey. Have a good day with the gee-gees tomorrow . . . yes . . . good night.'

He pressed the receiver down a moment and then dialled again.

'Gently here. Give me Copping.'

'Hullo?' came Copping's voice, 'have you had any luck? The chief super says that if you haven't—!'

'Never mind the chief super,' interrupted Gently

with a grimace. 'Listen, Copping. This is vitally important. I've just sent Peach home to his flat at 27 Sidlow Street with Dutt to keep an eye on him. Now I want Dutt relieved at midnight and your best man sent to replace him. And armed, you understand? Peach has got to be guarded from now on, day and night . . . and heaven help the man who slips up on the assignment!'

CHAPTER FOURTEEN

S TARMOUTH RACES – that colourful, moneyful, tax-free event – Starmouth Races, when a town already full to the brim began bursting at the seams. From early in the forenoon the train-loads started to emerge. By lunch-time you could hardly move on the road to the race-course, and as for getting a sit-down meal, you were lucky to pick up a couple of cheese sandwiches. But it was Starmouth Races and nobody cared. You came for the fun and the flutter and the sea-air, and if you went back skint it was all part of the outing.

They'd got a brass band from Norchester, a regular festival-winning affair. It had come out today in a fanfaronade of new grey and pink, with a man on the baton who really knew his business. Dutt was enthralled. He had always had a weakness for brass bands. When they went to town with 'Blaze Away' it touched a chord in his simple cockney heart . . .

'Worst day of the year!' moaned Copping to Gently, 'how can you police this lot with the men we've got? If we arrested all the dips and shysters who come up for the races it'd need a special excursion train to cart them back to town!'

The super was there, looking very spruce and commanding in his best blue with its rainbow of medal ribbons. He sharpened a glance for Gently's baggy tweed. 'I hope you know what you're doing, Gently . . . Gish is out for your blood if anything goes wrong.'

Gently tilted his head accommodatingly and the super passed with a sniff.

As a matter of fact, Gently was beginning to worry himself, just a little bit. The thing wasn't going to pattern at all. There had been no alarums and excursions, no rush for Sidlow Street in the quiet hours . . . Peachey had spent a restful night, said the report, or if not a restful one, at least a peaceful one. In the morning it was the same. The routine of 'The Feathers' had continued undisturbed. Louey had gone for his constitutional, Peachey had reported to the office, at lunchtime they had eaten together at a nearby restaurant and directly afterwards Peachey had fetched the car and driven Louey and two of the bar-regulars to the race-course. It was almost as though Louey were ignoring the situation, as though he were deliberately calling Gently's bluff. Certainly there was no anxiety in his aspect, and if Peachey was looking rather more like a boiled stuffed rabbit than usual it was hardly to be wondered at.

Gently's eye wandered through the busy crowd to the line of bookies' stands. Biggest of all flamed a great orange banner, set up on two poles, and licking across it like scarlet fire ran the legend: LOUEY ALWAYS PAYS! – Not that it was necessary, such a banner. You could hear the voice of Louey like distant thunder, over-topping crowd, band and competitors:

'FIVE TO TWO ON THE FAVOURITE . . . COME ON NOW . . . ONLY LOUEY GIVES IT . . . FIVE TO TWO ON THE FAVOURITE!'

His gold tooth shone, his diamond ring flashed, he loomed over the crowd like a genial Goliath. And they liked Louey. He was an institution on the race-course. Plump Peachey could hardly scribble slips out fast enough to keep pace with the money going into that gaping Gladstone.

'FIVE TO TWO ON THE FAVOURITE . . . TEN BOB TO WIN TWENTY-FIVE . . . HUNDRED TO EIGHT ON CAMBYSES . . . COME ON NOW, THESE ARE THE ODDS YOU'RE LOOKING FOR!'

Up beside him the sporty individual was taking signals from someone across in the stands and chalking up fresh odds on the blackboard. Down below a couple of bar-types were touting recklessly, yanking custom from the very shadow of rival stands.

'COME ON NOW . . . NO LIMIT . . . IF YOU WANT A FORTUNE COME TO LOUEY . . . YOU SEE MY BANNER – IT MEANS WHAT IT SAYS! . . . COME ALONG NOW AND DO THE INCOME-TAX COLLECTOR IN THE EYE!'

It was all so innocent, all so regular. Moral or immoral, book-making was legitimate business and watching Louey up there in all his glory tended to shake one's convictions. He looked so little like a murderous fanatic with the gallows threatening to yawn at his very feet.

But that was the situation and Gently had made sure that Louey knew where he stood. He was counter-bluffing, that was all; doing what Gently would have done himself if the positions had been reversed. But counter-bluff was a temporary measure. There would be a plan behind it, a positive step. What was it cooking now, that calculating mind, when was it going to happen, and where?

Gently moved over to Dutt, who had resumed his role as Peachey's protector.

'Keep your eyes on your man,' he warned him snappily, 'he'll be easy enough to lose in a crowd like this.'

'Yessir . . . of course, sir. But you got to admit it's a smashing bit of brass . . .'

'I don't admit anything – keep your eyes on Peachey.'

Dutt clicked his heels and did as he was ordered.

Gently wandered away with a frown on his brow. He was biting Dutt's head off now! The double strain of a waiting game with Louey and a checking game with Gish was beginning to fray at his nerves. Gish wanted action. He hadn't any faith in Gently. One had a shrewd suspicion that twenty-four hours would be the limit of his patience.

A slinking figure appeared to materialize out of the worn turf in front of him and Nits' pop-eyes strained up to his own. Gently summoned up a smile for the halfwit.

'Hullo! You come to see the races too, my lad?'

Nits gibbered a moment with his invisible mouth.

'You better get over by the rails – there's a race starting in five minutes.'

'You let her come back!' piped the halfwit, 'you let her come back!'

Gently nodded gravely. Nits chittered and gabbled under his staring eyes. Then he turned to cast a glare of hatred at the towering form of Louey.

'Him – he's a very bad man – very bad!'

Gently nodded again.

'He came to see her – frighten her!' Nits hesitated and crept a little closer. 'You take him away! Yes! You take him away!' He laid a hand on Gently's sleeve.

'I'm thinking about it, Nits . . .'

'He's the bad one – yes! You take him away!'

Gently shrugged and slowly released his sleeve. The halfwit gabbled away furiously, darting angry glances, now at Louey, now at Gently. Gently produced a coin and offered it to him.

'Here you are . . . but don't go making bets with Louey.'

'Don't want it – don't want it!'

'Buy yourself an ice-cream or a pint of shrimps.'

The halfwit shook his head violently and knocked the coin out of Gently's hand. 'You take him away!' he reiterated, 'yes – you take him away!' Then he jumped backwards with a sort of frisking motion and dived away through the crowd.

There was a stir now and a general surge towards the rails. The horses had come up to the tapes and were under starter's orders. Out of a grey sky came a mild splash of sun to enliven for a moment the group of animals and riders, the brilliantly coloured shirts, the white breeches, the chestnut, grey and dun of satin flanks. Tense and nervy were the mounts, strung up and preoccupied the jockeys. A line was formed, a jumpy horse coaxed quiet and almost before one realized what was happening the tapes flew up and the field was away. Instantly a shout began to rise from the crowd, commencing near the gate and spreading right down the track. Fifty thousand pairs of eyes were each magnetized by that thundering, flying, galloping body of horse.

Out in front went the favourite, Swifty's Ghost, and following it close came Cambyses and Rockaby, the latter at a hundred to one and scarcely looked at by the punters. Three furlongs, and the field was getting lost. Six furlongs, and you could almost draw your money. Seven furlongs, and Cambyses, a big grey, was making a terrific bid and going neck-and-neck. Eight furlongs, and out of the blue came Rockaby, fairly scorching the turf, a little dun horse with a halting gallop, but moving now like a startled witch. Could Swifty's Ghost hold them? Could Cambyses maintain his challenge? – The roar of the crowd ebbed up to a fever pitch. But Rockaby drew level with a furlong to go, Rockaby slipped through with a hundred-and-fifty yards in hand, Rockaby passed the post two lengths ahead of the grey and the favourite was beaten to a place by another outsider called Watchmego. The roar died away, the roar became a buzz. They'd done it again . . . another race to line the bookies' pockets!

Gently hunched his shoulders and turned away from the rails, and at that precise moment things began to happen. He had only time for a confused impression; it took place like a dream. There was a crash, some angry shouting, a sound like a quantity of coins being shot on the ground, and then somebody or something struck him heavily in the back and he was lying on his face on the bruised turf.

He wasn't hurt. He got up in a hurry. All around him a crowd was milling about a centre of attraction which was otherwheres than himself. Inside this centre a dialogue for four voices was developing with great verve.

'Of course it was on purpose – I bloody saw you do it!'

'I was shoved, I tell you.'

'You can tell it to the coppers!'

'I tell you I was shoved – some bastard tripped me up!'

'Do you think we're blind?'

'Well, you don't look too bloody bright.'

'Now look here, you dirty so-and-so!'

Gently shouldered his way through. The scene enacting was self-explanatory. A bookie's stand lay on its side amid a debris of betting-slips, notes and coins, about it four angry men. Three of the men were obviously allies. The fourth, a burly gentleman in a mackinaw, appeared to be the defendant in the case.

'Police!' snapped Gently, 'you can stop that shouting. One of you tell me what's been going on here.'

The gent in the mackinaw broke off a challenge to the opposition and stared at Gently with aggressive insolence.

'Police, he says! A snouting copper! You keep your

big nose out of this, mate, or it'll finish up a different shape from what it started this morning!'

'You hear him?' struck in one of the aggrieved, on his knees and trying to collect the scattered money, 'that's your man, officer – you don't have to ask! Come up and threw down my bleeding stand, he did, never as much as a word offered to him!'

'Mad!' snapped a little man with a big coloured tie, 'mad, I tell you – that's what he is!'

The gent in the mackinaw seemed about to resent this allegation when he was interrupted a second time by a new arrival. This time it was Dutt and he was propelling in front of him no less a person than Artie of the ferret face.

'I got him, sir!' panted Dutt, 'he's the one, sir – saw him wiv me own mince pies! Standing right close-up to you he was, sir, all during the race, and as soon as this lot here started he catched you a right fourpenny one and hooked it ... all he didn't know was that I was watching him!'

Gently stared at the scowling bartender as though he had seen a ghost. 'Get back!' he thundered at Dutt. 'Good God, man – *don't you understand*? The whole thing's a trick to get us out of the way – get back at the double, or there may be another body on the beach tomorrow!'

The odds were still being called under the orange banner, but it wasn't Louey calling them. The slips were still being scribbled and handed out, but the man with the book wasn't Peachey. It was the sporty individual who had taken over, with one of the touts for his clerk.

He welcomed Gently and Dutt derisively as they rushed up to the stand.

'Hullo-ullo! Coupla gents here getting in training for the selling-plate!'

'All right!' rasped Gently, 'where are they – where have they gone?'

'Gone, guv'nor? And who is it that's s'posed to have gone somewhere?'

Gently wasted no time. A brown hand flicked out and fifteen stone of sporty individual was picked off the stand like a pear. 'Now . . .! This may be fun for you, but it's murder to me, and if you don't tell me what I want to know I'll see you in dock for complicity. Where's he taken Peachey?'

'I don't know, guv, honest—!' He broke off with a yell as Gently applied pressure to his arm.

'*Where's he taken Peachey?*'

'I don't know – we don't none of us know!'

'That's right, guv!' broke in the tout with the book, 'he just said him and Peachey had got some business to see to what he didn't want you to know about.'

'It's the truth!' shrieked the sporty individual, 'oh, my bloody arm!'

Gently threw him down against the stand, where he lay massaging his maltreated limb and moaning. 'Find Copping!' rapped Gently to Dutt, 'tell him what's happened – tell him to issue a description to all his men – send one to "The Feathers" and one to Sidlow Street – the rest fan out and search the area round the race-course. Where's Louey's car parked?' he fired at the sporty individual.

'It's over there – right by the gate!'

'Check and see if it's gone – if it has, alert all stations.'

Dutt hesitated a moment and then turned in the direction of the gate, but before he could set off an animal-like form came darting and swerving through the crowds and threw itself at Gently's feet.

'He went that way – that way! I saw him! I saw him go!'

Gently's eyes flashed. 'Which way, Nits? . . . which way?'

'That way!' The halfwit made a fumbling gesture towards the north end of the enclosure.

'Gorblimey!' exclaimed Dutt, 'it's "Windy Tops" again!'

Gently rounded on him. 'Forget what I've been saying – just tell Copping to bring his men up there. And when you've done that, don't wait for him . . . I shall probably be in need of some help!'

'Yessir!' gasped Dutt, 'yessir – I'll be there with you!'

But by that time Gently was gone.

It was a hummocky bit of paddock separating the race-course from the lane to 'Windy Tops' and Gently, past his best sprint years, found it very heavy going. At the far side was a scrubby thorn fence in which he had to find a gap. Nits, frisking along at his side, went over it like an Olympic hurdler.

'You get back, m'lad!' panted Gently, 'there'll be trouble up there!'

'You going to take him away!' chuckled Nits. 'I want to see you take him away!'

'You stop down here and you'll get a grandstand view!'

'I want to see – I want to see!'

There was no discouraging him. Gently ploughed on up the slope of the cliff. By the time he reached the gates of 'Windy Tops' he was glad of the breather offered by a pause to reconnoitre and Nits, entering into the spirit of the thing, gave up his leaping and frisking, and slid away like an eel behind the cover of some rhododendron bushes. Not a sound had come from the house. Not a vestige of life was to be seen at any of the windows. Only the front door stood half ajar, as though whoever was within didn't mean to be there for very long.

Keeping his breathing in check, Gently moved swiftly across to the threshold. Inside he could hear voices coming from somewhere at the back. Silently he worked his way down the hall towards the baize-covered door of the kitchen, which was shut, and pressed himself close to it, listening . . .

'No, Peachey,' came Louey's voice at its softest and silkiest, 'we don't seem able to find that money anywhere, do we?'

'B-but boss . . . he give me the message,' came Peachey's whine in reply.

There was the sound of a cupboard door being opened and shut, and something else moved.

'Quite empty, Peachey . . . not a dollar-note to be seen.'

'Boss, he t-took it with him . . . you don't think I'd l-lie?'

'Lie, Peachey?' Louey's laugh sounded careless and easy. 'You wouldn't lie to me, now, would you?'

'N-no, boss, of course I wouldn't!'

'And you wouldn't tell tales, Peachey, would you . . . not even to save your own worthless skin?'

A confused noise was Peachey's answer to this sally.

Louey's laugh came again. 'You see, Peachey, we all have our value, looked at from a certain point of view. I have mine. Streifer has his. Stratilesceul had a value too, but unfortunately for himself he lost it. And now the pressing problem of the moment, Peachey, is your value . . . you do see what I'm driving at?'

A strangled sound suggested that Peachey saw it very plainly.

'Yes, Peachey, I thought you would. I don't want to be unkind, you know. I'm prepared to listen to any defence you may have to offer, but it seems to me that there can't be any real doubt about the matter . . . doesn't it to you? Here am I, on whom the forces of liberation in this country depend, and there are you, a small and expendable unit. Now I could betray you, Peachey, and that might be wrong. But if you were to betray me, that would be a crime comparable to the crime of Judas. You understand?'

'But boss – I never – I didn't – I told them I wouldn't!'

'SILENCE!' thundered Louey's voice, stripped in a moment of its silky veneer. 'Do you think I didn't know, you miserable worm, do you think you can lift a finger without my knowing it?'

There was a pause and then he continued in his former voice: 'I like to make these matters clear. I tried to make them clear to Stratilesceul. I'm not a criminal,

Peachey, in any real sense of the word. There's only one crime and that's the crime against the forces of liberation: when we, the liberators, proceed against that crime, we are guiltless of blood, we are the instruments of true justice. So I am not killing you, Peachey, from hatred or even personal considerations . . . I am killing you in the name of Justice, in the name of Society!'

'. . . No!' came Peachey's terror-stricken cry. 'Boss . . . you can't . . . you can't!'

'Oh but I can, Peachey.'

'No boss – no! It's a mistake – I never told them nothing!'

'And no more you shall!' came Louey's voice savagely, 'this is it, Peachey – this is the tool for traitors!'

Gently hurled open the door. 'Drop it!' he barked, 'drop that knife, Louey!'

The big man spun round suddenly from the sink, over which he was holding the helpless Peachey. His grey eyes were blazing with a malevolent light, strange, fey. '*You!*' he articulated with a sort of hiss, '. . . you!'

'Yes, Louey – me. Now drop that knife and take your hands off Peach.'

'. . . You!' hissed Louey again, and the light in his eyes seemed to deepen.

'Stop him!' whimpered Peachey, 'oh, God, he's going to do for me!' And with the energy of despair he twisted himself out of Louey's grip and made a dive for the back door, which fortunately for him was only bolted. But Louey made no move to restrain him. His eyes remained fixed on Gently.

'Let him go!' he purred, '*he* won't talk . . . I'm not so sure now he ever would have done, are you, Chief Inspector Gently?'

'He'll talk,' retorted Gently, 'there's a limit to what you can do with a knife. Now drop it and put your hands up. It's time you started thinking of your defence.'

By way of answer Louey let the knife slide down his hand, so that now he was holding it by the tip of the blade. 'My defence, Chief Inspector Gently; you are looking at it now. Isn't it a pity? I've let a miserable parasite like Peachey escape and in his place I must execute a man of your . . . attainments. Isn't – it – a – pity?'

With the last four words he had reached back with his gigantic arm and was now leisurely taking aim at Gently's heart. There was no cover to dive for. There was no prospect of a quick back jump through the door. The knife was poised and on a hair-trigger, it would reach its mark long before Gently could move to evade it. And then, at the crucial split second, the knife disappeared – one instant it was flashing in Louey's hand, the next it was spirited away as though by a supernatural agency.

'You take him!' piped the delirious voice of Nits through the back door, 'ha, ha, ha! You take him – you take him!'

With a roar of anger Louey recovered himself and leaped at Gently, but it was too late. A hand that felt like a steel bar smashed into the side of his throat and he collapsed on the floor, choking and gasping, a pitiful, helpless wreck of humanity. Gently snapped handcuffs on the nerveless wrists.

'It had to come, Louey,' he said grimly, 'there has to be an end to this sort of thing.'

'Ha, ha, ha!' giggled Nits, dancing around them and brandishing Louey's knife, 'we'll take him away now – we'll take him away!'

Gently put out his hand for the knife. It was a curious weapon. The hilt and blade were one piece of steel, the former heavy, the latter relatively light and narrow. On each side of the hilt was engraved the mark of the TSK along with a number of Egyptian hieroglyphics.

'Double-edged, about three-quarters of an inch wide,' mused Gently, 'it couldn't be any other . . . it would have to be this one.'

Louey struggled up into a sitting position. He was still gagging for breath, his face was grey. He stared at Gently, at the knife, at the discreet links shackling his enormous wrists. 'No!' he whispered hoarsely, 'you weren't big enough . . . *you just weren't big enough!*'

Gently nodded sadly and slipped the knife into his pocket. 'It's you who weren't big enough, Louey . . . that was the mistake. We're none of us big enough . . . we're just very little people.'

Half the Starmouth Borough Police Force seemed to be congregating in the garden as Gently led Louey out. There was the super with Copping and three or four plain-clothes men, at least ten constables and the complete Special Branch outfit. Dutt came panting up the steps, relief showing in his face at the sight of the handcuffs and an unmarked Gently.

'You're all right then, sir – he never give you any trouble?'

Gently shrugged faintly. 'About the routine issue . . .'

'And Peachey, sir – you got him away safe and sound?'

'Safe and sound, Dutt . . . all Peachey had was a scare.'

'By thunder, Gently, you've pulled off a splendid piece of work!' exclaimed the super, striding across. 'I have to admit it – I thought you were going to fall down over this fellow. I suppose it's unnecessary to ask whether you've got the goods on him?'

'I got him red-handed . . . he was going to stab Peach with a TSK patent executioner's knife. I think we'll find it adds up to the weapon which was used on Stratilesceul.'

'You're an amazing fellow, Gently!' The super gazed at him with honest admiration. 'You're not an orthodox policeman, but by heaven you get the results!'

There was a cough of some penetrative power indicative of the near presence of Chief Superintendent Gish. 'I'm sure you'll forgive me for interrupting,' he observed bitterly, 'but we, at least, have still some business to transact in this affair. I take it that Chief Inspector Gently no longer has any objections to my carrying out my duty?'

Gently signified his innocence of any such desire.

'Then possibly Peach can be produced to answer a few of my irrelevant questions?'

Gently deposited Louey with Dutt and took a few

steps towards the edge of the wildered garden. 'Peachey!' he called softly.

There was a rustling amongst some rhododendrons.

'Peachey ... it's all right. We've got Louey under lock and key. You can come out now.'

There were further rustlings and then the parrot-faced one emerged. He was still trembling in every limb and his knees had a tendency to buckle, but the sight of so many policemen reassured him and he walked shakily over to the front of the house.

'That's the boy, Peachey ... nobody's going to hurt you.'

'You got his kn-knife?' gabbled Peachey, darting a wild-eyed glance at his shackled employer.

'Yes, Peachey, we've got his knife ... everything's as safe as houses. All we want now is a little information – just a little, to begin with! I suppose you're in a mood to do some talking, Peachey?'

Peachey was. He had never been so much in the mood before. Shocked to his plump core by his experiences in the house, Peachey had learned the hard way that honesty was his only hopeful policy and he was prepared to give effect to that policy in all-night sittings, if that should be required. Chief Superintendent Gish, however, was more moderate in his exactions. He was obstinately and snappily interested in but one set of facts – a short-wave transmitter and some records – and when he had obtained the address of same he departed in haste, leaving Peachey to waste his sweetness on the East Coast air.

'But you wanted a statement about the m-murder,

didn't you?' asked Peachey aggrievedly, though with an anxious look at the silent Louey.

'We do, Peachey . . . don't you worry about that,' Gently assured him. 'We'll take you right back now and you can tell us about it over a cup of canteen tea.'

'Then there's Frenchy . . . she can b-back me up . . .'

'She hasn't been overlooked.'

'And I dare say some of the boys . . . it was only me what was sworn into the p-party.'

Gently nodded and urged him towards the gate. The super signed to his men and Dutt touched Louey's arm. From below them, through the scrub trees, came a murmur like a swarming of bees, a murmur that grew suddenly, became a frenzied roar. Louey stood his ground a moment. It was another race in progress.

And then there came a second sound, a rumbling, subterranean sound . . . like the first one and yet strangely unlike it. The roar of the crowd died down, but the second roar didn't. It seemed to be vibrating the air, the trees, the very ground itself. Yet there was nothing to see. There was nothing to account for it. It was Copping who suddenly realized what was going on.

'Run for it!' he bellowed, 'it's the house – it's going over – get the hell out of here, or we'll all be over with it!'

A sort of panic followed his words. There was a general and high-powered movement on the part of one super, one inspector, four detective sergeants, ten constables and a plump civilian in a down-hill and due south direction. This left a balance of three to be accounted for and a backward glance by Copping

261

revealed them in a snapshot of dramatic relation which rooted him to the ground. There was Dutt, sprawling on the pavement; Gently, racing up the path; and Louey, roaring defiance from the top of the steps. And the house was already beginning to move.

'Come back!' howled Copping, 'it's on its way – come back!'

Gently pulled up short some feet from the steps. A crack was opening like magic between himself and the house.

'What are you waiting for?' roared Louey. 'Come on, Mister Chief Inspector Gently – let's die together, shall we? Let's die as though we were men – let's die as though we were more than men!'

Gently measured the distance and poised himself for the leap. Louey rattled his handcuffs in ironic invitation. Then, as though his good angel had whispered in his ear, Gently flung himself backwards instead of forwards: and at the same instant 'Windy Tops', complete in every detail, lurched out frightfully into space . . .

They ran to pick him up, Dutt, Copping and two uniform men. As they pulled him to safer ground another chunk of cliff dropped thundering to the beach. Down below them a raw gap loomed, large enough to put the Town Hall in. There was a curiously unnerving smell of dank and newly-revealed gravel. On the beach was piled the debris, lapping into the sea, a cloud of dust and grit still rising from it. Gently tore himself loose from his rescuers and stared down into the settling chaos.

'Not so close!' shouted Copping, 'you don't know where it's going to stop!'

But Gently remained staring from the edge of the yawning pit. Then he turned to Dutt, a curious expression on his face. 'All right . . . fetch him up. Use that little path over there and fetch him up.'

'Fetch him up?' echoed Dutt. 'Yessir. Of course, sir. But we'll need some picks and shovels, sir, and maybe a stretcher . . .'

Gently shook his head and walked away from the edge. 'Not a single shovel, Dutt . . . not the strap off a stretcher. Poor Louey! This is his final tragedy. He thought he was big enough to play God, but when it came to the push he couldn't even commit suicide.'

'You mean he – he's *alive?*' goggled Dutt.

'Yes, Dutt, and kicking too. If we'd left the door unlocked he'd have been buried in the middle of that lot, but as it is he went down on top . . . he's sitting there now, shaking the muck out of his ears.'

CHAPTER FIFTEEN

I T WAS GREAT stuff for the press, the double arrest of Louey and Streifer. It sent the Body On The Beach rocketing right back into the headlines. There were encomiums for Gently and encomiums for the Borough Police – it was only Chief Superintendent Gish who got a cold and cautious mention. But Gish didn't mind. They were used to it in the Special, he told everyone.

All the same, it was a pity that the best angle on the story didn't come out. It drove the reporters wild to see so much delectable copy laid for ever in the freezer. There was that transmitter under a ruined pill-box down at South Shore, for instance, with its aerial cheekily installed on the Scenic Railway . . . and there were the mass arrests and deportations of agents all over the country, a major operation which the British Public had an undoubted Right To Know About. But it was no use arguing. Chief Super Gish had a heart of stone. As a result of his inhuman decree the British Public were left with the vague and erroneous impression that the Body On The Beach had to do with a gang of international counterfeiters, with an element of vice thrown in by way of a gift to the Sunday papers.

BODY ON THE BEACH – VICE KING ARRESTED declared one such. BEACH MURDER TRACED TO VICE EMPIRE said a second. And it was almost pure libel – Louey only did a bit of sub-letting. After all, even revolutionary parties have to get their funds from somewhere . . .

But it was a London Evening that produced the really telling caption. It caused Chief Super Gish to drop dark hints about people being friendly with editors. 'Body On The Beach' ran a small by-line and then, in a triumph of Cooper Black, GENTLY DOES IT AGAIN! – with one of Gently's better press photos cut in across two columns. Of course, Gently pooh-poohed it. He folded up his copy and stuck it in his pocket with scarcely a glance. But a little later, when he thought he wasn't being watched, Copping saw him perusing that paper with more than common attention.

'We didn't waste no time, when you comes to think of it, sir,' Dutt remarked with a tinge of regret, as they stood on the bridge by the station awaiting their train. 'We comes here on the Friday night to meet a stiff what nobody don't know about and by Tuesday tea-time we got the two geezers what done it, busted up a lot of bolshies and run in a sample of ponces and Teddiesall in a long weekend, you might say.'

Gently passed him a peppermint cream and took one himself. 'We certainly haven't been too heavy on the ratepayers.'

'And me, I was just getting attached to the place, sir. I reckon it beats Sahthend hollow for some things . . .

there's a bloke off Nelson Street as does a plaice-and-chips that knocks you backwards.'

Gently smiled at a distant tug with an orange funnel. 'Talking of plaice, there's some first-rate fishing goes on off the Albion Pier.'

'And them digs of ours, sir, they wasn't half bad neither. I reckon I could stand a week down here with the missus next Bank Holiday . . .'

A train-whistle sounded close at hand. Gently consulted the watch on his clumsy wrist. Beneath them an empty motor-barge came chugging past, its skipper lounging lazily by his wheel.

'But things change, Dutt . . . it doesn't take long to alter them. Do you know what struck me most while we were on this job?'

'No, sir. It ain't been like our other jobs, really.'

Gently took careful aim with his screwed-up peppermint cream bag and dropped it neatly on the barge-skipper's peaked cap.

'Well, Dutt, it was the donkeys.'

'The donkeys, sir?' queried Dutt.

Gently nodded and raised his hand in salute to the barge-skipper. 'They've done away with them, Dutt. There isn't one on the beach. If you'd known Starmouth when I knew Starmouth it would make you feel older . . . but something like that goes on all the time, doesn't it?'